KAIT

"Ballenger offe... ge
start to her series about ...
their adversaries."
—*Publishers Weekly*, starred review, on *Twilight Hunter*

"Paranormal fans have a new voice to check out with the
debut of Ballenger's terrific first book in her
Execution Underground series."
—*RT Book Reviews* on *Twilight Hunter*

"Debut author Ballenger shows awesome
potential and talent."
—*RT Book Reviews* on *Shadow Hunter*

"Kait Ballenger is a treasure you don't want to miss!"
—*New York Times* bestselling author Gena Showalter

"Nonstop action, pulse-pounding suspense, and red-hot
romance… Kait Ballenger's Execution Underground
series delivers in spades!"
—Jaime Rush, *New York Times* bestselling author

"Action and romance in one mesmerizing story.
A phenomenal start to the Execution Underground series.
Shadow Hunter will leave you breathless and
demanding more."
—Cecy Robson, author of *Sealed with a Curse*

"Taut with action, suspense, and romance that sizzles,
Shadow Hunter is an evocative prelude to what's certain
to be an exciting new series! Fans of J.R. Ward are going
to love the sexy warriors of Kait Ballenger's
Execution Underground."
—Kate SeRine, author of *Red* and *The Better to See You*

Also available from Kait Ballenger

TWILIGHT HUNTER
AFTER DARK
"Shadow Hunter"

Look for Kait Ballenger's next novel

MIDNIGHT HUNTER

coming soon

IMMORTAL HUNTER

KAIT BALLENGER

Published in Great Britain 2014
by Mills & Boon, an imprint of Harlequin (UK) Limited,
Eton House, 18-24 Paradise Road, Richmond, Surrey, TW9 1SR

ISBN: 978 0 263 913958

89-0514

Harlequin (UK) Limited's policy is to use papers that are natural, renewable and recyclable products and made from wood grown in sustainable forests. The logging and manufacturing processes conform to the legal environmental regulations of the country of origin.

Printed and bound
by CPI Group (UK) Ltd, Croydon, CR0 4YY

For my dad, Rick Schulz,
who has always supported me in everything I do, and
who has provided me with all the opportunities I needed
to succeed in life. I love you, Daddy.

Chapter 1

David Aronowitz unsheathed his dagger and steadied the weapon. The serrated silver blade glinted in the dim amber glow of a nearby streetlight as he slipped into the shadows. He ran his thumb over the edge of the knife. New. Spotless and unused. If he had his way, it wouldn't be unused much longer.

That demon piece of shit was going down.

He crept farther into the darkness, ears attuned to the slightest noise. The distant sounds of sirens from Strong Memorial Hospital echoed through the night, mixed with the sounds of occasional car horns and passersby. The damp scent of March's latest snowfall-turned-brown-slush filled his nose. He had only a few minutes until his target arrived, and he couldn't afford to mess this up.

He didn't want to leave Allsún. It *killed* him to leave her bedside. But he had no choice. Jace had agreed to take over his vigil. In his absence, David trusted Jace to keep Allsún safe.

He patted the pocket of his Harley jacket. As he felt his Beretta holstered beneath the leather, a grim smile curved his lips. If there was one thing he loved it was new weapons, and tonight he had two brand-new toys: his dagger and, his personal favorite, the new bullets he'd loaded into the Berretta. Months of trying and finally he'd crafted a bullet that exploded on impact, releasing holy water inside the demonic target. A small part of him couldn't wait to see the look on the monster's face when he tested those little beauties.

His current assignment was to trail a demon he suspected was an Abyzu. One of those sick bastards had popped onto the Execution Underground's radar when an infant girl was murdered two weeks ago. A dull ache pulsed through his heart every time he thought of the horrifying pain her parents had experienced, and would for the rest of their lives.

That baby-killing son-of-a-bitch would pay—no doubt about that, he'd make certain of it. But he had different plans for tonight. An Abyzu wasn't his target. This was personal.

He shifted behind the Dumpster. A sharp pain shot up his leg, reminding him—as if he could forget—of his last major job gone horribly wrong, and the price of his failure. He deserved the pain. It was a just punishment, because he'd failed her. The one time Allsún had needed him, and he'd let her down. Left his ex-fiancée to the mercy of a sick, sexual sadist.

He gazed in the direction of the hospital, picturing her as he'd left her. She looked so peaceful, lying in the hospital bed with her eyes closed as if she were sleeping, though he knew better. She'd been imprisoned and tortured, and he'd been helpless to protect her. Sure, there were circumstances beyond his control. And, as his fellow hunters liked to point out, he *had* been the one to save her. But she'd suffered. She continued to suffer.

And knowing her pain was driving him insane.

He kicked the Dumpster with his injured leg, welcoming the sting it sent through his leg. Discovering a demon had possessed the doctor caring for his suffering ex-fiancée while she helplessly lay in a coma had been the chocolate icing on the shit cake.

The demon/doctor was no fool. He surrounded himself with humans, keeping to the busiest sections of the hospital. Shit, David had come close to losing his fucking mind, waiting for the right moment to take the sucker down. He'd been watching the bastard for weeks, and his patience was about to pay off. Any time now the monster would be cutting through the alleyway after the end of his shift.

David paused, and listened. Footsteps approached. He forced himself to focus. It was time. In three, two, one. *L'chayim,* bitch.

His eyes locked on to the open mouth of the alley, illuminated by a nearby streetlight. As his target rounded the corner and moved toward him, David held his breath and raised his knife for the attack. The sound of footfalls filled the alleyway's narrow walls, and the whistling wind echoed through the backstreet. With his damaged leg, one wrong move and he would be toast.

The demon's steps grew louder as David waited to strike. He had one shot to pin the hell-crawler before the monster attacked, or, more likely, turned tail and ran like the little bitch it was. And if the bastard ran, David's jacked-up leg would make pursuit near impossible.

David focused on his enemy. Suddenly the demon halted mid-stride, on alert, as if sensing the threat lurking in the shadows. David froze, not a single muscle moving. He couldn't screw this up.

The demon took another cautious step forward. A ray of light from one of the nearby streetlights cast on to the doctor's face. Shit. This situation was a mess. David had no idea how long the physician had been possessed or, more importantly, whether or not he was still living somewhere inside that skull. He bit back his frustration and reminded himself of the plan. He didn't want to kill the thing, just pin it down, get the information he needed and exorcise the demon from the doctor's body. As much as he wanted to carve the monster's face up for even looking at Allsún, he couldn't bring himself to go for the kill. Not with the possibility of the body's original owner being alive.

The demon's eyes darted around the alley, scanning his surroundings. After several long moments it continued on its way. David smiled. Perfect. He allowed the monster to walk several feet past him, farther into the shadows. Shifting his weight, he prepped for a lunge. The side of his hip brushed the brick wall he stood against, making the slightest sound.

Fuck.

The bastard paused again and turned around.

David didn't have time to think. He threw himself on

to the demon. His torso collided with the lanky physician's, and he knocked the monster to the ground. He shoved the blade of his knife against the hell-crawler's throat. The demon struggled beneath him. It wriggled an arm free and clocked David square in the cheekbone.

David's head snapped back from the force of the blow. His vision blurred. Though the demon's chosen body was human, the monster's strength was still of supernatural proportions. The demon possessing the doctor packed one hell of a punch. Damn, that would hurt in the morning.

The hell-spawn seized the free moment, bucking David off and scrambling to its feet. Vision still blurred, David followed suit, quickly regaining his footing. He slashed his knife through the air, backing the demon into a corner between the Dumpster and the wall of the alley.

The demon laughed. "You think a blade will hurt me, hunter?" It put both arms out in a welcoming gesture. "By all means, carve up this nice doctor I'm wearing. You won't cause *me* any permanent harm."

David frowned. Now he was pissed. He hated demons, especially smart-ass ones. He slashed across the demon's face. A sharp hiss echoed through the alley as the blade seared through its skin. The creature clutched its cheek as steam billowed off the burning wound. David slammed the demon against the wall, pushing his knife flush against its throat.

He smirked. "A blessed blade, you sulfur-sucking fucker." David pushed the knife harder against the demon's skin. "And that's 'exorcist' to you."

The demon swore. David choked back a laugh. What kind of dumbass was this thing? He wasn't one to brag, but with a reputation like his, the demon should've known stepping foot inside Rochester put him smack-dab in the middle of David's hunting territory. If there was one thing demons hated more than anything, it was dealing with exorcists like him. He sent them back to hell every time—and every demon he'd ever encountered had been desperate to escape Satan's hellhole for good. It was no easy feat to get here, so they sure didn't want to be sent back.

David leaned the slightest bit harder into his blade, drawing blood. Another hiss sounded as the cut on the demon's neck burned and smoked. It writhed against David's weight.

First for the personal business. "What were you doing at Allsún's bedside, you freak?" David growled.

A small smile curved the demon's lips. "Who?" it taunted.

With his free fist David punched the demon in the face. From the crunch beneath his knuckles, he could tell the physician's nose had broken. The poor guy would have to deal with the pain of the injuries David inflicted, assuming he was still alive, but it sure beat the alternative. David threw another punch, and blood gushed from the demon's nostrils.

He needed answers, and he needed them now. "Don't get cute with me, princess. You know exactly who I'm talking about."

The demon's eyes shifted from a human brown to a burning bloodred. Its anger showed in the hint of its true form. "You mean the delicious girl I plan to gut from the inside out?"

"If you touch a single hair on her head, I will skin you alive and pour holy water across your open wounds until you've sizzled to nothing more than a piece of smoking, rotting flesh," David hissed. His blood was boiling. The thought of Allsún hurting any more than she already was sent pure rage coursing through his veins. He'd already failed to protect her once. He wouldn't let it happen again.

The demon grinned through the blood pouring down its face. "And kill this sweet doctor I'm wearing, a man who has saved countless lives? I don't think so."

David growled. "You underestimate my hatred for you hell-whores." He shoved the knife harder against the demon's throat. More smoke burned from the wound. "Tell me why you've been riding her doctor or I'll exorcise your sorry ass back to hell right this second."

The demon didn't respond.

"One last chance."

The demon grinned. Blood from the doctor's nose gushed into its mouth and stained its smile a putrid shade of crimson. No answer.

David clenched his teeth. Fine. If the demon wanted pain, he'd give it pain. He cleared his throat and began to recite the exorcism ritual. The Hebrew words fell from his lips with familiar ease.

The veins underneath the demon's skin darkened until the varicose lines covered the doctor's whole body. The demon's eyes blazed an even more fiery red, and he shook in uncontrollable jerks. David didn't stop chanting, not even to catch his breath.

The demon let out a strained cry. "All right already," it interrupted him. "Don't exorcise me and I'll tell you what you want."

David waited. The little shit had called uncle sooner than he'd expected.

The demon coughed blood as the blue-and-purple

veins covering the body it possessed slowly faded. "She's the last Fae creature outside the Isle of Apples. I came to kill her, and I would have, if you hadn't been permanently glued to her bedside."

Fuck. David fought back a long string of profanities. As if Allsún didn't have it rough enough already—lying there unconscious while her injuries healed. Now this demon knew what she had been hiding for years, her half-Fae bloodline. Her pixie bloodline, to be more specific. As earthly angels, the Fae were the demons' only true natural enemy. As one of the last of her kind remaining on earth, Allsún was a danger to them, and she'd gone into hiding several years ago during the last mass exodus of Fae from Earth.

David forced himself to remain calm for Allsún's sake. He couldn't let the demon know it was on to anything big. "Who sent you?" he asked.

The demon shrugged. "It's just me."

David let out another low growl and slid the edge of his blade across the demon's throat.

The monster yelled in agony. "I'm on my own. I swear it. I possessed the hospital janitor, and I was riding him for some fun when I came across her. I knew what she was right away, so I decided to toy with her and possessed the doc. I wanted to say *I* was the demon to kill the last faerie on Earth."

David met the demon's eyes and assessed the worthless piece of filth. From its mild strength he could tell it was no head-honcho. Just another lowly bottom-feeder. Probably a Belial demon, if he were to wager a guess. A Belial *would* be dumb enough to go after someone as valuable as Allsún without orders from its superiors.

"Did you tell anyone else about her?"

The hell-spawn shook its head. "No, no one. You have my word. Just let me go."

David scoffed. "Your word is worth less than a dead man's ball sack. I know you demons chatter like gossiping schoolgirls with one another, so unless you can tell me something useful about the demon that murdered that poor infant girl two weeks ago, you're taking a one-way trip back to hell." David began to recite the ritual again, his words slow, deliberate.

The veins throughout the doctor's body bulged again, and the demon shrieked. "Send me back to hell and I'll tell every demon there about her!"

David froze. Rage filled him as he considered the demon's words. He was so not in the mood to play around with this sulfurous piss-ant.

The demon grinned from ear to ear. "Looks like you're just going to have to let me go, exorcist."

David laughed. "In your dreams." He punched the demon in the gut. The demon/doctor let out an audible "oof."

He would exorcise the demonic piece of shit as painfully as possible. He reached for the chain around his neck, pulling the Star of David he always wore from underneath his shirt. He pressed it into the demon's forehead as he mumbled the ancient words of the ritual.

The demon's body seized. The screams that reverberated from its throat were anything but human. "For that, I'll spread the word about the faerie *and* I'll kill the doctor, too. He may need to breathe, but I don't."

The doctor's chest quit moving as the demon intentionally stopped breathing, suffocating the body it wore. David quickened the pace of his chanting, mumbling the words as fast as he could. He prayed the doctor was able to fight somewhere in there, was able to force the demon to take a breath.

He was halfway through the ritual and still the doctor wasn't breathing. Playing out all the possible scenarios in his mind, David calculated his next move. He was damned either way. If he exorcised the demon, he would be putting Allsún's life in danger once again.

Allowing the hell-spawn the opportunity to share the news of her existence was not an option—though for all he knew the others were aware of her existence already. Still, could he take the chance? His only other choice was to kill the demon for good, but that meant he would be killing the doctor, too.

His loyalties clashed—his duties as a hunter to protect the innocent, and the loyalty and devotion he felt for the woman who'd once been the love of his life, even if she no longer returned that love. David gritted his teeth.

Shit.

He shoved the Star of David harder against the demon's forehead and recited Psalm 91 in Hebrew as fast as he could. Three times. That was all he needed. Just three recitations, and then the ritual would be finished. Allsún would want him to save the doctor if he could. He knew it, but how could he knowingly place her in danger again? And would the doctor already be dead by then anyway?

The demon gasped. The doctor's face cleared for barely a second. His eyes flashed to their normal shade. The red disappeared as he fought against the demon. "Kill it! I don't care if you kill me, too!"

For a moment David hesitated. Then, without thought, he plunged the blade into the doctor's heart.

The man's body seized and shook beneath David's hold. Blood gushed from the wound in thick spurts. The veins darkened beneath the doctor's skin as the demon fought unsuccessfully to hang on to its existence. A pulse of energy emanated from the doctor's body, a signal of the demon's death. The doctor's veins faded. The red of his irises transitioned into his normal brown color. His body went limp, but the light hadn't left his eyes. He coughed up blood, the red liquid oozing down his chin and face.

He opened his mouth to speak. "H-he already told the others," he rasped. "About…h-her." The doctor's body jerked one last feeble time before his eyes went dark, and the muscles in his face slackened.

Blood poured on to the cement as David lowered the doctor to the ground. He stared at the man's limp form as guilt rushed through him. Shit. He'd wanted to save the doctor. Damn. In situations like this, he always knew it wasn't his fault, and that he needed to get the job done, which he had. But it didn't matter. He always blamed himself anyway. Damn it all. Following his first instinct, he clutched the Star of David at his neck and muttered the Mourner's Kaddish. As the last words fell from his lips, he released his necklace and stepped away from the body.

Chapter 2

Thirty-six hours of torture wasn't exactly easy on the body. Neither was waking up after nearly a month in a trauma-induced coma. Allsún O'Hare found that out the hard way. A pulse of energy shot through Allsún's body, and she jolted upright, gasping for breath. Every inch of her body ached with a dull throbbing pain. The smell of too much sterilization and cleaning agents assaulted her nose. An incessant beeping sounded like a siren inside her head. She covered her ears as she stared at a white-washed room, her vision blurred.

Shite. Where in Morgana's name was she? She blinked several times until her eyes cleared, then she took in the scene around her.

"Paging Nurse Robson to the labor and delivery

unit," a female voice echoed over nearby loud speakers. Labor and delivery? She knew there was no way in hell she was in labor and delivery, that was for sure. The last time she'd been there had been when… Oh, God.

Her head spun, and she clutched the sheets over her. Labor and delivery…that meant she was in a hospital, right? Her vision blurred again. Holy faerie dust. No. No hospitals. She hated hospitals. She needed to get out of here. Now.

Her vision spun again. Boy, was she feeling loopy or what? What the hell had they given her? She glanced down at her arm and saw an IV sticking out from the back of her hand. Her eyes followed the tubing up to a clear bag. She squinted at the small printed label on the side of it. Ativan. What kind of drug was that? Nothing she was familiar with from the humane shelter, that was for sure.

She flopped back on to the not-so-fluffy pillow propped behind her head. Why was she in the hospital anyway? Slowly her eyes drooped, as if the lids weighed more than her muscles could bear to handle. How had she gotten here? She…

The image of David's handsome face flashed through her mind.

With a fresh round of determination, she sat upright

in bed again. Though it felt as if she'd lost all muscle control in her hands, she pawed at the IV. She grasped at the tubing in desperation, until finally she ripped it from her hand. She let out a sharp yelp at the pain. A heavyset nurse walking by her room paused at the sound, then turned to see Allsún fiddling with the IV.

She hurried to Allsún's bedside. Clara, as her badge read, sported platinum blond hair up to the two-inch roots at her scalp, which showed a dark, sharply contrasting brown—clearly her natural color. She smiled with lips that had a little too much burgundy lip liner and placed her hand on her hip. "Oh, no, you don't. You have to leave that in, honey."

Allsún shook her head. No way was she letting that human poison run into her veins for another second. Clara left her bedside for a moment, searching a nearby cabinet for supplies. Supplies she wouldn't need. Scooting to the end of the bed, Allsún swung her legs over the edge. She dangled on the side of the hospital mattress until finally her tiny feet touched the cold, hard tiling of the floor. Still clutching the bed, she stepped forward. Her knees wobbled beneath her and…shite. She crumpled to the floor, her legs so weak she couldn't even support herself. How was she supposed to escape like this?

At the sound of Allsún hitting the floor, Clar… Clarese?—Allsún's mind went fuzzy. What was the nurse's name again? Before Allsún could think about it much longer, the woman was at her side, hooking her under the arms and hauling her to her feet as if she weighed no more than a doll. Maybe she did weigh that little…she couldn't remember the last time she'd eaten.

"All right, honey. Let's get you back in bed, okay? We don't want you falling again. I'm already going to have to fill out a nice big pile of paperwork just because of that little spill. So let's take it easy, okay?" She eased Allsún back toward the bed.

Allsún planted her feet as firmly on the ground as she could. With every ounce of strength she had, she pulled against the woman's hold. "No, I'mmm not ssstaying here," she said, suddenly very aware of her slurred speech.

The nurse frowned. "I know you don't want to, but you really need to lie down and rest."

Allsún pulled against the nurse's hold again, trying her hardest to make her voice sound firm. "No."

The woman grabbed hold of Allsún's left wrist, gentle but commanding. "You have to—"

"I said *no*." Allsún wrenched her arm away from the

nurse. She stumbled several steps sideways, away from the woman's hold.

The nurse stepped toward her again. Her frown twisted into a look of frustration as she reached for Allsún. "Look, I only have so much patience. You need to—"

Allsún lifted her hand and made a throwing motion. A cloud of sparkling faerie dust emanated from her open palm, as if she'd thrown a handful of glitter straight into the nurse's face. Immediately the woman crumpled to the floor. Her mouth gaped open as she fell into the best sleep she'd probably had in years.

Allsún blinked two times, the movement slow and sluggish from the weight still forcing down her eyelids. "Thass what you get for m…m…messing with a pi…pixie." She was slurring worse than a college frat boy on a Saturday night.

Concentrating on keeping her balance, Allsún stumbled out of the room and into a long hallway. After what seemed like an eternity of thinking, she deduced that it had to be nighttime. The lights were dimmed, and no one was in sight. She inched down the hall for what seemed like hours before reaching the nurses' station directly next to the elevators. Her escape.

A night nurse perched at her desk looked up from a mound of papers. "Miss, are you all right?"

Allsún didn't answer. She walked up to the desk, made a throwing motion with her hand, and watched the nurse slump onto the desktop with a thud in response to her natural faerie dust. She shuffled past the now-incapacitated woman toward the elevator.

Allsún jabbed the blurry elevator button three times until the doors finally opened. Using every ounce of brain power she could muster through her drug-induced haze, she selected the star button for what she hoped was the ground floor.

The elevator closed with a high-pitched ding. After four floors the elevator finally reached the bottom, and as fast as she could, she stumbled out and booked her way through the sliding glass doors of freedom.

When the doors opened, a huge burst of cold air hit Allsún straight in the face, sending a chill racing through her entire body. She wrapped her arms around her torso in a useless attempt to keep herself warm. She needed to get home before she got hypothermia. Her bare feet stung from the light layer of snow still coating Rochester's streets. The prickling sensation helped clear her head, like what she imagined a sobering cold shower after a long night of way too much drinking would be like. Not that she would know for certain, since she'd never been the partying type. Not too much to celebrate when you're spending your days chasing after…

Demons.

The scent of sulfur hit her nose as she passed by an empty alleyway. All at once her senses came alive, and she could feel the natural instinct in her Fae blood calling her. She turned in the direction her instinct indicated, the instinct that told her where demonic activity was, the instinct she hadn't used in years. Not since *that* night…

Since then she'd found herself capable of ignoring the call. She knew that the city would remain safe without her. Though David couldn't be everywhere at once, he was the only human she'd ever encountered who was capable of exorcising demons back to hell instead of just killing them. He could save the victims in a way that not even she could.

But somehow this time was different.

The pull inside her, like a rope tugging hard at the center of her chest, compelled her forward. And how could she not listen to such a strong command? She took another step, and then her head began to clear.

She was thankful for her supernatural metabolism. It was burning up the drugs nicely, but…

How had she ended up in her current situation? What had put her in the hospit—

She staggered as the memories rushed back to her in one overwhelming burst.

That *thing,* the monster that did this to her. The thought of his disgustingly handsome face twisted in a look of pure hatred and malice flashed through her mind. Robert. That had been his name, before the hunters killed him.

She'd been in the hospital because that monster had kidnapped and tortured her, left her for dead. And then David had saved her. The memory of his arms wrapped around her warmed her to her core.

No, she couldn't think like that.

She shook her head, trying to erase both Robert and David from her thoughts. She shouldn't be thinking this way. Robert was dead now, and she'd done her best to push David from her mind years ago. David had made his choice. When she'd left, he'd never come after her, so that was that. Sure, he'd saved her, but that was his job. Nothing more. She was certain of it.

Shuffling to the edge of the busy street outside the hospital, she waved her arms, hoping to flag down a taxi. Someone out there needed to be saved, her instincts told her that much, and after the torture she'd so recently been through herself, she couldn't just leave them to that same horrifying fate. If she could just get a cab to stop, she could follow her instincts. The coldness in the air continued to seep into her body, and slowly her feet tingled to numbness. After several minutes with no taxis in sight, she ran into the middle of the street the minute she saw one barreling toward her. The driver slammed on his brakes and pounded the horn. The sound reverberated in her ears, pulling her further from her drugged haze.

The cabbie rolled down his window. "What the fuck are you doing, lady? Get out of the street."

She inhaled a deep breath and called back to him over the busy sounds of the city. "I need a ride." Rushing to the side of his cab, she fumbled her way into the backseat, apparently still slightly dizzy from the remaining Ativan.

The cabbie leaned back in his seat and sighed as he stomped on the gas pedal. "Where to, lady?"

"Listen, this is an emergency, and I don't have any money on me."

The cabbie glanced in the rearview mirror, eyeing

the hospital gown. "Look, lady. I don't give free rides. Either you pay or you get out of my—"

Before he could finish his sentence, Allsún shoved her hand in front of his face, releasing another swirling puff of faerie dust. She cleared her throat. "So, about that free ride?"

The man blinked as if in a haze before he said, "Free ride? Sure, I can do that. Where to?"

She smiled. "Head toward the south end of the city, and hurry. I don't know where we're going, exactly, but as we get closer, I'll figure it out."

The pull deep inside her chest increased with every mile, her senses sharpening the nearer they came to their destination. She marveled at how quickly she had burned off the drugs. Her head cleared more with each passing moment. No wonder they'd had her hooked up to the stuff. She'd probably needed a dosage more appropriate for someone three times her size.

When they reached the edge of the city, the tall buildings and industrial sprawl faded into quiet suburbia. Out here the bright lights of the skyscrapers shimmered from a distance, but the streets were dim, lit only by the occasional streetlight. She directed the cabbie through a series of turns until they were fully surrounded by rows of small brick houses. The view of the city disappeared. She would search all night if she had to. Because maybe, just maybe, she could save someone tonight.

Disposing of a body was never pretty. The metallic odor of the doctor's blood invaded David's nose, and he fought not to gag as the scent mixed with the smell of rotting garbage. The open Dumpster smelled more like decaying flesh than the actual dead guy did. Better get this over with. Lifting the doctor's corpse, he hefted the limp body into the trash. God forgive him. It went against every fiber of his conscience every time, but he always got the job done. A part of him wished he could call up the guy's family or at least take him to the morgue, make sure he had a proper funeral, but unless he wanted witnesses, that wasn't a possibility.

Boy, how much fun would it be to explain to the police that he'd killed a man because the guy was possessed by a demon? That one would really go over well with the cops—about as well as fat-free doughnuts and decaffeinated coffee.

After closing the Dumpster lid, he pulled an old black bandana from inside his jacket and wiped down everything he had touched. He couldn't leave his prints around. Once he finished, he slipped down the alley, hobbling through several back passageways until he reached his parked motorcycle. A sharp pain shot down his leg with every step, and he winced. Damn it.

He let out a long breath and unlatched the saddlebag on his black 2011 Harley-Davidson Dyna Super Glide, a piece of perfect machinery, if you asked him, and the one beauty who never failed him. He dug around the inside of the saddlebag, then frowned as he uncapped the bottle of hydrocodone. He shook two of the white horse-sized pills into his hand and dry-swallowed them, then placed the prescription bottle in the saddlebag once again. He hated taking the pills, but they were the only way he could operate with his leg as jacked up as it was. At least the doctor insisted the limp and the pain were only temporary, and he'd be healed soon.

Every four to eight hours, depending on his level of pain and the amount of strain he'd put on his muscles, he was reminded of his most recent failures and misgivings.

Robert, that sadistic skinwalker, had tortured the only woman David had ever loved. Kidnapping and torturing Allsún had been pure fun and games for Robert, and because the sicko had torn up David's leg, leaving him with a limp, David had been humiliatingly unable to save Allsún himself and had been forced to watch as his friend and fellow hunter Jace McCannon did it for him—but not before Allsún had incurred the kind of physical and mental damage she might never recover from. Sure, he'd been the one to actually get Allsún out of the building and to safety, but Jace had been the one to kill Robert.

If only David had been stronger, a better fighter, he could have bested Robert to begin with, and Allsún would have remained safe. He would never forgive himself for all the pain she'd endured. Her suffering was *his* fault for not protecting her.

He knew nothing good would come from blaming himself, but it didn't matter. The guilt was enough to hurt him until the day he died. But hell, he had already failed her in so many other ways, what was one more thing added to the list?

A muffled buzzing noise broke his train of thought. His phone was vibrating in the pocket of his jeans. He slipped his hand underneath the edge of his leather bike chaps and pulled out the sleek new phone—courtesy of his fellow hunter Shane Gray. The name "Damon Brock" flashed across the screen. His division leader calling could only mean one of two things: either there was another bitch-fest meeting he would have to attend or a demonic possession had been reported.

Having grown up in Rochester, David had the advantage of knowing all the rabbis in the city, so once he had grown old enough to begin his work as an exorcist, the rabbis had introduced him to the pastors, the priests and the imams, until he had an entire network of holy men aware of the work he did. When people figured out a family member was possessed, their religious leader was always the first person they called. Any time a parishioner reported a possession, someone in the network called Damon or reported it directly to David.

Sure, the system wasn't perfect, but it definitely helped David find the monsters. He had been called in a few times for some druggies who had taken one too many tabs of the brown acid and were spouting all sorts of demonic bullshit, but for the most part the system worked.

Knowing he couldn't avoid Damon's call, he finally hit the talk button and pressed the phone to his ear. "Yeah?"

"Father O'Reilly called. Someone needs you," Damon said without so much as a hello. Cold and straight-to-the-point, as always. He wasn't one to fool around with pleasantries, especially where the Execution Underground was concerned.

"What's the address?" David asked.

"South side of the city. Almost out in the suburbs." Damon rattled off the info.

David quickly committed the address to memory, pulled out the keys to the Super Glide and mounted his bike. "What's the situation?"

"A woman from O'Reilly's parish called him," Damon said. "She's certain her husband is possessed by the devil. The Father heard her scream, and then there was a gurgling followed by…nothing."

"Poor old bastard was probably scared shitless." David shoved back the bike's kickstand with the heel of his boot and jammed his key into the ignition.

"There's a meeting tonight. Come here once you're finished."

"Anything else?" David asked.

Damon hesitated before he said, "You know I don't agree with your theory that there are going to be more murders, but O'Reilly said to tell you the family had an infant."

"Shit." Without another word, David hung up the phone.

He turned the ignition key, and the engine rumbled to life. Within moments he was zooming through the streets, cutting in and out of traffic. He needed to get there—and fast.

This night was going great. One dead body was bad enough, and now he had another possession and a bitch-fest meeting to boot. Somehow he doubted things were going to get any better.

He didn't care what the other members of the Execution Underground said or that Damon didn't support his theory; something big was about to go down with the demons in Rochester, and he was determined to find out what that was. It had been two weeks since the infant girl's murder, and he'd been expecting more to come. Since he'd found the victim, Rochester's demons had been quiet—way too quiet for his comfort. He'd never seen such a drop in demonic activity in all the years he'd been hunting. Since the decline in possessions, a feeling of dread had been slowly building inside him. Something in his gut told him these past two weeks had been the calm before the storm.

Beyond the sheer horror of the baby's death, something just wasn't right about the situation. Demons rode humans like disposable cattle, but they didn't kill them for sport. They used them for pleasure, to get their rocks off and escape the hellfire for a while, and if the human happened to die in the process of their twisted games, so be it. But they didn't set out to kill normal humans, and there was no way a demon would have a good ol' time possessing a sixth-month-old baby. The little girl's death was more than collateral damage. Demons were sick dipshits to begin with, but it took a special kind of evil to kill an infant.

Initially, he'd had no leads on the case. During an examination of the infant's corpse, he'd found little indication of what type of demon had orchestrated the murder, let alone its motivation. Demons left messes behind them, but this one hadn't. That set off more red warning flags than heroin track marks on a cheap hooker. Those warning signs told him one thing: something bad was about to go down. His best guess had been an Abyzu. The awful little shits were known for preying on infants, using their life force for energy and power. But Abyzu's, who *did* set out to kill, weren't common—at least not since the decline of so-called SIDS.

The whole case was a mess. No evidence, no indication of what was to come, just a dreaded gut feeling things were about to become even messier.

Chapter 3

Within fifteen minutes David reached the address. Shutting off the ignition and setting the kickstand, he parked his bike on the street several houses away. He quickly jogged toward the house, ignoring the shooting pain coursing through his leg.

As he crept up the porch steps, the hairs on his arms and the back of his neck stood on end. His senses heightened, he listened for the sound of screams or yelling from behind the door. Nothing.

He breathed deep, preparing himself, then froze. The smell of rotten eggs hit his nose, and he swore under his breath. David knew that smell.

Sulfur.

Without hesitation, he slammed into the front door

with his full weight. It caved in after two hits from his two-hundred-plus-pound frame. Thank God for flimsy locks and no dead bolts. When his leg still functioned well, one kick would've done the trick. He frowned at that thought. As he stepped through the broken doorway, he pulled his gun and cocked the hammer, preparing to shoot. He was *so* ready to try out those new bullets. Holy-water-filled bullets wouldn't kill a demon, but they would definitely slow it down for a few moments, and that was all he needed.

He listened intently, trying to get a sense of where the demon was.

After a quick scan of the ground floor, he called out, "Is anyone home?"

An eerie silence answered. The quiet was too absolute. No sounds of talking or movement. His stomach dropped, and something inside told him he wasn't searching for a demon anymore. He was searching for its victims. Its dead victims.

He charged up the stairs. Agony seared through his leg as he climbed the steps faster than his pain-in-the-ass physical therapist would have approved of, but he wouldn't allow that to hold him back. Not again. Three bedrooms to scan. Slowly he pushed open the door to the first and stepped inside. From the size and décor, definitely the master bedroom, probably where the wife, who'd called Father O'Reilly, and her husband slept. Unlike the rest of the pristinely organized room, the comforter and bedsheets lay in a twisted bundle, as if someone had shoved them off in a rush to jump out of bed. Otherwise, no signs of anything out of the ordinary. But there was no way he had the wrong house, not with the sulfur he smelled. Even old rotting Easter eggs that the kids hadn't found for months didn't smell that potent.

He moved to the next bedroom, gun still drawn. He peeked inside: the room of a teenage boy. Sports memorabilia and a game system, but nothing unusual, just another messy bed. Turning toward the last room at the end of the hall, David stared at the open doorway. A shiver ran down his spine. Most people would have run in the other direction. It didn't matter what dumbasses movies made the average citizen look like; in the real world, when people felt threatened, they ran, which honestly was the smartest thing to do. Instincts served a good purpose. But it was David's job not to run.

With a deep breath, he stepped inside. Immediately he lowered his gun. He was standing inside a baby's nursery. He turned on the light and blinked rapidly as his eyes adjusted to the sudden brightness. From the pale pink molding on the white-painted walls and the small onesies lying in a neatly folded pile on a changing table near the crib, he could tell the room was meant for a baby girl. His stomach twisted into knots.

Not again. Dear God, not another baby.

Adrenaline coursed through him, and he fought back panic. He needed to find her, find the whole family, but to do so he needed to stay calm, collected, no matter how much the situation primed him to leap into action.

Where was this family? No signs of a struggle, yet they weren't here, and the disarray of their beds in comparison to the rest of the immaculately clean house suggested they hadn't planned on leaving. No, David could tell something had woken them and forced them out of their beds.

Tucking his gun back into its holster at his hip, he limped over to the baby's crib and peered inside. A single bloodied thumbprint dirtied the white-painted wood. Shit.

As quickly as he could manage, he jogged down the stairs. There had to be something he'd missed. He stopped as he reached the bottom of the staircase. Light shone faintly underneath the door of what he'd initially thought was a closet. He wrenched the door open.

Carpeted stairs descended down into a basement.

Several drops of blood stained the tan carpeting. One painful step at a time, David negotiated the stairway. His heart thumped against his chest. The sound rang in his ears in the silence.

Though he'd known as soon as he reached the porch steps that something was wrong, nothing could have prepared him for the sight before him. A large lump crawled into his throat as he surveyed the gore-covered scene. The basement looked as if someone had taken the contents of an entire blood bank and used them to set off an explosion with a messy homemade bomb. Blood soaked the walls, ceiling and floor, seeping into the carpeting.

The whole family…slaughtered.

David stood for several long moments, surveying the scene. There was something not right about this on so many levels. Demons were assholes, and they loved to use humans and leave them for dead, but this? The carnage in front of him made the victims Robert had left in his wake look as if they'd died in their sleep. But the lingering smell of sulfur mixed with the overpowering odor of freshly spilled blood told David he wasn't imagining things. This was demons' work.

If someone had told him that a demon had murdered an entire family in cold blood, he wouldn't have believed it. He scanned each of the family members. The mother lay slumped against the corner of the far wall, her throat slit. Blood covered the front of her nightgown. Her mouth remained open, and her lifeless eyes stared upward to where her attacker would have stood. The cell phone she must have used to call Father O'Reilly sat a foot away from her outreached hand, the screen covered in cracks like spiderwebs.

Across from the wife, her husband lay facedown on the floor, the murder weapon still clutched in his hand after he'd slit his own throat. The wife had been right. From the looks of the scene, the demon had possessed her husband, who'd murdered her and their children before he'd turned the knife on himself.

A sharp pang of sadness hit David in the heart at the sight of the couple's teenage son. A gaping hole in the middle of his chest showed the brutality of what the demon had done to him. The sulfur-sucking monster had slung the kid's intestines around his corpse as if they were nothing more than sausage links. This had to be the most sickening scene he had ever laid eyes on, and he had seen some seriously messed-up shit during the year he'd served in the Brooklyn division.

The next thought that came to his mind made him cringe. Where was the baby?

Cautiously, David rounded the staircase to another section of the basement. His stomach flipped. Bile rose in his throat and burned his esophagus. He ran to the nearest trash bin and hurled the contents of his stomach into the small plastic bag. He didn't have a weak stomach by any stretch of the imagination, but even he couldn't handle the sight of what had been done to the once beautiful infant girl. He blinked back tears on the family's behalf.

A dangerous mixture of sadness and pure unadulterated rage rushed through him. He would find the demonic piece of shit that did this. He would find the bastard and painfully torture it for days, weeks, until it was begging to be put out of its misery. Then he would do more than send it back to hell, where it had the potential to crawl its way out again decades later. He would find some sort of spell, some ritual, something to ensure it was tortured in the most painful way possible for the rest of eternity.

David stood in the middle of the basement amidst the dead bodies and the lingering smell of sulfur mixed with the metallic scent of the family's blood. With robotic movements, he removed his phone and snapped photos of the crime scene for HQ to process and analyze. One step at a time.

He would get the job done, just like he always did, and each time he emerged as a stronger, better hunter... and less of a human being. A normal person wouldn't have been able to handle seeing something like this and still function. And that was exactly the problem: he could.

Every Fae sense Allsún possessed blazed to life when the cabbie finally turned the corner on to the correct street. Immediately she knew they were in the right place, the exact house. Her Fae senses rang like a sounding school bell, alerting her that she had reached her destination. Peering out the front window of the cab, she eyed the broken-in front door. She leaned forward from the backseat. "Stop here," she said to the driver.

The cabbie had barely braked to a smooth stop before Allsún darted from the car, practically leaping from the vehicle. She burst into a full-on sprint toward the house as the cabbie drove away.

Shite. Was she too late?

As she neared the threshold, the rotten scent of sulfur assaulted her nose. She ran inside, hands up and prepared to blast any demons she encountered with a burst of faerie dust. The place reeked of demonic activity, and she could practically feel the power seeping out from the basement. Were the demons still down there?

She padded lightly down the steps, careful not to make noise. Her stomach flipped as she reached the bottom of the stairs and took in the sight before her. She couldn't even gasp, couldn't yell, couldn't scream, couldn't cry. Her heart thumped against her ribs, and a wave of anxiety washed over her. She was in way over her head.

She had seen demons do some horrific things in the years she had spent freelance hunting alongside David before he joined the Execution Underground, but nothing she had ever seen then remotely compared to the carnage that lay before her now.

A shiver rushed down her spine at the thought of what kind of creature could have done this, and then she froze as a small click sounded from behind her. The click of a handgun's hammer.

Chapter 4

David had been waiting all night to test these new bullets, and finally he was being given a chance. He held the Beretta steady, pointing it at the base of the woman's skull. His voice came out in a low, aggressive rumble. "Don't move."

She froze.

He gave one slow deliberate nod as he told her, "Good. Now—slowly—raise your arms."

Moving carefully, she did as she was told and lifted her hands from her sides, fingers spread so he could see she had no weapons. Holding the Beretta in his right hand, he quickly used his left hand and frisked her, patting down the thin material covering her.

"What's your name?" He eyed her up and down.

From behind, all he could see was her long curled brown hair. She wore a hospital johnny coat that opened in the back, exposing just the thinnest peek of a round, firm ass. Wait a second. He knew that gorgeous hair and that sweet behind all too well. What the—

Her voice shook as she spoke. "David?"

His heart came to a screeching halt before starting to thump double-time in his chest. The blood pounded in his head. He knew that voice, but…no. It couldn't be.

She shifted, and the robe moved ever so slightly to reveal a small orange freckle right above the curve of her butt. He knew that freckle. He had run his fingers over it so many times as they made love. Incredibly sexy and perfectly adorable all at the same time.

It couldn't be…but she *was* in a hospital gown.

After a long moment, he finally managed to choke out her name. "Allsún?"

She lowered her hands to her sides again and turned around.

David's eyes widened, and for a moment he forgot to breathe. He took in the familiar contours of her beautiful face. Large green eyes the color of the Irish countryside, full pink lips, high cheekbones and a small button nose that made him want to kiss every inch of her. Man, seeing her alive and well was a relief beyond anything he'd known before. She had lost weight in her already slender face and body during her time in the hospital, but aside from the minor detail, she was as perfect and divine in her beauty as she had always been when they were together. The kind of beauty most women envied. Allsún didn't need makeup to enhance her looks. She had a natural aura about her, the kind that couldn't be replicated.

A wide grin spread across his face, and at the sight of her, all the horrors surrounding him melted away. His heart continued to pound. He couldn't believe what he was seeing. There she was, alive and healthy. Weeks had passed since he'd last seen her that way, and even then it had only been for a handful of minutes. It was hard to believe that five years had passed since they'd broken off their engagement. There were times when the wounds of her leaving still felt fresh. Hell, he would be lying to himself if he said he was anything but lonely without her around.

"Hey, gorgeous," he said.

Allsún opened her mouth as if she wanted to speak, only to close it seconds later. She didn't say a word. Instead, she ran.

Shit.

She bolted up the stairs faster than David would have

thought possible. Throwing aside any concern for his injured leg, he raced up the steps after her. How the hell could she move so fast? She'd just come out of a trauma-induced coma, and she'd been drugged on top of it, for Pete's sake. Then again, when *didn't* Allsún surprise him? Hell, he sure as shit hadn't expected her to show up in the middle of the crime scene, still in full patient garb. Only two hours ago he'd been sitting at her bedside while she rested peacefully.

Though Allsún was fast and he was hurt, his legs were still significantly longer than hers. He reached her just as she was about to rush straight out the front door. Grabbing her from behind, he circled his arms around her waist, lifting her clean off the ground.

She struggled against him, feet kicking wildly and hands shoving against his hold. "Let me go!" she shrieked.

David hauled her back into the house, closing the broken door behind him.

Allsún beat her fists against his grip, her words in rhythm with each blow. "Let. Me. Go."

David fought back a laugh. She was so tiny compared to him and always had been. Did she really think that would work? "Are you kidding me? You wake up from a coma after being tortured, then you show up at a crime scene littered with bodies, and you expect me to just let you run off?"

She tried elbowing him in the shoulder. "Yes."

"Don't be ridiculous, Allie. You're not going anywhere. How the hell do I know if your sanity is even intact?"

"I'm perfectly fine." She pushed against him, grunting as she fought to break his hold.

But no matter how powerful her Fae powers were, she would never match him in the strength department. Their difference in size alone was enough to give him an unfailing advantage.

Loosening his hold, he quickly rotated her to face him. She weighed so little, even less than she used to.

"Let me go." She kicked hard and caught him straight in the shin. Holy shit, that stung. He bit his lower lip and fought back a curse. Allsún had never had much in upper body strength, but, man, did she have loads of power in her legs. Holding her out in front of him, he walked over to the wall, then pinned his body against hers, holding her in place with his weight so she couldn't kick him.

But now he had other problems. Shit, if the feel of her body against his wasn't enough to undo him completely. His cock stiffened as her hips pressed against him. He wanted to kiss her hard and deep, slide his hands down to truly remember the feeling of her body.

No. He couldn't do that. She didn't want him like that, not anymore.

"Let me go," she said again.

He held on to her tight. It didn't take much for him to subdue her, and frankly, he wanted to keep her pressed against him forever. "I'm not letting you go until you agree not to run off."

She continued to shove against him. "I won't make any promises."

When he didn't release her, her sweet face twisted into a scowl, and he knew what she was gearing up to do—what she always did when she was beyond pissed at him. Use his full name.

She inhaled a sharp breath, and as she spoke she punctuated each of her words with pure irritation. "David Jonathan Matthew Aronowitz, you let me down this instant or I swear I'll—"

"Allsún, you need to listen to me. This is really important," he interrupted her.

Refusing to listen, she continued to scowl at him, and he knew her stubborn side had set in. If he didn't cave, at least a little, she would keep going for hours, and if he got her pissed off enough, boy, would he regret it. Allsún might be only half-Fae, but that half was of pixie heritage, and while pixies were sweet little things most of the time, you really didn't want to piss them off. Allsún held true to that rule.

Slowly he loosened his hold, allowing her body to slide down the wall until her feet touched the floor. But he didn't release her completely, just enough to placate her temper.

The scowl faded slightly. "I can't stay here, David. I came to help that family, and you know I'm all for saving live victims, but the dead ones are your thing, so since you have this covered, I really need to go and get out of this hospital gown."

No way was he letting her go when there were demons out there who knew what she really was. "Allie, listen to me. We need to talk."

Turning her head away, she refused to look at him. "There's nothing for us to talk about."

He scoffed. "Really? Nothing? How about the fact that you've been in a coma the last month, and now you're suddenly awake and at a crime scene? How the hell did you get here? How did you get out of the hospital? Jace was heading to the hospital to watch over you as soon as I left."

Finally she met his gaze again. "No one was there but

me when I woke up, so I just left, okay? All of a sudden I woke up. I was lying in a hospital bed, connected to an IV, and when I woke up I didn't want to be there anymore, so I took the IV out and I left."

David stared at her for a long moment. She wasn't serious, was she? "So you woke up, pulled out your IV, decided 'I don't really need to be here,' and then walked out in a hospital gown into the freezing cold Rochester night and decided to follow me to a crime scene? Why wouldn't you wait for clearance from a doctor to make sure you were okay?"

She ignored his last question. "Followed you? I didn't have any idea you would be here, okay? I woke up, and I had one of my feelings. I knew that somebody in the area was in trouble, that they were having problems with demons. I listened to my senses. I flagged down a cab, and I got a ride here. I didn't expect you to be here, that's for certain. If I had, I wouldn't have come."

"I'm the only demon hunter in the city, and you didn't expect me to be here?"

She flashed him a look that said don't-be-an-asshole.

David's eyes widened, and he stared at her in disbelief. Clearly she hadn't thought a single bit of this through. All the more reason she needed to stay with him. She needed time for her head to clear. "Last I knew, you weren't hunting demons. What happened to that?"

She frowned. "I haven't been hunting demons, okay? I haven't been hunting anything in the past five years, but when I woke up, this feeling of someone being in danger overcame me and I couldn't ignore it. I've never felt a pull so strong. I knew I had to track it to the source, and my senses led me here."

"What exactly were you expecting to do when you got here? Single-handedly take down a demon with no weapons and protected by nothing but a hospital gown?" he asked.

He loosened his hold enough for her to wiggle free. As soon as she left his arms, he missed the feel of her body pressed against him. He grabbed her hand to keep her from leaving, but she wrenched away from him.

"I hadn't thought that far through it, okay? Get off my case. What does it matter to you, anyway?"

David's jaw dropped. "What does it matter to me? *I'm* the one who's been stationed at your bedside nearly 24/7 since you were hospitalized. *I'm* the one who carried you out of that awful warehouse where Robert tortured you. You *do* remember that, right?"

She met his stare. "There's no way I could forget that, even though I want to."

A lull fell between them. There were so many things he wanted to say, but he wasn't even certain where to begin.

Allsún broke the silence first. "Once the drugs wore off, it all came back to me pretty fast."

David couldn't believe what he was hearing. She'd simply snapped out of her coma? That was it? On the very night he'd found out that her life was in danger?

No. It was too coincidental. Her senses were clearly trying to tell her something.

Allsún dropped her hands to her sides in exasperation. "Look, I get that it was dumb, okay? And I can clearly see that I'm not needed here. The carnage that's down there—" her eyes flicked to the staircase leading down to the basement "—well, you can take care of that. Now that you have the Execution Underground on your side with all their fancy equipment, I'm sure that sort of thing is no problem for you."

He could hear the slight contempt in her voice at the mention of the Execution Underground. Did it really still piss her off after all these years? She'd left him after he joined the Execution Underground. She hadn't approved of him signing on. Not that he could really blame her. Hell, he should've considered her feelings more back then. He knew that now. He'd been young, naïve and so ready to save the world that he'd failed her in the process. For the first year, every day without her had been worse than the last. He tried to tell himself that things had improved since then, that he wasn't constantly longing for her to be by his side, and that he was really okay, but who was he kidding? Even being with her like this now was killing him. He shoved the feelings inside, boxing them away where they wouldn't be so painful. He couldn't allow himself to go down that road.

She wrenched her eyes away from the stairs and spoke again. "Anyway, I'm out of here," she said. She moved toward the door.

David stepped in front of her. "I can't let you do that."

She crossed her arms over her chest. "Why not?"

"Because I need to watch over you."

She scoffed. "I'm perfectly capable of taking care of myself. In case you hadn't noticed, I wasn't kidnapped by a psychotic killer until you and Jace barged into Frankie's pack. Before that I was fine."

He winced. He knew it was his fault. He knew that before he and Jace had shown up at K9's, the club run by Frankie Amato, Rochester werewolf packmaster and Jace's girlfriend, Allsún had just been hanging out with the werewolves. He had brought Robert into her life. She didn't need to point that out to him. "Yeah, I know it was my fault, but that's all the more reason I need to keep you protected now. I know you've always been capable, but give yourself at least a few days to recover from what you've been through, Allsún. Allow me to watch over you."

She tried to move around him, but whatever way she turned, he blocked her path. "I don't need you to watch over me. Robert's dead, right? If I remember correctly, Jace killed him."

David nodded. "Yeah, Jace killed him."

The tense muscles in her shoulders relaxed. "Good. Then, as far as I'm concerned, I'm perfectly safe."

Without warning, she ducked underneath his arm and started to walk out of his life yet again.

"A few days ago a demon possessed your psychiatrist."

Allsún froze. She lingered in the doorway for a moment as if she couldn't decide whether she wanted to leave or not. Finally she turned around. "You have my attention now," she said.

Relief washed over David. Maybe he could actually convince her to stay. "I went after that demon tonight."

Allsún wrapped her arms around her body as if she

was trying to hold herself together while she listened to him speak. "And?"

His face hardened at the thought of that demonic piece of shit threatening Allsún. "And I killed him."

"Good," she said. She turned to leave again.

"But it knew about you, Allie. It knew you're the last Fae outside the Isle of Apples."

Allsún turned back toward him. He could see in her eyes that she realized the ramifications of the news he'd just told her. If that demon had told even one other demon about her—and according to the doctor, it had told far more than one—the word would spread amongst them.

As the natural enemy of the demons, the Fae had been engaged in a constant war with them for centuries. But not long before David and Allsún separated, there had been a mass movement of Fae back to the Isle of Apples, an alternate dimension inhabited exclusively by the Fae, a completely different world. Since then David had done plenty of searching, and as far as he could tell, all the full-blooded Fae were gone, and Allsún was the only remaining half-breed outside the Isle. When she stopped hunting, she had gone undetected by the demons. Now that the demons knew she was still here, they would all be gunning for her.

A slight note of panic crept into her voice. "B-but I'm only a half-breed. He must have realized that I—"

"Allie," he said, cutting her off before she could get herself worked into a tizzy, "you know that doesn't make a difference to demons. You're a faerie all the same. You're still their enemy. Plus, you don't think it's strange that on all the nights you could have woken up, this was the one? I don't know about you, but that's a little too coincidental for my tastes."

"Shite." Allsún swore under her breath. The slightest bit of her mother's Irish accent crept into her voice. That always happened when she was upset. "What do I do now?"

He stepped forward again. He was barely a foot away from her. He towered over her small frame and scanned the length of her body. She was hardly covered in the hospital gown, and being this close to her still electrified him. His desire for her came rushing back, though he was certain it had never truly left. God, how he'd missed her.

"Stay with me. Allow me to protect you." He said the words as if the situation were only temporary, only until they could find a way to get her off the demons' radar again, but deep down he wanted so much more. Being so near her when he knew she didn't want him anymore was the sweetest form of torture—painful and divine all at once.

She shook her head. "You know I can't do that, David."

"Why not?"

She glanced at the floor, refusing to meet his gaze. "Because forgive me if I'm the only person in the world who doesn't want to spend time with my ex-fiancé."

Damn. That stung. His face remained calm on the surface, but inside he wanted to scream in agony. He was tormented by so many emotions he couldn't let out. He wanted to say that he didn't have to be an ex-fiancé, that nothing in the world would make him happier than getting back together with her again, but instead he settled for, "You know it's necessary, at least for a few days until you're back to normal again and can fight off demons on your own."

"Fine," she said. "But I want to make it clear that this is *not* a chance to mend things between us."

A sharp pain hit him straight in the heart, but he held on to his poker face.

When he didn't respond, she continued. "I assume that's not what you're going for here, but let's both be adult enough to agree beforehand that dredging up our past is only going to make both of us miserable.

So, if I stay with you for the next few days, just until I'm on my feet again and we've figured this situation out, we'll agree to be just friends and nothing more, okay?"

She stuck out her hand to shake on it. He stared at her and couldn't help but wonder how they'd gotten to this point. How had their relationship gone so wrong? They'd grown up together, been friends since they were young.

It was the summer in between David's junior and senior years in high school that changed everything. Allsún had been away all summer in Ireland with her mother, while David had spent his free time acting like an idiot and getting into trouble with Jace, who was home for a brief summer break from training with the Execution Underground. Once Jace had shipped off again, the rest of David's summer was spent watching too many bad cartoons. With Allsún not scheduled to return until the day before school began, David had anticipated the first day of class like a starving man staring at a juicy hamburger. He had never been a book-worm, much less enjoyed school, but Allsún had gotten him into reading, which was the extent of his interest in learning. His excitement for that first day of classes had been solely because of the chance to see Allsún again. He had counted down the days all summer long until he could tell her his thoughts on the books she had left him to read.

But all of that had been blown to hell as soon as he saw her.

The once gangly Allsún who wore glasses a little too large for her face and a retainer, and possessed an unruly amount of curly, slightly frizzy hair, had blossomed into the gorgeous girl who every guy in high school wanted. Over the summer she had filled out in all the right places. Her hips had widened, and her formerly nonexistent breasts had developed and then some. She'd ditched her retainer, giving her the perfect smile, and her mother had finally caved and bought her contacts. Even her once-crazy curls had now fallen in smooth, perfect ringlets without a hair out of place.

Whatever was in the water in Ireland, David was a major fan.

Really, he hadn't been sure if he was seeing correctly at first. Hell, he'd always thought Allsún was beautiful, even despite all her geeky attributes, but she'd been transformed overnight from his best friend to the girl he couldn't stop thinking about.

Sure, even to this day he still felt a bit shallow that he wasn't interested in Allsún romantically until her inside and outside matched in beauty, but he had been a teenage boy then, and he knew now, as a full-grown man, that even in her nerdlike state he would have fallen in love with her.

When she'd walked into the hallway of Brighton High School after that summer, he'd dropped the three textbooks he was carrying, just like a total idiot.

A smile had blossomed across her face at the sight of him, and she'd thrown her backpack to the ground and run down the hallway to launch herself into his arms. "Hey, jerk. I've missed you."

It had taken him a minute to respond. He'd still been trying to process the fact that his best friend, someone he'd never been nervous around, was suddenly the one girl in school he wished he could take advantage of. Shit, that was so not good.

They'd danced back and forth in an overly flirtatious tango throughout the year. They would go from being comfortable with one another one minute to avoiding each other for days the next, because in some way the thought of wanting to kiss and touch the girl he had once considered to be like a sister made him sick to his stomach with anxiety. He hadn't wanted to hurt her, and he hadn't wanted a romance between them to mess up the friendship they'd shared for so long. But that friendship had already changed as soon as his attraction to her had made itself evident. He'd been certain Allsún had noticed the different way he looked at her.

He wished he could say that he'd swept her off her feet on prom night or something equally cheesy, like *Sixteen Candles* or all those other '80's movies that she loved to watch. But he hadn't shown up with a birthday cake at her house to declare his love, he hadn't ridden a lawnmower across her front lawn, held a blaring boom box outside her window, or any of the other ridiculous things that Allsún fawned over in those films.

One night, when she was at his grandmother's house for dinner and his grandmother had gone to bed, leaving the two of them alone, he'd just done it. Mid-sentence. Without any warning signs.

Allsún had been talking about how his grandmother had offered to teach her to cook, and before he knew what was happening, his hand had been on the back of her neck. He'd pulled her into his lap and was kissing her with so much force the world seemed to spin. She'd kissed him back, and that sealed the deal.

They'd never been "just friends" since.

He'd thought that year of school had been pure unadulterated torture—wanting her but being completely unable to make his move—but that would be nothing compared to the torture of being around her now. Because now he knew her in *every* way he possibly could, wanted her more than anything, loved her more than anything, knew how great it was to be with her, and he knew how much he wanted to stop boxing all that up and allow himself to go back to the way things had been when they were together.

Back then he hadn't known what he was missing, but now he knew *exactly* what he was missing—and the longing was going to kill him.

But he didn't care.

He would torture himself every day if it meant he was able to see her.

With as much fake enthusiasm as he could muster, he forced a smile on to his face and stuck his hand out to meet hers. They shook.

"Friends?" she asked.

He gritted his teeth. "Friends," he lied. "And nothing more."

Chapter 5

Friends? Friends? Why the hell did she have to label it like that? She had regretted the words as soon as they came out of her mouth, and David's willingness to agree had hit her like a sucker punch to the gut. She was fooling herself if she thought she could ever be "just friends" with David. She'd always cared for him, from the time she thought boys didn't have cooties anymore until she was old enough to realize her true feelings: that she loved him.

She ran her eyes over his frame. Towering over her at a whopping six foot six, with muscles that put most of the male population to shame, he was quite literally tall, dark and handsome, sporting the bad-boy look to boot in his leather Harley gear. His deep brown eyes were so close to black she could almost drown in their darkness, and the feel of his large masculine hands holding her moments earlier was as divine as it had ever been. Heat rushed between her legs as she thought of all the things he could do with those hands.

No. She shook her head to shove the thoughts away as the handshake ended. She didn't love him, not anymore. She had moved on from that chapter in her life, left all the memories, both the good and the bad, behind her. She did not love David. She didn't even know David anymore. Until they'd recently met again, it had been years since they'd last seen each other for any extended period of time, much less spoken to one another. Her gaze traced over his sharply defined features, his prominent cheekbones and jawline. She was forced to admit to herself that David was like a fine bottle of top shelf whiskey that only got better and better with age.

A sudden feeling of self-conscious awareness hit her hard. She doubted he was thinking the same thing about her. She glanced down at herself, unable to ignore her appearance. A hospital gown wasn't flattering on anyone, and from the lovely breeze she was getting back there, she was certain that her behind was bared for anyone's viewing pleasure. And her curls probably hadn't been combed through in ages.

But there she was, standing in front of David looking like something one of her cats had digested and then hacked up all over her brand new carpet. She knew she shouldn't care, but somewhere a part of her still hoped that David was the same man she'd once planned to marry. The one who would take care of her when she had the flu or comfort her when she was sick, and tell her she was beautiful all the same. He thought he'd been seeing her at her worst then, but damn if she wasn't vain enough to have put on just a touch of makeup every time before he'd come over.

Pulling his cell phone from his pocket, David began to text a message. "Let's get you to my place and cleaned up as soon as possible."

"Who are you texting?" she asked.

"Jace. He's been blowing up my phone with calls for the last twenty minutes, probably wondering why you weren't at the hospital when he showed up, and someone needs to watch over you while I finish up here. He can take you back to my apartment."

"Wait a second. I agreed to stay *with you,* not to be kept under lock and key."

"I don't want you to get another look at what's down in that basement."

She rolled her eyes. She wasn't some fragile china

doll that was easily broken, and he knew that. "It's dead bodies, David. I've seen them before."

"You didn't see what was around the other corner, and believe me, Allie, you don't want to see it."

She crossed her arms. "I've seen some pretty gruesome things over the years, David, and you know it. I doubt there could be anything down there that I haven't seen worse. Remember when that Imp decided to prey on teenage girls?"

A grim look crossed his face. "It's worse than that."

Allsún's eyes widened. She wasn't certain she could imagine anything worse. She wasn't weak, but she couldn't detach herself from the victims the way David could. She had spent hours crying once that case was over with. It didn't matter that they'd earned justice for the victims. The pain of the victims' loved ones and their horribly unfair deaths was still with her.

"David, whatever it is, after everything with Robert, I'm sure I can handle it." No matter her feelings, she wasn't about to let him baby her. The sooner she could prove to him that she was strong, fully recovered both mentally and physically, the better. She needed to get the hell out of there as soon as possible.

David shook his head. "Allie, I know you, and believe me when I say you can't handle this one. We both know you're one tough chick, so you don't need to prove it to me. Not this time."

"Fine. If you're not going to let me help and just plan to keep me...keep me prisoner, then I'm leaving."

She needed to get out of here and away from him anyway. She shifted to move past him, but he grabbed hold of her wrist. Another wave of electric power shot through her, straight to her heart and the growing warmth between her legs. The energy that flew between them just from his touch was mind-blowing and sexy and a massive reminder of everything they'd once shared. She could have sworn that from the brief look of shock in David's eyes that he felt it, too.

She forced herself to pull her wrist away and fixed him with a stern glare—the same stern look that had always let him know that he was pushing the envelope with her, and if he kept it up, he would regret it when her anger peaked.

They both knew that hell hath no fury like a pixie pissed off. The last thing she needed was the heartache he still brought her, even all these years later.

David let out a long sigh and tried to renegotiate. "The point is that you shouldn't be here. You need to be resting. You need to be healing."

"I've been healing for a month, David. I feel fine

now that the drugs are wearing off. All my injuries from Robert are gone." She cringed a little as she said his name. The thought of what Robert had done to her still haunted her. "Besides, I want to get to the bottom of all this, too. I want to know why I was drawn here."

The pain in his face pierced through her. She saw the guilt he felt written all over him.

He pressed his lips together until they formed a thin line before he sighed. "If you want to stay, then fine, but you're not leaving my sight. I'm not letting anything happen to you. Not again."

David stared down at Allsún with resolve in his eyes. He had agreed to let her stay with him, but he still didn't want her to see the atrocities in the basement. After all she'd been through, she didn't need something like that seared into her memory.

The buzz of his phone interrupted their argument. She turned away from him as he pulled out his cell. Jace's name flashed across the screen.

He hit the talk button. "Yeah?"

"So I have something to tell you that you're not gonna be happy to hear." Jace delivered the words slowly, as if he wasn't certain he wanted to say them. "Frankie and I are at the hospital, and…Allsún's not here."

David eyed Allsún as she paced anxiously around the foyer. "Yeah, I know, J. She showed up here—at the crime scene."

A string of profanities sounded from the other line. "And you couldn't have fucking called to tell me that? Frankie and I were scared shitless that a demon had gotten to her before we did. I've been calling you repeatedly."

"Sorry. She just now showed up."

"Well, that's a fucking relief. Aside from that, did you find anything?" Jace asked.

David bit his lower lip. He'd found something, all right. Something not fit for human eyes, something so evil it made his stomach churn and his heart hurt. "Yeah, I found something. I'll tell you about it at the meeting."

Silence answered from the other end of the line. David could tell Jace was waiting for an explanation.

"J, I'm sorry, man. I can't even… This is just so evil. I'll tell you when I get there."

The images of what lay one level beneath his boots flashed through his mind. Those poor people.

"I'll see you at the meeting, then. Get the job done, David. For their sake."

David nodded. "Yeah."

With a small click, the line went dead.

Allsún stopped pacing and faced him again, arms crossed over her chest. "So, are you going to tell me what else is down there or keep me in the dark?"

"You don't want to know what's down there, Allsún."

"If I'm going to help you, I—"

He held up a hand. "Who said anything about you helping me?"

With a frown, she pointed to herself. "I did. If you refuse to let me leave your side, then you're going to let me work the case with you."

"I can't let you do that. This is different than usual."

"How different can it be, David?"

He shook his head. He knew Allsún, and he understood completely why she wanted to be a part of this. Back in the day, she had been amazing at hunting demons. They'd partnered together and had been damn near unstoppable, between her Fae power and his exorcist abilities, but that had been before he was a member of the Execution Underground, before Allsún decided she didn't want to live a hunter's lifestyle anymore. "Allsún, the demon massacred this family. You know that's not typical."

"It's not typical for me to have premonitions about upcoming demon activity, either, not since I quit hunting. But somehow, in this case, I did—to the point that it woke me up from a drug-induced coma. That means I'm supposed to be involved somehow. If you were in my position, you'd want to be involved, too."

She had a point with that one. He would definitely want to be a part of the investigation. Well, "want" was the wrong word. No one *wanted* to be involved with demons, but they did so because they needed to, because they felt it was their duty. Allsún had given up that duty long ago.

"What happened to 'It can be somebody else's job'? You told me that it wasn't my duty to protect people from demons, despite the fact that I was born with this gift. Now, just because you have a feeling, that means that you're meant to do this? You're being a hypocrite."

"Quit dredging up the past." Allsún pushed past him and marched down the stairs before he could stop her. When she reached the bottom she turned and surveyed the side of the basement that had been blocked from her view before. David heard her breath escape in one large gasp. Shit.

His bad leg burning at every step, he hurried down the stairs as fast as he could.

As he reached her side, he saw that tears were rolling down her cheeks. He wrapped his arm around her and pulled her close to him. Though the sight of her tears made him ache inside, he relished the feel of her in his arms. God, he had missed holding her like this, being this close to her. They stood together for a few moments before she pulled back, wiping vigorously to erase the streaks from her tears.

He cleared his throat. "I told you it was a horror show."

Horror show. Talk about a massive understatement. The things the demons had done to the humans before their deaths were sick and despicable, twisted. Only pure evil could have been responsible for something like that. Anyone with an ounce, even a shred, of humanity, would have shown at least some mercy.

She looked toward him. The barest quiver still shook her lip. "So, what do we do now?" She was fighting to get hold of herself. He could see her face visibly change as she transitioned into work mode.

She took a deep, steadying breath. "Back when it was me and you, we would have taken the evidence we needed, called the cops and then continued the investigation ourselves, but…you know. Now that you're part of the Execution Underground and all…"

"Similar protocol," David said. "We take photos of the crime scene that will be processed and sent off to

Headquarters, if necessary, but in the meantime the Rochester division begins the investigation. We need to be quick, though. We'll take the samples and leave. We don't want to hang around in case a neighbor heard something and contacted the cops."

"I doubt they've been called, since they haven't shown up yet." She lifted her shoulders in a small shrug. "So, once you gather the evidence, then what? Do you take me to your meeting place, too?"

"Yeah, and I debrief the rest of the hunters."

Her nose wrinkled in disgust. "The rest of the hunters? How many of them are there? Jace and you make two, obviously."

He'd forgotten her bias against hunters. While Allsún was all for hunting demons, her natural enemy, as a supernatural creature herself, she was wary of the Execution Underground and its policies. That was one of the many reasons why she hadn't wanted him to join. "There are six total, me included."

Allsún's eyes widened slightly, as if she couldn't believe what she was hearing. "I wasn't surprised to find out Jace is one of you. I knew you two would eventually find your way on to the same team, or whatever your unit is called. I know he played a part in getting you to enlist."

"Don't be bitter toward Jace. It's not his fault I joined the Execution Underground."

"He and Frankie are together now, right?"

He nodded. "Yeah, they're together."

Allsún nodded in return. "Good. I'm glad he's making her happy. Frankie has been a good friend to me." She paused, carefully considering her next words. "I don't feel any resentment toward Jace. It's been…what? Five years now."

He opened his mouth to tell her exactly how many years, months and days it had been, but she lifted her hand to silence him. "Don't give me the exact count. Just get your evidence. I don't know how much longer I can stand to be here. These poor people."

He closed his mouth and swallowed down the words he'd been about to say.

David scanned the scene. He wasn't even sure where to start. As awful as the thoughts would be, he needed to re-create the events in his head. The way in which the demon had carried out the murders might give him some insight into its sick motivations. Part of him felt it would be like reading tea leaves—trying to understand remorseless violence was hardly ever fruitful—but on the off chance that something, anything, might give him a hint that would help him catch this murderous hell-crawler, he needed to do this.

According to the information Father O'Reilly had relayed to Damon, the mother had called, claiming that her husband had been possessed by a demon. David walked over to the corner of the basement where the woman's body slumped against the wall. The cell phone with the cracked screen lying a few feet from her hand was evidence of the truth of that assumption. The husband had died last. From the knife lying in his hand, it was clear the demon had made the man slit his own throat, then undoubtedly hightailed it in untraceable spirit form to the nearest human it could possess. He would put his bet on one of the family's poor next-door neighbors being its latest suit of flesh. Thankfully demons never changed hosts unless they had to. The process weakened them and was painful as hell. In a way, they were like a parasite that grew attached to its host, never wanting to let go.

Knowing the way the parents had died was helpful, but in what order had the children been killed, and was there any significance to that? And why *this* specific family?

His eyes darted from the disgusting atrocity on the other side of the basement to the teenage boy spilled across the floor. From the things that had been done to the infant, he could tell that she had been the demon's main focus. The innocence of the child was clearly an important part of the demon's plan. What else could draw a demon to a child that way? He stood and crossed the room, though it took everything he had in him not to toss the remaining contents of his stomach into the garbage bin again. In fact, he would need to find a way to dispose of that evidence so he didn't leave his DNA at the crime scene.

Eyeing the surrounding area, he paused when a glimpse of red caught his gaze. A small spot of blood on the edge of a nearby chair. He moved closer to examine it. A small clump of blond hair was caught in the clotting fluid. Yes, this was what he was looking for. The mother was the only blond in the family, but she was several strides away. Crossing the room again, he pulled a handkerchief from his pocket. No gashes on her forehead, but no one else was blond. He quickly wrapped the fabric around his hand before slowly tilting her head, which fell forward with an awful flop in the way only dead weight can. He tried to ignore the anger he felt on her behalf and focus on the situation at hand.

Leaning forward, he examined the back of her head until—bingo. A bloodied gash on the back of her skull confirmed what he had suspected. Like any mother would instinctually do, she had tried to save her child. The horror of the scene flashed before his eyes. That poor woman, witnessing her husband doing those awful things to her sweet baby girl. The thought made him sick with pain for her, and he all too vividly imagined the sounds of her uncontrollable screams at the sight of her husband hurting her child. She would have tried to save her baby, but with its supernatural strength, the demon had undoubtedly shoved her away with ease, causing her to fall back and hit her head on the chair. But why not just kill her then, when she was trying to interfere? Her body and phone were on the other side of the room, with no smears of blood across the carpet leading to her to indicate she had died elsewhere and her body had been moved, so clearly the demon had chosen not to kill her right away? Why leave her alive?

Because the demon had *wanted* her to see….

The pieces of the puzzle fell together in his mind as he played his theory out step by step. But another question nagged at the back of his mind: Why had the woman thought her husband was possessed? Undoubtedly she hadn't wanted to think her husband was capable of such atrocious violence, but she had been so specific. She hadn't said he had gone mad or crazy. She'd said he was possessed, which meant the demon had done something to give away its identity. It wouldn't have shown its demonic red eyes unless she'd somehow managed to hurt it, which she wouldn't have been able to do unless she had holy water or a blessed relic at hand, which didn't seem likely, even though the family had been religious.

He thought back to all the crappy B-movies he had seen over the years, which had portrayed demons in some of the most absurd ways and most likely would have been the extent of this woman's knowledge of the demonic. What could the creature have done that would have…

The thought clicked into place. Latin. The demon must have been speaking Latin or some other dead language her husband wouldn't have known. That was one thing the films got right, and if the demon had been speaking Latin, that meant it had performed some sort of demonic ritual. That explained the desecrated state of the infant's body. The horror of the situation hit David like a punch straight to the balls.

The point of the demon's ritual hadn't been spilling blood, it had been creating fear. The demon had forced the mother—and the father, while he was possessed and unable to control his body—to watch the deaths of their two children so it could feed off their fear.

David shoved his anger down inside, balling it up in a way he was certain would kill him one of these days. He needed to remain focused. He had already taken photos of the crime scene. Now he needed samples to send off to the lab. If he could find some trace of sulfur the monster had left behind, forensics could analyze it and give him some idea of what type of demon fucker he would be torturing. He made quick work of taking the samples. After pulling the small lab kit from inside his leather jacket, he swabbed the victims' wounds and underneath their fingernails, and took samples of their hair, anything that could give him insight.

When he finished, he glanced one last time at the bodies.

Sickening, intense rage built inside him as he thought of the horror these poor people had gone through. He would find the demon piece of shit that had done this, and when he did, he would enjoy every moment of making it suffer.

Sammael poured the spilled blood across the altar, mumbling his incantations. The ancient symbols painted on the wall in front of him flared to a bright glowing orange at the sound of his words. Hellfire incarnate.

"Speak to me, Mistress," he purred.

A moment of silence passed before a sweet, satisfied hiss filled the room. His master was powerful enough that no words were needed. He could feel her presence intensifying. Her arrival was growing nearer and nearer.

Once Mistress was here, they would slaughter their enemies slowly, one by one, when their victims would least expect it. The Mistress would take on the little Fae bitch herself, and finally, after all these years, when the Mistress was done with the girl, he could rip her open and feed on her insides for the pure pleasure of it.

The pain on the exorcist's face would be priceless.

The exorcist would be angry at the loss of his love, and he would put up a fight, but they would win. David Aronowitz was powerful and deadly against most demons, himself included, though he hated to admit that, but the pathetic excuse for a hero would never be capable of taking on a being as great, as deadly, as the Mistress was.

A pity that the Mistress wanted the exorcist all to herself.

Sammael would have loved to do the deed himself—

slay the only mortal man who struck fear into the hearts of all the children of hell.

He remembered fondly the feeling of the family's pulses beating beneath his fingertips, their last few breaths before slipping into darkness, releasing their power to him. The sweet feeling of their deaths, and the terror in the eyes of the parents as they watched their children die, would be nothing compared to the rewards for doing his Mistress's bidding. He had been waiting, biding his time until the moment was right, and now the time was finally here. They would escape. They were *all* going to escape, and when the gates of hell opened, it would be chaotic paradise on earth.

A whisper of power filled the room, and the presence of his Mistress moved closer to the surface. He could feel her power beneath his feet.

And then he knew what he needed. Two more families. Only two more, and then the Mistress would be free to rise from hell.

Chapter 6

Only about a quarter of the way through their trip to David's division headquarters, Allsún was already certain there were icicles dangling from her nose and toes. Though he had given her his leather Harley jacket and removed the socks he wore underneath his massive motorcycle boots to cover her feet, she was hardly bundled up. As he phrased it, it was colder than a witch's tit outside. The winter wind whistled in her ears despite the slight cover of David's spare helmet. A shiver ran through her body as they rounded another corner, but this time it wasn't from the cold.

The image of that poor innocent baby wouldn't leave her mind. How could anyone, any *thing,* ever do something so cruel to a child? What had been done to the adults and the teen was disgusting and evil enough, but the baby…

She shook her head. She had never seen that kind of carnage at a crime scene. David was right. This was by far the worst she'd encountered, at least on scene. She couldn't imagine anything more terrifying. A knot tangled in her stomach and anxiety gripped her insides until a wave of nausea rolled through her.

No, that wasn't right. She *could* imagine something more terrifying, something she didn't need to imagine at all, but instead remembered. Something she couldn't bear to tell David. She inhaled a breath of crisp air in an attempt to calm her nerves. She would do whatever it took to help David. She didn't know if she could bear to see another innocent mother lose her child. Unintentionally, she clung more tightly to David's waist.

"You okay back there?" he yelled.

She leaned in close to his ear from where she sat behind him on the area David and other bikers referred to as the "pussy pad." She could have complained about how sexist the term was, but she knew she would be preaching to the choir when it came to David. She couldn't count how many times he had tried to convince her to get a bike of her own, so he could teach her to ride. But nerdy girls like her weren't meant to be badass biker babes. She didn't even like riding on the back without the "sissy bar," which she'd been grateful David had taken off his old Honda and installed on the new Super Glide, even though she knew it hadn't been intended for her use. She frowned. She didn't want to ponder exactly whose use it *had* been intended for.

"Yeah, I'm fine," she called over his shoulder.

Deep down, though, she was far from it.

She couldn't shake the awful images from her head. She knew from so many previous crime scenes that often the memories of the atrocities faded over time. But some things were just inescapable. She had experienced a few of those instances in her life—events so awful that memories never faded. This would be one of them. Another shiver shot through her. The situation was already so messed up on so many levels. When she'd awakened earlier in the evening, the last thing she would have expected was to find herself on the back of David's motorcycle, riding to his meeting with the Execution Underground. Yet she was doing exactly that. Throw in the unexplainable pull that had roused her from a drug-induced sleep and brought her to that sickening crime scene, plus David's news of demons being on her trail, and she was a royally screwed cookie. She closed her eyes as she continued to hold on to David. Just a few days. Once she was back on her feet, things would go back to normal. She and David would part ways again, and the only problem she would be left with was the horde of demons tailing her. Maybe she could even patch things up with Tom.

They rounded another corner before quickly pulling to a stop outside an abandoned-looking warehouse. They parked behind a Hummer H3 with its engine still running. David shut off the bike, before tearing off his helmet. She followed suit and removed her own helmet as the front doors of the H3 opened.

Jace and Frankie stepped out of the vehicle, and a look of relief crossed Jace's face as he spotted her and David. He sighed. "I was out of my fucking mind with worry until I talked to you," he said to David. The two men walked toward each other and embraced in a quick half hug.

"Sorry, J. I was kind of dealing with my own shit. Thanks for going to the hospital to check on her, even if she wasn't there." David shot a glance in her direction that was half admonishing, half playful.

"All water under the bridge now. No harm done." Frankie stepped around from the other side of the car. A smile spread across her face as she stepped forward and pulled Allsún into a hug.

Allsún hugged her back. It was so good to see a friendly face. Well, one that wasn't her ex's, anyway. Frankie released her, the smile still on her as she pulled away. Allsún examined her friend's features. Though she couldn't quite pinpoint the change, something was off with Frankie. The slightest trace of dark circles colored the skin underneath her eyes as if she'd been losing sleep, and a faint line of worry cut deep between her eyebrows.

"Thanks for going with Jace to try to look after her, Frankie," David said.

Allsún shook her head. "Jeez, way to make it sound like I need a constant babysitter." She shot David a glare. She hated being treated like a helpless victim.

Frankie placed a hand on her shoulder. "It was really no trouble. Besides, who wouldn't need some help after being left with Robert for so long?"

David cringed, and Allsún could see the guilt behind his eyes.

"I'm headed inside, so I don't have to listen to any more of Damon's bitching than we're already in for." Jace threw the keys to his H3 to Frankie. He grinned from ear to ear as she caught them in one hand. "Love you, princess."

Frankie blushed, and Allsún glanced away. The love

flowing between them was staggering. A small pang of jealousy shot through her. Shite. She wished she had something as beautiful as that in her life. Her heart hurt as David's eyes met hers. There was a time when she *did* have something that beautiful in her life, but now only painful memories were left.

The moment passed as quickly as it had come, and Jace jogged inside.

David turned toward Allsún. "I'll try not to be too long. Will you stay with Frankie until I'm finished?"

She nodded.

He gave her a pointed look. "No running."

"If I was going to run, I wouldn't be here."

He looked toward Frankie, and she gave him a reassuring nod. Without another word he turned and headed into the warehouse.

A breath Allsún didn't realize she had been holding escaped her as he disappeared from sight. A few seconds of silence passed as she stared at the closed door.

Frankie cleared her throat. "I can't imagine hanging around with your ex-fiancé is a comfortable situation."

Allsún nodded. "Yeah, tell me about it."

"Let's get you in the car. You've got to be freezing."

Allsún allowed Frankie to usher her inside the H3, suddenly realizing she could no longer feel her toes.

She climbed into the backseat, with Frankie following close behind her. As soon as Frankie closed the door and heat filled the car again, Allsún sighed in relief. A slow tingling sensation filled her as her limbs came back to life.

"I'm so glad to see you're all right after the whole Robert ordeal."

"If it wasn't for you, he would've killed me. You saved me."

Frankie waved her hand in dismissal. "No way. All I did was get kidnapped right along with you. It was Jace and David who saved the day."

"Well, regardless of how it happened, I'm still thankful."

"David was out of his mind with worry. Jace said he'd never seen him so crazy with rage before. It didn't help that his leg injury stopped him from saving you sooner."

Allsún raised a brow. "What leg injury?"

"Oh, that's right. I guess you wouldn't know. Before you were kidnapped, the three of us got into it with Robert." She paused, as if she wasn't certain she wanted to continue. Finally she sighed and went on. "Robert threw David off the platform in Manhattan Square Park."

Allsún knew how long and hard a fall that was, one

that would be fatal to the average human. All she could manage to choke out was, "I'm glad he's all right."

"I'm not sure how okay he is, given that he has a permanent limp. I'm sure you've noticed. From what Jace tells me, David hasn't been handling the injury too well. He's almost healed now, but he's probably trying to tough it out when you're around. You know, the whole macho man thing guys do."

She nodded, though she hadn't noticed, and bit her lower lip. If she was being honest with herself, it was because she'd been trying hard not to notice how ridiculously sexy David's ass looked in his leather motorcycle chaps. She placed her hands between her knees in order to warm them. "So...you and Jace, huh?"

Frankie smiled, but a bit of sadness crept into her eyes. "Yeah."

Allsún debated whether to ask her next question, given all the upset feelings Frankie was giving off, but she considered Frankie a good friend, someone who had been there for her when she needed it most. This was her chance to return the favor. Frankie clearly needed someone to talk to. "Want to talk about it?"

Frankie folded her hands across her lap and stared down at them, refusing to meet Allsún's gaze. "It's hard to say. I love Jace and I know he loves me, but I'm just wondering if that's enough."

"Why wouldn't it be? If you both really love each other, I think even if there are some bumps along the road, ultimately you'll always find your way back together."

Frankie glanced in her direction, sadness visibly weighing on her shoulders. "Like you and David?"

Allsún bit her lower lip.

Frankie had a point. She and David had been in love—madly in love, just like she could tell Jace and Frankie were—and perhaps even more so, because she and David had been together for so long. Yet somehow they hadn't ended up together. Things had gone so sour so fast.

She pushed the thought from her mind. No, that was different.

"I guess you have a point, but just because David and I couldn't hang on, that doesn't mean the same thing will happen with you and Jace."

"I don't even know the details of what happened with you and David."

"Believe me, you don't want to know."

"I'm just so uncertain about the future." Frankie's shoulders slumped even farther.

"Whatever you're uncertain about, I'm sure you'll overcome it."

Frankie shook her head. "It's not the sort of thing you overcome. It's permanent."

Allsún eyed Frankie in the light flooding the car from the nearby street lamps, trying to speculate what her friend was going through. Despite her obvious sadness, Frankie was still so beautiful.

Wait a second.

The whole thing with Frankie and Jace had started when Frankie had skipped out on her ritual mating ceremony and the fellow pack member she'd been destined to mate with that night. To the best of her knowledge, Jace and Frankie had met that same night. Allsún's eyes widened. Oh, damn. The point of that ceremony was to breed potential Alphas for the pack. No wonder Frankie had a certain glow about her despite how upset she seemed.

Allsún's gaze shot down to Frankie's midsection. She wasn't showing by any means, but her normally flat, toned stomach had a new roundness to it. Allsún covered her mouth to stop from gasping, before slowly lowering her hand. "Oh, my God. Frankie, are you pregnant?"

Frankie pulled at the flaps of her coat, wrapping the material over her belly. She nodded. "With twins."

Allsún gasped, and for a moment she struggled to find the right words. "Congratulations! How do you know it's twins?"

Frankie stared at the car floor and shrugged. "A wolf just knows."

"Does Jace know you're pregnant? Is that what's upsetting you?"

Frankie shook her head. Tears clouded her dark brown eyes. "I'm afraid to tell him. It's not like we've been together that long, you know? One baby is a big enough commitment, but *two?* I don't know how he'll react." She placed her hands on her stomach. "I'm only about eight weeks along by my calculations, but already I can't fit into any of my salsa dresses. I'm going to be huge." She smiled a little, but it quickly faded amidst her growing tears.

Allsún scooted toward her on the seat, wrapping her arms around Frankie and pulling her friend into a tight hug.

"You're not going to be huge, you're going to be pregnant. There's a difference. You're creating life. It's going to be an amazing experience—scary, but amazing. You love Jace. Yes, this journey is going to change your lives and your relationship, but for the better. It will be hard, but you'll come out stronger. And honestly, I think Jace will make an excellent father, don't you?" She pulled back from the hug. "He's loyal to a fault, and that's a good quality for a family man. I'm sure he'll be fiercely protective of you and your babies, and I know he'll take great care of all three of you."

A small smile crossed Frankie's lips. "Yeah, I do think he's going to be an amazing dad."

Allsún smiled. Deep down, she wished she could be in Frankie's position. She'd wanted children when she and David had been together. That had been five years ago. Now, that ache to have a child of her own had grown and become so intense, she couldn't see any pregnant woman or newborn baby without filling up with envy. Despite her happiness for Frankie, she was filled with a jealous longing. Man, she was an awful person.

She grabbed hold of Frankie's hands, gripped tight and met her friend's eyes. "I'm really happy for you, Frankie. Don't be afraid. Jace will take it much better than you think he will." She gave Frankie another squeeze.

She wasn't lying. She *was* happy for her, but a

sick twisted side of her couldn't help but feel sorry for herself.

Such cruel irony. If only Frankie knew the real reason she'd left David, aside from him joining the Execution Underground.

"Are you going to tell Jace soon?"

Frankie nodded. "I can't avoid it much longer. I'm tired all the time, eating everything in sight, and since I'm having twins, I'm certain my stomach is going to pop at twelve weeks and there will be no more hiding it." Frankie let go of Allsún's hands. She stared out the window at one of the glowing streetlights, wrapping her arms around herself as if to stop herself from falling apart. "I'll tell him, but what if he leaves? It's not like we've been together that long. He may love me, but I doubt anyone would be ready for the commitment of having children this soon in a relationship. Hell, I don't know that *I'm* prepared, but I don't want to give these little ones up. Still, what if this scares him away? What will I do then?"

"You really think he'll leave? Jace isn't that type of man—I know that much just from David. From my understanding, he had a pretty shady childhood. An abusive, then absent, father. Jace would never do that to his own kids, and he'd never leave you like that. I can tell how much he cares for you."

A small smile crossed Frankie's face. "I never thought I'd be able to love someone so quickly and so deep. It seems unreal at times how fast things have happened."

Allsún placed a hand on Frankie's arm. "It's going to be okay. I promise."

For the first time in all his years of hunting, David was late to a division meeting, and Damon was not going to be happy. Normally David was the first one there, ready to follow orders. He was also unofficially responsible for getting Jace to show up no more than twenty minutes late, something that generally took a long series of nagging phone calls and texts. This time was different.

He pushed open the door to the warehouse.

"You're late. Better be for good reason," Damon said.

David walked around to the far side of the table. He sat down, leaned forward and placed his elbows on the table, then rested his head in his hands.

His fellow hunter Trent Garrison, who specialized in hunting non-werewolf shapeshifters, placed a hand on David's shoulder. "David, you all right?"

Without answering, David unholstered the Beretta, placed it on the table, then quickly removed his other weapons. No matter how he tried, he couldn't push the images of the victims from his mind. All the spilled blood and the way the demons had mutilated that poor baby girl. His stomach churned. The thought of it made him sick.

"Well, I'll be damned." Ash—short for Ashley—Devereaux, the division's resident ghost/poltergeist hunter and medium, leaned back in his seat and eyed David. "If you're actually carrying a gun, I'm a bit concerned," he said, his thick Louisiana drawl drawing out the words.

"Enough," Damon said. "Now that David and Jace are here, we need to get started." He grabbed David's weapons off the table and placed them in the large plastic container they used to check their weapons before entering the control room, a small hidden space that held all their supercomputers and the technology that connected them to their division's underground ops center.

A chorus of screeching sounded as the men pushed back their chairs across the concrete floor. As they stood, Damon met David's gaze. His eyes narrowed.

David wasn't certain whether it meant Damon was pissed off or concerned.

"You all right?" their boss mouthed silently.

David gave a single nod. Everything that had happened in the past hour weighed heavily on his shoulders. He was glad when Damon took the hint and didn't ask any more questions.

David followed his fellow hunters through the warehouse. He helped Ash move seven crates aside until they cleared a path to the key panel hidden in the wall. Damon typed in the code, placed the weapons in the containment drawer and entered first, passing through the scanner. They followed one by one until they were all crammed inside the small control room. Everyone took their usual seats. When all six men were settled, Damon cleared his throat and turned to David.

"You want to go first, since clearly you have something important to share?"

David shook his head. "Save the shitty news for last."

Surprisingly, Damon obliged and didn't push further. He turned his attention toward Jace. "You have anything for us?"

Jace shook his head. "*Nada, mi capitán*. Nothing to report. The wolves are behaving under my watch, with Frankie's help. No rogues have come into the area, since the rumors of Robert are still pretty rampant. After hearing what happened to him, they don't want to be met by the badass that is Jace McCannon." He flashed a smug grin.

Damon didn't look one bit amused. "You're certain you have them under control?"

Jace crossed his arms over his chest. "Yeah, you doubt me?"

Damon ignored his question. "How would things be in your absence?"

Jace uncrossed his arms and sat forward aggressively.

There they went again, David thought. Another pissing contest. He let out a long sigh. He had more important things to think about than this. Like the fact that some sort of demonic shit-storm was about to go down, and his ex-fiancée was the last Fae outside some weird otherworldly faerie dimension, so all the demons were going to be coming after her.

"What the fuck are you saying?" Jace asked.

Damon growled. "Just answer the damn question."

Jace scowled. "They'd be a bit more unsteady without me, but nothing Frankie couldn't handle. Why?"

Damon met Jace's gaze head-on, and if David hadn't known better, he would have thought he was going to fire Jace right then and there.

Despite the cold fire in his eyes, Damon kept his tone calm and even as he spoke. "Headquarters requested you make a trip down to New York City to assist in a hunt there. They need someone with your experience to lead. Can I count on you to do that without fucking up?"

Jace's frown deepened, but he nodded. "Yeah, I'll get the job done."

Damon twisted in his office chair and looked toward Shane, clearly happy to done with Jace. "Anything?"

Shane straightened his glasses. "Well, actually something's brewing—no pun intended—with the witch covens. There's been some activity, but nothing I can really pinpoint. I don't know the definite significance yet."

Damon tapped his pen against the stack of reports in front of him. "Anything you need?"

"Not at the moment. No. I'll keep you posted," Shane said.

Damon scribbled notes on a blank sheet of paper. "What about you, Ash? How is everything going at the asylum?"

"Slowly," Ash replied. "There are enough souls that need to be put to rest to keep a hunter busy for years."

Damon raised a brow. "Mostly benign spirits?"

Ash gave a low chuckle. "Hell no. The mentally ill

are tortured souls, treated badly enough in life as it is. Their problems only get worse when they become spirits. I've got poltergeists coming out my ears."

Damon shook his head as he continued taking notes. "Not what I wanted to hear, but keep working at it. Just make sure no teenage assholes decide to show off and take their girlfriends in there again."

Ash gave an ironic salute. "You got it. That place ain't safe for anyone."

Damon's gaze flicked toward Trent. "You?"

Trent grinned like he was the cat who'd just swallowed Tweety Bird. Whatever he had to share, he wanted to tell it. "You're not gonna believe this, with all the normal nasty monsters I have to deal with, but yesterday I found a pig shifter."

A moment of silence passed before Jace, Shane and Ash all burst out laughing. Even Damon cracked the smallest of smiles.

Trent chuckled, his own grin stretching from ear to ear. "No joke, and I'll be damned if that guy didn't have the most pig-like nose I've ever seen when he was back in human form."

In between laughs, Ash managed to choke out, "You didn't kill the poor motherfucker, did you? Sounds like he's got it bad enough as it is, bein' a hog and all."

Trent waved his hand in dismissal. "Nah, I didn't kill him. There was no point. He wasn't hurting anybody. Poor guy didn't even have those badass tusks like some wild pigs do." Trent faced Damon again. "Jimmy from the police department called me in on that one. Apparently they raided some pig slaughterhouse just outside the city and found the guy covered from head to toe in mud inside one of the pens. Jimmy figured it qualified as strange enough to call me. I got everything sorted out, though." He shrugged. "Aside from that, I'm getting some of the aftershock of Jace killing Robert, too. Non-werewolf shifters seem to be steering clear of Rochester right now."

A smug grin spread across Jace's face.

Once the snickering over Trent's pig-shifter encounter settled, all eyes turned toward David. No one spoke, not even Damon. A wordless understanding hung in the air. It didn't take David saying so for his fellow hunters, the only men he called his friends, to know that what he was about to show them was tragic.

He reached inside a pocket and removed his cell phone, then handed it over to Shane. "The crime scene photos are on there. Can you bring them up on the big screen so everybody can see what we're dealing with here?"

With a nod, Shane took the phone from David's hand and pulled a cable from his messenger bag. He quickly hooked the phone to the main system, then started pulling up the photos. David immediately knew when Shane had seen them, because his fellow hunter's eyes widened and the blood drained from his face. Shane passed the phone back to David once he'd uploaded the photos.

Shane shook his head as he spoke, as if he didn't like what he was about to say. "Uh…guys, brace yourselves." He hit a button, and the first of the crime scene photos appeared on the screen.

"Oh, shit," Ash mumbled.

Trent swore under his breath.

Jace slammed his fist on the table. "Demon motherfuckers."

Damon stared intently at the screen. His eyes iced over into a stare that was purely professional. David could always tell that Damon distanced himself from the reality they dealt with as much as he could. He tried to see things objectively. But David couldn't be objective when it came to gruesome acts like this. No matter how hard he tried.

The rest of the photos flashed across the screen in succession, one every few seconds.

David massaged the edges of his temples. "The worst is the last one."

Another round of cursing and disgust raced through the small control room as the final photo, a close-up of the baby girl, filled the screen.

"Turn it the fuck off, Shane. Turn it off." When Shane hesitated, Jace stood and stalked across the room. He hit the power button, and the screen faded to black. He let out a long string of profanities before he turned to face the rest of the group again. "Well, David may be too much of a good guy to say it, so I'll say it for him." He pointed at Damon accusingly. "That's the second dead baby we've had to deal with. And David told all of us—" Jace pointed to each of them in turn "—after the first one that he thought it was going to happen again. He fucking told us so, and we didn't listen."

"Damn straight," Trent said. He glanced over at David. "Sorry we didn't listen to you, man."

David nodded. "Aside from finding that shit storm earlier this evening, I've got other news, too." He let out a long sigh. "Allsún's awake again."

"That's a *good* thing, right?" Shane asked.

David debated whether or not to lay all his cards on the table. So far, Jace and Frankie were the only ones who knew Allsún was part Fae. It wasn't that he thought his fellow hunters would go after her—the Fae weren't an enemy of the Execution Underground; they protected humans from demons the same way the EU did—but did he really want Headquarters to get wind of her situation? All the possible scenarios flashed through his mind, and finally he decided that yes, he *did* want Headquarters to get involved, because maybe, just maybe, they could help him find a way to better protect her.

"Yeah, but before I found that mess, I was tracking a demon who'd possessed the psychiatrist who'd been taking care of her. She woke up on the very night that little piece of shit told me it knew…it knew she was half Fae."

Damon stared at David as if he'd grown five heads. "She's a Faerie? And you neglected to tell me this?"

David decided to try brazening it out. "What does it matter? We don't hunt faeries."

"What did you do with the demon who told you that? Did you exorcise him?" Jace uncapped his flask and chugged a swig of the Bushmills Irish Whiskey he always drank.

Damn, this was the part David had really been dreading. "No, I didn't exorcise him. I had to kill him. There was nothing else I could do. It was either exorcise the demon and risk him telling all his buddies about Allsún or kill the thing and take out the doctor in the process. The doc told me to just kill him and the demon, because if I didn't kill him, the demon was going to, so I did what I had to do. Turns out I was too late anyway. The last thing the doc said was that the demon had already told all the other hellspawn."

"Kill an innocent man? And not just any man, but a well-known and respected psychiatrist?" Damon swore. "What the fuck were you thinking? The family being murdered is going to cause enough media trouble as it is, but another dead innocent? I thought you were more professional than this, David."

David rested his face in his hands and sighed. He was so not up for listening to Damon's anger. "There was nothing I could do. The demon was killing him anyway, and you think I should have just let that thing get away with it? Better to kill it than let it get away with murder, then waft off to take over another body."

He could feel his anger rising. Damon had no right to rip him to shreds in front of his fellow hunters.

Damon let out a low growl. "That's not the point, David. What about his family—or the police, for that matter? To them, *you're* the one who killed him, *not* the demon. If the police manage to crack this and point the finger at you…"

"The doctor was able to push through the possession momentarily. He *told* me to kill him." David clenched his fists.

Damon shook his head. "I expect this kind of behavior from Jace, but from you?"

"Hey. What the fuck did I do to get drawn into this?" Jace spun in his desk chair to face Damon. "In case you forgot, I just bagged a fucking serial killer last month. Why are you on *my* case?"

"Shut up," Damon barked. "If Headquarters finds out about you and your Berserker shit, all of us are fucked. You're still on my shit list." Damon pointed a finger at David. "And now, thanks to you, HQ is going to be all over my ass."

Damn it. Frustration rose up in David's chest. He'd put up with a lot of Damon's crap, but this was pushing it. He fought to hold his tongue as Damon went on.

"If *anything* goes wrong because of what you did, I'll—"

Enough.

David stood and stepped toward Damon. "Look, I don't care if HQ is so far up your ass their heads are poking out your mouth. I won't let a demon walk away free. It was gonna murder that poor man, so I killed it. The doctor would've died either way, and if you and HQ can't understand that, you can bend over and kiss my hairy ass."

The two men stared at each other in silence, as if daring each other to speak.

Trent cleared his throat in an attempt to lighten the mood. "For the record, I've seen his ass, and it *is* just the slightest bit hairy."

Jace busted out laughing.

Damon shot Jace a death glare. "You think this is funny?"

Ash raised his hand, moving as slow as his Louisiana drawl. "Actually, it *is* pretty damn funny."

David ignored them all and started in on Damon again. "I've got so much shit to deal with right now that I don't need you getting on my back to top it all off. You're the one who wanted to be a division leader. That means you have to deal with Headquarters and their shit regardless of whether the team members that *you* picked are fuck-ups, which we're not. I'm not going to deal with your bullshit right now." He pulled the samples from the crime scene from his coat and dropped them in front of Damon. "Send HQ the photos and the samples, and if they're pissed off about how I do my job, then either fire me or tell them to get the fuck over it."

Anger and frustration raced through him as he turned and stalked out of the control room. He didn't care that Damon hadn't said the meeting was over. He was leaving.

Dr. Shane Grey wasn't sure which group of animals showed more overt aggression toward each other: hungry wolves fighting it out for food or his fellow division hunters. His gamble was on the hunters.

Shane watched David storm out of the control room in a fury. He couldn't say he blamed him. He hated drama and conflict, and both of those figured in roughly eighty percent of the Rochester division meetings. He supposed it came with the territory. Damon had hired a group that was comprised of some of the most elite men in their fields, all of whom behaved like the alpha males they were. Just like in the animal world, they were bound to clash.

Shane really couldn't say much on this one. As an occult specialist, witch hunter and the division's unofficial tech-head, taking care of all the division's electronic gadgetry, he didn't see many dead bodies unless he was aiding in one of his fellow hunter's cases.

Jace was the first to break the silence. "Well, if nobody else is going to go after him, I guess I will." He stalked toward the door, then paused and turned around, shooting a pissed-off glance at Damon. "You know whose side I'm on for this one," he said before leaving.

"Well, damn," Ash said. "I guess the meeting's over." He eyed Damon cautiously.

Damon waved his hand in dismissal. "Yeah, whatever. Get the fuck out."

Ash and Trent didn't need any more of an invitation. They hightailed it out of there.

When Shane and Damon were left alone, silence fell over the control room. Shane pulled up the photos again, arranging them in rows on the screen. Once they were up, he stood resting his chin in his hand as he examined them. His eyes paused on the final photo of the innocent baby girl. His stomach churned. Such vile hate released on such a small innocent baby. From the corner of his eye, he noticed Damon watching him.

Shane's gaze trailed over the blood smears on the wall next to the victim. "Do those look like anything to you?"

Damon stared at the screen. He remained silent for a moment, then finally answered, "Not at all."

Shane crossed his arms. "Hmm. I can't help but wonder if maybe they're a symbol for a demonic ritual of some sort that we're just not recognizing. That level of violence among humans usually indicates passionate hate, so I suppose it could be the same for demons. I'd have to dig further into the family's background, though. I doubt they were involved in any sort of demonic activity. From the looks of them, they seemed pretty white bread. Your normal nuclear household."

"Not to mention this was the second murder of an infant, which implies a less personal motive," Damon pointed out.

"True. So if it wasn't hate, why such violence?"

Damon didn't respond. He eyed Shane as if he was assessing his abilities. Knowing Damon, Shane thought he probably was.

Shane turned back to the screen. "I'd like to make a copy of these to take with me, if that's okay I want to look further into that symbol. It's possible there's a relation to a similar occult ritual. If I can find that relationship, I might be able to help David figure out the demon's motivation."

"If you want to aid in David's investigation, you have my full support."

"Thanks," Shane said, pressing several buttons. He made quick work of copying the photos on to a USB drive, which he threw into his messenger bag. "I'll keep you posted if I come up with anything."

"Yeah, sure," Damon replied.

Shane took the obvious hint that Damon needed to decompress after the meeting. He grabbed his messenger bag, left the room and retrieved his standard nine mm and his book from the weapons bin. He held the heavy book in his hands. Whenever he opened it, he could smell the old crinkled pages, slightly yellowed with age. He'd found it at a yard sale back home in Las Vegas when he was a teen. Not only did it contain loads of invaluable information about the occult, it also contained all his personal notes about the encounters he'd had with witches, warlocks and their spells throughout the years. Not that he'd had many years, considering he was the youngest member of the Rochester division, but he was a thorough note taker.

If there was any relation between the recent demonic activity and the occult, he would find it. He was certain of it.

Chapter 7

A loud creak sounded from the warehouse, startling both Allsún and Frankie. David stepped outside, with Jace trailing close behind. Frankie quickly climbed out of the car and headed in his direction, and Allsún followed suit.

At the sight of Frankie, Jace's mouth went from a tight stern line to a genuine smile. "Meeting's finished," he said. "Ready to go, princess?" He walked over and wrapped his arm around her shoulders before planting a quick kiss on the top of her head.

"Yeah, I'm ready." With a small wave goodbye, the two turned back toward the H3.

"Frankie!" Allsún called after her.

Frankie glanced over her shoulder. "Yeah?"

"Give me a call if you need anything."

Frankie smiled. "Will do."

A grin crossed Allsún's face as she watched Frankie take hold of Jace's hand. If her supernatural hearing served her right, she was sure she'd heard Frankie whisper to Jace, "Hey, can we talk?" as they slid into the car.

David mounted his motorcycle and buckled his helmet as Jace and Frankie drove away. He passed Allsún the spare helmet, and as she put it on she watched him release the kickstand. With a nod, he gestured for her to get on behind him. She understood him well enough to read his expression and know he was pissed.

"Meeting didn't go well?" she asked as she swung her right leg over the bike.

Man, was she thankful David's jacket was so long on her. Otherwise her ass would be hanging in the wind for everyone to see, courtesy of the hospital gown.

"Downright shitty," he replied. "But the main point is the samples were sent off to HQ, so we'll have an analysis on them by tomorrow evening."

"And until then?" She clung tight to him as he started the engine.

"We don't really have any leads, so until then we wait at my apartment."

A lump crawled into her throat. David rolled the bike

forward and eased it on to the street. Seconds later they were speeding downtown toward his apartment. No matter how much she tried, she couldn't shake the nervous feeling in her gut. Her? Inside David's apartment again? The night just kept getting better and better.

Completely stunned didn't begin to explain how she felt when she walked into David's apartment a little while later. She took in the clean countertops, uncluttered by empty beer bottles. The floors had recently been vacuumed, and she was pretty sure there wasn't a single speck of dust anywhere. She wasn't quite sure she believed her eyes. She lingered in the doorway for a moment. This apartment held so many memories for her, memories she didn't care to think about. She wasn't sure which was worse: to recollect the happy memories—the ones that made her miss what she had before—or the bad ones, which were a painful reminder of how wrong everything had gone.

"Apparently you learned to use basic household cleaning tools," she said. She pulled the door closed behind her and walked farther into the living room. Why couldn't he have been this clean when she was dating him? Men.

"I always knew how to use them. I just preferred to watch your cute little butt as you danced around the apartment flittering away with your duster cleaning everything. That's why I never cleaned on my own."

She blushed, and even though he wasn't looking at her, she tried to hide her face. She didn't want him to know that hearing him say that, thinking about him wanting her, sparked a fire in her that hadn't been lit in years. She scolded herself. They were just friends now, and she had ended a different relationship with a different boyfriend not long before she'd been kidnapped. She wasn't ready for another commitment. Not yet.

"I never knew you were a chauvinist," she teased.

"You always did like using big words to try and confuse me, at least when we were kids."

She laughed. "Like you haven't heard me use that word hundreds of times before in other contexts."

He grinned, before gesturing to the couch.

She crossed the room and sat down.

"You want something to drink?" He walked into the kitchen, fully visible thanks to the open floor plan, and wrenched open the door of the stainless steel refrigerator.

"Water would be fine."

He pulled a pitcher of water from the fridge, then removed a glass from the closest cabinet, filled it with ice, then poured in the water. He grabbed a beer for himself, then headed back to her. Dogfish 90-Minute I.P.A. Dogfish had always been his favorite brewery since he'd developed an interest in craft beers back in college. He uncapped the bottle with a fish-shaped bottle opener on his key ring, took a sip, then sat on the coffee table across from her. She drank her water.

Man, this was awkward already.

He cleared his throat. "So…we need to discuss what we're going to do about this demon situation."

She shrugged. "I don't know that there's much to discuss. It was interested in me because I'm the last Fae outside the Isle of Apples, right?"

He nodded and took another sip of his beer. "As far as I could tell, anyway. I had to kill the little fucker before I could find out more. Didn't want him getting back to hell to pass on any more information to his sulfur-sucking buddies. Turns out I was too late, though the only reason I found out he'd already told others is because the doc told me before he died."

Allsún shook her head and fought back a curse. She felt awful for the poor doctor, but she couldn't shake the fear gripping her, knowing she was going to be followed by demons everywhere she went. That was certainly going to screw with her life. She wouldn't be able to go anywhere without being on guard. She tried to tamp down her growing sense of panic and maintain a level head the way she'd always been able to do back when she hunted demons. "Is there really anything we can do? You know how demons are when it comes to the Fae. They're so intent on seeing our demise, they'll drive themselves into the ground in order to destroy us. They won't stop until they have me or I'm dead. I don't know how I'm going to manage to avoid them. It's not like you can protect me every minute of every day—not that I even want you to. There's no place to…" Her sentence trailed off as the idea hit her.

She'd been about to say there was no place to hide, but she was wrong. There *was* a place to hide, the same place all the other Fae were hiding: the Isle of Apples.

"Allsún, are you okay? Allie?" David waved a hand in the front of her face.

She snapped back to attention. "Sorry. The weight of the situation just finally hit me."

And, boy, had it ever. The only place she would truly be safe was the Isle of Apples. The only problem was that getting to the Isle required magic she didn't have. She needed her full magic, her "light," in order to get to the Isle, and she had unknowingly gifted part of hers to David nearly seven years ago. A faerie's light was their essence, their source of power that they drew from to create their magic. After she and David had separated, she'd briefly considered relocating to the Isle permanently, to get away from Rochester and all the memories it held, and to be with creatures of her own kind. She'd discovered the hard way that she wasn't able to enter the Isle anymore. When she'd tried, she hadn't been able to conjure up the magic she needed to open the portal. Apparently one aspect of being Fae, an aspect her mother had neglected to tell her about before her death, was that half of a Fae's "light" passed to their "life mate"—their life mate being the first person they ever slept with. It worked out great for Fae who mated with other Fae, a pairing that was always for life. They expanded their powers by swapping half their magic with one another. But for a half-blooded Fae like herself, who mated with a human man, it didn't work out so well. Getting her light back would be easy—if she wanted to sleep with him again. Which she definitely did *not.*

She was caught between a rock and a hard place.

Renew a past romance that had placed her life in potential danger at its end or be chased by demons for the rest of her life.

Either one would eventually be the end of her. It wasn't as if she could tell David about the situation.

Not after the threat she'd received so long ago. A shiver ran over her skin.

David cleared his throat again. "I think the best course of action would be to gather as much information as we can before we make any rash decisions."

"How do you suggest we go about doing that?"

"Well, I think all of this has to be connected somehow. I said this earlier, and I'll say it again, you waking up on the same night a demon tells me he's after you and then showing up at the crime scene where I'm working can't be a coincidence. This all has to be connected. I think the more we learn about what happened to that poor family, the more we'll learn about the situation with you and the demons."

She nodded. "Yeah, I'm inclined to agree with you on that."

David held up his beer in a toast. "Here's to agreeing on a strategy."

Allsún raised her glass to meet his bottle. "Well, we did used to hunt together all the time. It doesn't surprise me that our minds are still in sync."

He took a swig of his beer, then set the bottle down on the coffee table next to him.

Her eyes followed the movement, and she noticed a novel sitting not far away. "You're still reading?" she asked.

"Of course. You taught me to love it."

She laughed. "I always kind of wondered if maybe you were just doing it to impress me or get my attention."

David grinned. "That was it at first, but I did eventually grow to enjoy it."

"So, what have you been reading?"

"Romances."

She laughed again. "No. Really…what are you reading?"

"I'm serious. I've been reading romances." He pointed to the book on the coffee table. She looked closer and smiled. A Nora Roberts novel. Good choice. When they'd been together, he'd always seemed to like suspense novels and adventure, sometimes even literary fiction, and an eclectic selection of nonfiction. Romance, though one of her personal favorite genres, just didn't seem like his thing.

"Huh. Why romance?"

He shrugged and glanced down at his feet. "Because it's so different from real life. It's like an escape. In romance, there's always a happy ending. The guy always manages to get the girl, sometimes not in the way he expected, but he still always gets her." He met her gaze.

An electric pulse jolted through her as their eyes

met, and she quickly looked away. She picked up the book and examined it more thoroughly, anything so she didn't have to stare into those dark brown eyes of his. "I bet Jace gives you a lot of hassle for that."

"I don't tell him about it. I only read here at home. I can't focus if it's not silent. If he asks what I've been reading, I make up some shit about a crime novel or some sort of literary fiction that bores him out of his mind, so then he won't ask anymore."

She grinned. "I bet it's a real hit with the ladies, a guy who's sensitive enough to read romance novels."

He looked at her head-on, almost as if he wanted to be certain she heard him. "There aren't any women in my life."

"Oh." She wasn't sure what to make of that. "So you're not seeing anyone?" She knew she was prying, but she didn't care.

"No. No one since you."

Her eyes widened. "No one?" The words came out a little more flabbergasted than she intended.

A slight frown tightened his lips.

She quickly tried to cover her tracks. "Sorry. That came out wrong. I mean, I'm just surprised. It's not like you're not a major catch. I know that firsthand."

His frown faded, and he took another sip of his beer.

"I'm not with anyone by choice, not because there haven't been offers." He chuckled. "There've been *plenty* of those. More than I can keep track of."

"Way to be humble," she mocked, trying to be lighthearted. She bit her lower lip. Lighthearted, her ass. Deep inside she was really thinking about how she wanted to beat down any woman who even looked at him twice.

"What about you? Have you been seeing anyone?" he asked.

Briefly, she considered telling him she'd been single since they separated, but that seemed like a truly shite-filled idea. What was the point in lying? "Yeah, actually I have, but we broke it off just before Robert abducted me."

"Oh." A deep sadness swept into his eyes, and the look on his face nearly killed her.

"It was nothing serious," she added. That *was* a lie, but she would say anything to wipe that pained expression from his face, and, well, despite Tom's proposal, it wasn't very serious. At least not on her end, anyway. That was why it had ended when he'd asked her to marry him. She and Tom couldn't be serious.

How could they be, when she was still in love with David?

She shook her head. No, she didn't love him. She couldn't. She'd *loved* him—emphasis on the "ed." But she hadn't been *in love* with Tom. She had been trying to convince herself she was in love with him for the past year, but his proposal had blown her charade to smithereens. The head vet at Rochester's main animal shelter, where she worked as a veterinary technician, Tom Dodd was good man, average and unobjectionable in every way.

That was exactly what she disliked about him, actually, and also exactly what she needed: the antithesis of her relationship with David.

She had tried to force herself to focus on Tom's good qualities, all of which had been apparent from the moment they'd started dating. He was kind and sweet, friendly and a fabulous animal doctor. He loved animals as much as she did, particularly dogs, though she was more of a cat person. He liked to take her out to dinner on Friday nights, and he was good in bed, even if he never matched the fireworks David had been able to set off. She enjoyed spending time with him, doing ordinary things like watching TV and playing cards. She should have felt lucky that he'd asked her to marry him.

Instead of feeling lucky, though, she'd told him that she couldn't marry him, that she needed time to think about it, that she needed to be absolutely certain before she took such a big step. He'd said that if she couldn't marry him, then their relationship wasn't going anywhere and they were through. And that was that.

Every logical part of her brain wanted her to say yes and marry Tom. She could have the life she'd always wanted: a steady stable relationship with a husband who loved her, a white picket fence and a minivan full of kids. But every idiotic, stupid part of her brain told her that was the absolute wrong thing to do, because if she was really honest with herself, as nice as Tom was, he was exactly that. Just nice.

Average.

David was anything but average. David was unique. David rode badass motorcycles, spent his spare time playing with greased-up engines and shiny new weapons, not playing pinochle. David liked classic rock and drank craft beers. Tom liked soft jazz and tonic water. Tom was a veterinarian. David was a demon hunter and an exorcist for a top-secret organization.

But the biggest difference was that Tom loved her as Allsún, the quiet, soft-spoken, human vet tech. David had loved her as Allie, the feisty, fun-loving pixie who battled hell-crawlers on a regular basis.

No. She couldn't think like that.

"That's too bad, I guess," David said, breaking her train of thought.

What the hell did he mean by that? Her hand shot to her hip, and she gave him just a little more attitude than necessary. "Why?"

"Well, I know how much you always wanted to get married and have a family, so it just seems like something that's not very serious wasn't going to make you happy, so I guess it's good that it ended."

You're right, I wasn't very happy. I haven't been very happy since I was with you. She shook the thought from her head. "I get by just fine. He and I had a good relationship, even if it didn't end up lasting."

"That's good." A moment of silence passed, and he shifted uncomfortably as if he wasn't sure what to do with himself. "Umm…so I guess, if you want, you can take the bed for the night and I'll just stay out here on the sofa."

"Uh, yeah…sure. That's fine."

"I still have some of your clothes here, so you won't have to swing by your apartment."

She nearly choked. "You kept all that stuff?" She had to get away and stood to take her empty glass to the sink. Reaching out with her free hand, she silently offered to take his now empty beer bottle. He handed it to her with a quick "thanks," and she walked into the kitchen.

"I couldn't bring myself to get rid of them. It would've felt like I was getting rid of you, and I didn't want that."

You're the one who caused this. "Well, given the situation, I guess I'm lucky you kept everything."

He nodded. "Yeah, I guess. Make yourself at home." He stood, kicked off his massive biker boots and flopped on to the couch, grabbing the romance novel off the coffee table.

"You look funny reading that."

"Hmm, you called me a chauvinist earlier, but who's being sexist now?"

She gave him a half grin. "Ha. Guilty as charged."

"Do you need anything before I settle into reading? There's an extra toothbrush in the drawer, if you need it, and you can wear any of my shirts to sleep in if you like."

"That should be all I need. Thanks. I guess I'll just, uh…go back into the bedroom now."

"Feel free to pick something up off the bookshelf in there." He leaned back on the couch and went back to his book.

A sinking feeling filled her chest as she sulked into

the bedroom. She felt so out of place, so wrong, mainly because this had once practically been her home, but now she didn't feel at home here, didn't feel as if she had a place. She walked into the bedroom, eyeing the closet that still contained her clothes, the open bathroom door, and… Her heart sank.

There it was, the bed she and David used to sleep in. The bed she would have to sleep in alone now. Goose bumps prickled over her skin, and her breath caught. Anxiety flooded through her. It was all too much: David in the other room and all the memories piling up on her. Her eyes darted to the bedroom window.

What should she do? Should she go down the fire escape? She knew it wasn't true, but she felt that if she left now, she would be without her light and running from demons for the rest of her life, and that if she stayed she would have to seduce him if she could. As much as she wished it were as easy as telling him the situation, she knew it wasn't. She couldn't tell him without risking his safety, and she would never allow that to happen. Not after the threat she'd received.

If she could go back in time, there were so many things she would change about the night they broke up, but especially *that.* She and David had never kept secrets, but this was one thing he couldn't know—for both their safety. And yet she wanted—*needed*—her light back, and the only way she could get it would be to intentionally seduce David without ever letting him know why she was doing it. The emotions it would bring up inside her and the pain it would cause David would be devastating for her, for both of them, but if she wanted to escape the demons chasing her for good, she needed to do it.

Going home to the world of the Fae, the Isle of Apples, where the demons wouldn't be able to reach her, was her only solution. And yet sleeping with David was the last thing she wanted to do. Or, if she was honest with herself, maybe the first thing. On a physical level she still wanted him just as much as she ever had—more so now, since she'd been without him for so long.

But he'd made it clear that he no longer had an interest in her romantically. Just friends. Sleeping with her would be a result of pure lust on his part, nothing more, but even so, she couldn't live with the thought of being with him one more time, only to have to give him up again.

Forcing herself to take a deep breath, she sat down on the edge of the bed, allowing her weight to sink into the mattress. She buried her face in her hands.

The smell of David rose from the sheets and filled her nose, her heart. She inhaled deeply. Where had it all gone so wrong?

Chapter 8

David remembered Allsún bouncing into the apartment, piles upon piles of shopping bags slung over her shoulders and hanging from her arms. His eyes widened as he took in the sight of his five-foot-tall, hundred-pounds-when-soaking-wet girlfriend buried beneath the overwhelming results of her "retail therapy," as she called it.

"Do you need any help with that?"

She shook her head as she dumped all the bags on to the large island in the middle of his kitchen. "No, thanks. I think I've got it."

He stood and walked to her side anyway. Wrapping his arms around her from behind, he planted a kiss on the top of her head, then her cheek, snaking his kisses down her left arm until finally he reached the large diamond ring on her finger. He held her hand in his, lifting it up to the light. The rays caught on the multi-faceted two-carat diamond, sending sparkling rainbow light on to the walls.

He covered his eyes and faked being in pain. "Watch it, Allie. You could blind someone with that thing."

She laughed and stared at the perfect diamond. "Three months. Can you believe it? In just over three months from now we'll be walking down the aisle." She grinned from ear to ear. "Mrs. David Aronowitz. I like the sound of that."

He smiled. "I'm so glad you decided to take my last name. You know it will make my grandmother ecstatic."

Allsún ducked out of his hold, an easy move for her, considering the top of her head reached only to his chest. She dug inside one of the shopping bags, searching through its contents. "You know I could never do anything to displease your grandma. Not after she's treated me like one of her own for all these years."

David flashed a small smile, before heading back to the couch.

"I have something to show you," she said, once he'd flopped on to the sofa again.

He picked up the Dogfish he'd been drinking and took a swig. "Oh, yeah, what's that?"

A mischievous look crossed Allsún's face. "Close your eyes."

He leaned farther back into the sofa. "Do I have to?"

She gave him a stern look, her lips pursing into an adorably perfect pucker. "Yes. If you don't, I'll be heart-broken." She laughed.

He rolled his eyes. "Oh, yeah, I'm sure I'll completely break your heart."

She stomped her foot, though the smile remained on her face. "Seriously, David. Close your eyes."

He sighed. "Sure, sure." He closed his eyes, relaxing back into the cushions. The sound of rustling shopping bags filled his ears before he heard Allsún's light foot-steps pad across the carpet.

"You ready?" she said, excitement filling her voice.

He nodded.

"Okay, then open your eyes."

David opened his eyes and stared at the small items in Allsún hands. A single pair of little girl's boots sat in the middle of her extended palms. Pink stitching lined the little black boots. The tops sported a ring of black fringe.

He opened his mouth to ask her what in the world she

was doing with a pair of baby shoes, but she quickly interrupted him.

"Shelley from work bought them for us. Aren't they so adorable? We were talking at lunch the other day about the wedding, and I told her that I've always dreamed of having a daughter. So she brought these into work today for me. She said she didn't know whether we planned on having kids soon, or whether we'd have a daughter at some point, but she was out shopping for her niece and just couldn't resist getting them because they made her think of me. They look just like that pair of boots I wore to the Christmas party a few weeks ago. Just black instead of brown, you know?"

She pushed the boots toward him until he took them from her hands as she continued chattering. He could listen to her voice for hours on end, but he had something he needed to say.

"So it got me thinking about us settling down, you know, what with the wedding being so soon and all, and—"

"Allie," he said.

She didn't hear him and continued with what she was saying. "I don't know whether I want to stay living here directly in the city if we start a family and—"

"*Allie,*" he interrupted her again, raising his voice slightly so she would hear him.

She stopped and met his gaze. "Yeah?"

He cleared his throat and tore his gaze from hers. "We've talked about this before, Allie, and the more I think about it, the more I think kids aren't a possibility." He saw the light fade from her eyes and the grin slip from her lips.

"You've always known I want lots of kids. This isn't new news. I—"

David shook his head. "I just think we need to sit down together and reevaluate whether or not kids would be a logical choice for us, given our careers."

Allsún blinked several times. "Our *careers?* For fucking Morgana's sake! I'm a vet tech. How would that stop us from having children?"

David fixed her with a hard stare. "You know that's not the career I'm talking about."

She stared at him, mouth open in disbelief as if she didn't understand what he was saying.

"Demons, Allie. Demons. We both hunt demons. How can we have kids and knowingly place them at risk? If we had children together, you know demons would be after them from before they were even born."

Allsún crossed her arms over her chest and sighed.

"David, we already talked about this. We don't have to hunt demons for the rest of our lives. Why should the burden be placed solely on us to protect the rest of humanity? There are others out there protecting the public. Why can't we have a little slice of happiness?"

David sat up straighter and leaned his elbows on his knees. "You know why, Allie. There's a reason we were born with the gifts we have. We're meant to use them. It would be selfish of us not to do whatever we can to save others."

She gaped at him. "Selfish? Are you calling me selfish?"

"That's not what I meant. What I mean is—"

"No." She pointed a finger at him accusingly. "What you said was perfectly clear. You think it's selfish of me to want to marry you and settle down and have a happy family out in the suburbs. Everyone else gets a white picket fence if they want one, but I can't. I have to be saddled with being half human, but yet I get none of the benefits of that? What's wrong with us chasing our own happiness? Haven't we done enough for the world already? We've been hunting demons together since we were in high school."

"I know. It's not fair, but that's how it is. The demons are never going to stop. They're always going to keep possessing people, keep using them and riding their bodies until they're dead. Nothing but an empty shell left behind. We can't let them do that, Allsún."

She shook her head and tore her gaze away from him. "I can't believe you, David. You know what this is? You're letting the recruiters from that stupid Execution Underground organization go to your head. You've had dreams your whole life. You've always wanted to do something big, live a life worth living, and now these guys come along and you get it in your head that you're not allowed to have an ounce of happiness. All because you were born with a 'gift' that you never even chose. There are other people out there with the same abilities—other people who can fight the demons. Leave it to people who actually want to join the Execution Underground. They can handle it."

David couldn't believe she didn't see his point. The Execution Underground was right. He couldn't turn his back and leave innocent people to die. "My abilities are rare, and you know it."

Allsún walked over to the island and began unpacking the items from her shopping trip, placing them on the counter a little more forcefully than necessary. "You want to tell me about rare? I'm the only freaking faerie left in this dimension, David. How's *that* for rare?"

He clenched his teeth and fought to keep calm. He wasn't angry at her. He was angry at their situation, that they'd been dealt a shitty card in life, one that left them with this burden. How could he blame her for wanting a normal life? Hell, he wanted that, too. But how could she not see that he would never be able to live with himself, knowing that innocent people were being hurt, dying, families were being ripped apart by demon possession, when he could be out there preventing it, doing something about it? Most people's greatest achievement in life was building up a worthwhile 401k and retiring happy, but he had a chance to really make a difference. His ability was the card God had dealt him, and he could do something with it.

He moved to stand across from her at the island. "That's all the more reason you should be able to see where I'm coming from. I can't just ignore the lives of others, Allie."

"Yet you can ignore mine. What about *me?* What about what *I* want out of life? I'm going to be your wife, David. Regardless of whether you think it sounds selfish or not, you have to be willing to put me first, before everything. You won't be able to do that if you're too busy saving the world every day. You don't have to be a hero. Screw fate. Make your own damn destiny. Practice some free will."

"I have," he said. "I've made my choice."

Allsún stopped what she was doing and glanced up at him. "What do you mean?"

David inhaled a deep breath. He knew she wouldn't be happy about this, but all he could do was hope that she would support his decision in the end. He cleared his throat. "I have something to show you."

Her eyes widened as she watched him in silence. Slowly he turned around. Gripping the hem of his shirt, he pulled the black muscle tee over his head and tossed it aside.

Allsún gasped. He couldn't imagine the look on her face at that moment. Her eyes were probably trailing the edges of the dark black tribal tattoo ringed with slightly swollen red skin from the freshness of the artwork. The symbol that openly labeled him as an active member of the Execution Underground. Sure, he wasn't a full member yet. He'd just finally agreed to go into training, but once you signed with the Execution Underground, you were with them for life. You didn't give up on training or decide it was too much. Only the most elite men were chosen to join, and none of those men were quitters. It had been a major decision, but ultimately, one he knew he had to make.

With the resources the Execution Underground provided and the training they would give him, he would be able to hunt demons more successfully than ever, hone his abilities to near perfection. Not to mention that the generous pay would allow him to hunt demons full-time, saving people, while still helping to provide Allsún with the life he knew she deserved.

Sure, they might not be able to have everything they ever wanted—mainly children, because he couldn't bear the thought of placing any child in potential danger—but they would live comfortably. Allsún could continue working as a veterinary technician and care for all the animals she wanted to without having to worry about how much money she was or wasn't making. Lord knew, her heart was big enough that she wanted to take in every stray out there, and hell, he would happily let her if that would bring her joy. They could have the perfect life while also knowing they were creating a difference in other people's lives with the sacrifices they were making.

He spoke without facing her. "I signed the recruitment papers today. There's no turning back now. I have to do this, Allie. It's what I was meant to do." He finally turned to meet her eyes, and what he saw sent his heart plummeting to the floor.

Allsún's eyes were clouded; she was teetering dangerously on the edge of tears. She bit her lower lip. "You joined the Execution Underground without telling me?"

His shoulders fell. Why did she have to put such a negative spin on it? "I *am* telling you. I'm telling you now. It's not like I've kept it a secret from you."

She rolled her eyes and let out a forced laugh. "Ha! Oh, yeah, you haven't kept it a secret from me. That's for sure. You just neglected to tell me, when I left for work this morning and told you I'd be going shopping with Linda afterward, that in the meantime you'd be joining an international covert organization that would change our life and our relationship forever. No, you weren't keeping secrets."

David reached for her hand, but she pulled it back. "Allie, I didn't *know* earlier today, okay? Not for sure. You've known I've been thinking about this the past few months, and then this morning, after you'd left for work, I finally made up my mind."

"Yeah, I knew you were considering it—and you knew I didn't approve. What happened to my say in the matter? If we're going to be married, then I need to be included in any major life decisions you make." The tears finally brimmed over and rolled down her cheeks.

He imagined his heart shriveling into a crinkled raisin. It always killed him when she cried. Sure, they didn't fight a lot, but like all couples, they butted heads occasionally. And any time those tears came, especially when he knew they were because of him, he could barely take it. "Allie, please don't cry. I thought you would understand my decision. I made a choice, and I hoped you would support it." He walked around the island toward her, but she stepped back, keeping the distance between them.

"You've made your choice, all right. You chose your own need to fulfill your fucking hero complex and save the damn world over the woman you supposedly love."

"Supposedly? What do you mean 'supposedly'? Of *course* I love you."

She glared at him, the look in her eyes accusing and full of pain. "Do you? Could have fooled me. Last time I checked, if you love someone you include them in major decisions that affect both of you, you're honest and you consider their needs, not ignore them."

"Allsún, would you please listen to me?"

"No, *you* listen, David Jonathan Matthew Aronowitz. You know how much I want a family with you, how much I've *always* wanted a family with you. Either you call up the Execution Underground right now and tell them to shove it, or you suck it up and agree to let us have a normal life together—one filled with white picket fences and happy babies."

David shook his head. "Allsún, you know I can't do that. I can't go back on my word to the Execution Underground now, and I won't raise a child while I'm working in such a dangerous profession. I won't put my children—our children—in jeopardy, and if that means not having any, then so be it."

"So you can't go back on your word to the Execution Underground but you can go back on your word to me?"

"Allsún—"

"You're telling me that your promise to them is worth more than the promise you made to me when you gave me this ring?" She held up her hand, shoving the ring on her finger into his face.

"Gorgeous—"

"No!" Allsún yelled. "Don't you 'gorgeous' me. I want children, David. I want a big happy family and I always have, and if you won't give that to me, then..." Her voice trailed off, as if she wasn't sure what she would do then.

As much as he wanted to give in and make her happy,

he knew that it was out of the question. Aside from their kids being in constant danger, there was no way he could be home with her 24/7, and being pregnant would make her vulnerable. His heart ached. How could she not see that he wanted all those things, too? But they were also things he knew he couldn't have. "You know I can't, Allsún."

She met his gaze. The look in her eyes was full of a mixture of unadulterated rage and pain. The emotional punch to his gut was staggering. "It's not that you can't, David. You *won't.* You call me selfish for wanting to live a happy life, yet you're willing to sacrifice the happiness of the ones you love all so you can save the world."

She turned on her heel and walked toward the door. He started to follow her, but she raised her hand to stop him. "Don't bother," she said.

His heart shattered like a glass mirror someone had taken a sledgehammer to as she slipped her engagement ring off her finger. She placed it on the side table near the doorway, her back still facing him. "To them you may be a hero, but to me, you're just the man who broke my heart."

Without another word, she opened the door and walked out of his life.

Chapter 9

David closed his eyes and let out a long sigh as he tried to stop the barrage of painful memories flooding his mind. He wasn't sure how much more he could take. He closed the book he'd been attempting to read and dropped it on to the coffee table with an audible thud. Normally, especially after a shitty night's work, he could easily fall into one of the stories of romance and happily-ever-after he enjoyed reading, but now, with Allsún in the other room, all the book did was remind him of exactly what he was missing out on, the very demons he attempted to keep at bay by reading romances in the first place.

Damn. Lying on that couch with all the shit he had on his mind was about as fun as taking a buck-naked ride on a seriously pissed-off bronco with a cattle prod aimed straight for the balls, and he didn't mean the bronco's.

David blamed himself. For all of it. It was his fault she'd ended up hideously tortured and in the hospital. If he hadn't been such a jerk the night they broke up, maybe she wouldn't have left, and if she'd never left, then he would've been able to protect her better. And she would still be his. He'd been so foolish back then. So caught up in his own stupid hero complex and desire to save people that he hadn't even realized he was pushing away the only woman who mattered to him, denying her the life she wanted. All of it was his fault. Once she'd been taken by Robert, if he'd just gotten to her sooner, if he hadn't been so weak, babying his leg, maybe she would be fine by now. Back to normal. Maybe she wouldn't be in danger. Because now, with the demons knowing there was still someone of Fae blood left outside the Isle, they wouldn't leave her alone until she was dead.

Add that to the shit-storm he'd found in that family's basement and he hadn't thought the night could get any worse. But he'd been wrong. Knowing Allsún was lying in his bed, the same bed where they used to make love, made everything far, *far* worse. All he could hope was that tomorrow the samples he'd sent to Headquarters turned up something he could use, something that could lead him to the demon that had murdered that poor family and that also gave him some clue as to how to protect Allsún from all the demons that were about to start knocking down doors to get to her.

Silence deafened him as he lay on the couch, staring at the ceiling. Was she lying awake reliving the past, too, or had she gone straight to sleep in there? Not that he could blame her. Some nights he came home and crashed when the hunt had gone badly; other times, he found himself unable to sleep at all. He wasn't sure which was worse: the racing thoughts or the nightmares about the atrocities he saw on a regular basis.

"Did you find something to read?" He said the words just loudly enough that she could hear him from the other room, but hopefully not loudly enough to wake her if she was asleep.

"Uh, yeah. I did. Thanks," she called back to him. From the clear sound of her voice, she was still very much awake. A lull of silence passed before her voice came from the bedroom again. "Hey, David."

"Yeah?"

She paused for a second before continuing. "I lied to you."

He frowned. He couldn't imagine what she could possibly have lied to him about. Their conversations since she'd shown up at the crime scene had been pretty straightforward. "About what?"

He heard her sigh. "My last relationship wasn't really all that great, even though I wanted it to be."

David blinked several times, not quite certain what to say. Holy fuck, was the universe giving him a sign? If not, this had to be some sort of incredibly cruel joke. Because there were no ifs, ands or buts about it—he wanted to get back together with Allsún and would jump at any chance to hold her in his arms again. But he hadn't expected this. This was practically an open invitation to inquire further into her love life, to show her that he could be just as loving and caring toward her as he'd always been, that he wanted her in any capacity he could have her. He wanted to say to her then that he still loved her and she didn't need any other man in her life, because he could be everything she needed and more. Instead, all he could manage was, "Why are you telling me this?"

He swung his long legs over the side of the couch, stood and rounded the corner into the bedroom. Allsún was sitting on the edge of the bed, leaning back and using her arms to support her weight on top of the white-and-black comforter.

"I don't know. I guess because at one point you were my best friend, and I hoped that maybe we could still talk that way, you know?"

He crossed his arms and leaned against the door frame. "Yeah, sure. So what exactly weren't you happy with about that guy?" Though he knew it wouldn't be her answer, deep down he prayed she would say, "Because he wasn't you."

She shrugged. "It's kind of hard to put my finger on."

He cracked a grin. Oh, she'd set that one up perfectly for him. "If it's so small that it's hard to put your finger on, he might want to see a plastic surgeon."

She shot him a glare, but it quickly faded into a grin. "You know that's not what I meant."

He chuckled. "Come on. It was a little bit funny."

Her grin widened slightly, but she didn't respond.

"From the sound of it, the relationship lasted awhile. If you weren't happy, why not end it right off the bat?" he asked.

"I don't know. I guess I didn't want to be lonely, or maybe I felt like he was someone I *should* love, but for some reason I just *didn't.*" She patted the spot beside her, inviting him to sit down.

He crossed the room and sat down next to her. “There’s no ‘should’ about love. You either love someone or you don’t. Either way, you can’t blame yourself for feeling the way you did. Love isn’t an emotion we can control.”

“I know that, but it’s just…everything about this guy was what I always thought I wanted in a man, but once I had it, I realized it wasn’t what I wanted after all.”

“People are allowed to change their minds. No one says you have to always want the same thing. We change over time. We grow as people. We’re changing every minute. Change isn’t something you should fear.”

“It’s not that I fear it. I guess I’ve just found that I want something I know isn’t very good for me, and I’ve already made a lot of decisions I’ve regretted over the years.”

He gave a half laugh. “Unless its heroin you’re wanting or some other thing that inevitably leads to self-destruction, I think that what you want will always be what’s best.”

She glanced in his direction. “You’re wrong. It would be self-destructive. I know that from experience.”

“In that case, I guess it’s something you should avoid.”

“I suppose so.”

"You going to elaborate or keep being cryptic?" He lifted his hand and debated placing it on her shoulder, then thought better of it. He didn't want to make her uncomfortable or make her feel as if he was putting the moves on her when she was vulnerable, even though God knew that was what he wanted. Anything that would get her back. Hell, if he'd been the type of guy who thought with his dick, he would have played every card in his deck by now, courtesy of the near perpetual hard-on she always gave him. Damn, he wanted her, and there was nothing but the David Bowie T-shirt she'd slipped into between him and every bit of flesh he wanted to caress.

She turned toward him. "Do you remember when we first met?" she said, changing the subject.

He smirked. "I suppose it's a cliché if I say 'Of course I remember,' but, yeah, I do. What about it?"

She shrugged and smoothed the edge of the old T-shirt over her knees. "I don't know. The thought popped into my mind. I don't think I ever thanked you for that."

He chuckled. "No need to thank me. That kid deserved to be socked in the face. Little douchebag."

"He'd been picking on me for weeks, you know. It was such a relief for him to leave me alone." She allowed herself to fall back on to the bed, stretching her arms out beside her. "I had a rough time in school in general."

He lay down beside her and rolled on to his side, so he could see her face, her perfect pink lips, her delicate cheekbones, those big emerald eyes that he could stare into for days. "I know you did."

She looked toward him. "The worst was Lindie, though."

He frowned at the mention of his ex-girlfriend, a girl he'd dated in high school and always regretted. "I thought she was only a bitch to you that one time."

Allsún shook her head. "Not by a long shot. She tortured me the entire time you guys were dating. I just never had the heart to tell you." She turned away again and stared at the ceiling. "I know you loved her."

He propped himself on one elbow, so she could see the confused expression on his face. "What are you talking about? I didn't love her."

"Then why were you with her for so long?"

He chuckled. "Allsún, I was sixteen and a jock. What do you *think* I was with her for? I wanted to get in her pants."

Allsún blushed. "Oh. I just always thought you felt the same way about her as you did me."

"No way. I was never that way with you."

Her mouth fell open, and she gaped at him. A sheen filled her eyes, and he could have sworn she was about to cry. A pang hit him in the heart. It physically pained him every time he saw her tears. He scrambled to amend what he'd said. "What I mean to say is that our relationship was about more than my teenage sex drive. You were my best friend, and I was crazy in love with you. Don't get me wrong, though. I definitely wanted you."

I still want you. I miss you every day. Damn, how he wanted to tell her that.

She swiped quickly at her eyes. "It sure did take us a long time to get around to that, though."

"I didn't want to rush you into anything you weren't ready for."

"That probably wasn't much fun for you, was it?"

Without thinking, he reached over and tipped her chin toward him, guiding her to meet his gaze. "Can I be honest with you?"

She nodded.

"The wait was awful, but so worth it in the end. Before we finally made love, though, I wouldn't have been surprised if I sprouted hair on my palms."

She laughed hysterically, a laugh so hard she was

sure her stomach muscles would ache afterward. He chuckled along with her as she gasped for air. Tears poured down her face as she fought to control herself, clutching at her stomach to hold herself together.

David grinned from ear to ear. "Totally worth it, though."

As her laughter calmed, she turned toward him. The tension in her body had visibly relaxed. He loved making her laugh. It was always one of his favorite things to do.

"We did have a phenomenal sex life," she said.

He glanced away, forcing himself to not allow the longing he was feeling to creep into his voice. His cock hardened, and he prayed to God she didn't notice his obvious arousal. "Don't tempt me."

A rosy blush blossomed across her cheeks. Gorgeous. "What do you mean, don't tempt you?"

He ran a hand over his buzzed hair. Man, he needed to get hold of himself. "You know exactly what I mean. Don't tempt me into asking if we can be 'friends with benefits.'"

She laughed. "You would want that?"

He raised a brow. "Do you even need to ask?"

She turned away from him. "I didn't know."

He didn't believe that for a second. How could she

not know that he still wanted her? It was so obvious. At least he'd always thought so. He hadn't been the one to break things off. She had. "It's not like we broke up because the attraction went away. You don't spend that long sharing a bed with someone only to all of a sudden stop wanting them. Not unless you suddenly start wanting someone else. And as I already told you, I'm not with anyone else."

She shook her head, still refusing to look at him. "I don't know what to say to that."

"You don't have to say anything." He paused, not certain whether to go ahead and ask what he wanted to know. He knew it wasn't really any of his business, but his curiosity got the better of him. He cleared his throat. "So…how was the ex in bed?"

Allie's head snapped toward him, and she pegged him with an annoyed look. "It's none of your damn business."

He knew he shouldn't have asked, but he couldn't help but wonder. "Sorry. I'm not trying to be crude, but at one point the happiness of your pussy *was* my business. Old habits die hard."

"David!" She hit him in the arm, not hard, just enough to be playful.

A sly grin crossed his face. "Sorry, I couldn't resist. I was just curious, I guess."

"Well, keep your curiosity to yourself."

He nodded. Silence fell over them, but he couldn't hold himself back.

"No, seriously, how was he in bed?" he asked.

She folded her arms over her chest, and he could tell from the look on her face that if she'd been standing instead of lying on the bed, she would have had her hands on her hips. "Why do you think I would tell you that?"

He shrugged. "Well, you want to talk like we're best friends again, right? You wouldn't tell your best friend how your ex-boyfriend was in bed?"

She rolled her eyes. "But you're *not* just a friend, you're an ex. Talking about my sex life with you is hardly how I wanted to go about rebuilding our friendship."

He threw his hands up in mock surrender. He played it cool, but he had to be honest with himself. When she called him her ex, it stung like hell, a knife straight to his heart. He forced a chuckle. "Okay, point taken. I do still want to know, though."

"It was good, okay?"

He winced. "Ooh, good. That's a word you only want to hear describing the weather."

She pointed a finger at him. "Be nice."

"I wasn't being a jerk. I was just telling the truth."

She flashed him a coy smile. "Yeah, well, everyone can't do amazing tricks with their tongue."

David couldn't help but laugh. "Yikes. He gives shitty oral?"

"Going *way* too far into the details there."

"Okay, I'll stop asking."

She sat up on the bed. "Can't you ask me normal things? Like maybe how my career is doing?"

"If I asked you normal things, I wouldn't be me."

"You'd still be you, just a less vulgar version."

He sat up beside her. "Vulgarity mixed with humor has always been my thing, but if it makes you feel better, I'll ask—how's your career going?"

She stood and slowly paced in front of him, arms still crossed over her chest. "Fine. I'm working at the same veterinary clinic."

"Still ignoring that head vet you swore 'wasn't actually making a pass' at you? I never liked that guy. I know you said he was just being friendly, but I always had a sneaking suspicion he was into you and too scared of me to act on it."

Allsún chewed on her lower lip before she finally

spoke. "Last I checked, he's still scared shitless of you, but not enough to stop him from being with me."

David couldn't stop himself from swearing. Seriously? He didn't want to imagine her with anyone else, let alone that damn vet. He'd never liked the guy, mostly because of the I'm-so-in-love-with-you eyes he'd always made at Allsún, at *his* girl. He tried to hold himself back and find something nice to say for her sake, but he couldn't bring himself to do it.

"Fuck, Allie. *That's* the guy you were sleeping with? Of all people…"

She stopped pacing and glared at him. "Hey, Tom is a good person. You don't know him."

He fought back another curse. He knew it was her choice, but really, of all the people she could have dated… "I may not know him, but I *do* know that he was always eyeing you at the office Christmas parties, even when I was there with you and we were engaged. In my book, that makes the guy a total sleazeball."

"He was never a sleazeball. He just had a crush on me, and you didn't like it. But once you and I separated it was kind of nice to have someone pay attention to me, so when he asked me out I said yes."

He pushed off from the bed and walked toward the living room, running a hand over his buzz cut. Part of him wished he had enough hair left to rip out. Anything to calm the emotions plaguing him at the news. "Man, I never thought he would be the one to end up with my woman."

Before he could anticipate what she was doing, she grabbed hold of his arm, forcing him to turn and face her. "Your woman? Since when have I been your property?" She released him in disgust.

"I'm not saying you're my property. I know you're your own person and you're free to do whatever you want with whoever you want, but can't you understand how I would still see you as mine? I loved you for years, Allie. Longer than that loser has even known you."

She jabbed a finger into his chest. "He's not a loser, and he was good to me."

Gently, he caught her wrist. He cradled her hand against his heart. "Even if he was good to you, you didn't love him like you loved me."

She wrenched her hand away from him. "You're putting words in my mouth. Just because I said we weren't serious, that doesn't mean I didn't care about him."

"I'm not trying to be an ass, I'm just trying to get you to admit the truth. You just said a few moments ago that your relationship with him wasn't serious. You're not together anymore, so clearly, you weren't happy."

She shook her head. "You don't know what my relationship with him was like just from a few minutes of talking about it."

"Maybe I don't, but I do know *you,* and I can tell when you're happy—and when you're talking about him, you're not happy."

"Maybe I just don't want to talk about him with you," she said.

"And why is that? Because it reminds you of the great thing you and I used to have together? Because I know you miss that?"

She stared at him in disbelief. "You're putting words in my mouth. I never said I missed what we had." She stepped back, but he took a step forward, closing the distance between them.

She swatted at him in an attempt to shoo him away, but he caught her hand in his and pulled her closer. "Maybe not in so many words, but I can see it in your face, Allie. I'm not saying you want to get back together, there's too much bad blood between us for that, but don't try and tell me that what we had wasn't an amazing and beautiful thing. We were crazy in love. Look me in the eye and tell me that some part of you doesn't miss that."

She met his gaze and opened her mouth, but no words came out. He knew they wouldn't.

Pulling her closer, he wrapped his arms around her, leaned down and kissed her hard. Her mouth was warm against his. She tasted like sweet strawberries. For a moment she didn't respond, just allowed him to take control, but soon she leaned farther into him, kissing him back feverishly. A wave of desire rolled through him.

Suddenly she pulled her mouth away as quickly as he'd captured it. "I can't do this to you."

"Do what? I want this, and I think you do, too. We're both consenting adults. What's so wrong about it?" he whispered.

Placing her small hands on his chest, she pushed away from him slightly. "Because I know how you are, David. You're not the kind of guy who has sex with no strings attached."

"What do you mean by that?"

She looked away. "I mean that you always want a relationship, and we've already tried that and it didn't work."

He tried to pull her closer, but she eased farther back. "Maybe I've changed," he said.

"I don't think you have." She stepped out of his embrace.

Instinctually, he reached for her, but she only moved farther out of reach. "Well, if I haven't, then it will be my problem, won't it?"

"I can't do it. I'm sorry."

He dropped his hands to his sides, and his shoulders slumped. Shit. He knew when to admit defeat. He'd been wrong, so wrong. Too confident in thinking that maybe she still loved him the way he still loved her. "It's okay, Allie. It was my fault for pushing the issue. If you don't want to, then I don't want to, either. I'd never pressure you."

"Thank you."

"How about I let you get to bed, huh? We've both had a rough night."

She nodded. "Yeah, I think that would be for the best."

A large lump formed in his throat. Damn. Having her so close like this when he wanted her so badly was the sweetest and worst kind of torture. He forced himself to nod in return. "Okay. I'll let you be. Feel free to use anything you need."

He bit his lower lip and fought back all the frustration, all the pain, all the anger. It was his fault they'd come to this, his fault she didn't love him anymore. He wanted to tell her that he couldn't live without her, that he would rather die than do anything to make her hate him. But instead all he said was "good night" before he walked from the room, resigning himself to yet another night of sleeping alone.

Chapter 10

At the click of the bedroom door closing behind David, Allsún fell onto the bed, tears pouring down her face. She clutched the soft bed linens in her hands. How had this happened? She had enough on her plate as it was, but here was David, pushing all her buttons. Part of her hated him for knowing her so well, knowing exactly what to say to make her heart melt and make her miss him more than anything.

But how could she be with him after everything that had happened?

Of course she wanted him. But she had to be honest with herself now that the emotions were staring her right in the face. There was one thing in this world she wanted more than anything—more, even, than David: a child of her own. Ever since she'd been a little girl she'd dreamed of the day when she could be as wonderful a mother to her child as her own mother had been to her. She loved David, but she couldn't give up the aching need for a child that burned in her chest. Not even for him, and in some ways she blamed him. If it wasn't for the fight they'd had, the things he'd said the night they broke up, maybe she wouldn't have run from his apartment, maybe then the most awful night of her life wouldn't have ensued. She tried to keep the memories at bay, but they were inexorable and flooded over her despite her efforts.

Allsún's feet crashed against the pavement as she ran full force down the street with tears pouring down her cheeks. She hadn't bothered to grab any of her shopping bags, and she didn't care. The wind stung against her face, but she didn't slow down until she managed to catch a cab and the door was firmly closed behind her.

Slowly she turned around as she grabbed the handrail. Her eyes scanned the platform, and her heart sank even further, something she wouldn't have said was possible a moment earlier. He hadn't come after her. He hadn't followed her or tried to stop her. With seemingly not an ounce of remorse for his actions, he'd let her walk right out the door, right out of his life. She choked back a sob. This couldn't be happening. It couldn't be. She couldn't manage anything but lifeless mechanical movements until she reached home.

Though she wasn't quite sure how, as fatigued as she'd been feeling lately, something kept her going until finally she reached the front door. She jammed the key into the lock, then jiggled the knob left, then right, to undo the ancient lock, which her mother had discussed replacing countless times. Finally she stumbled into the old building.

It didn't take her long to realize that her mother wasn't home. An odd stillness throughout the house told her that much. But it didn't matter. The only thing that *did* matter was that she'd stupidly assumed David would come after her, and he hadn't. She knew what assuming did. It made her look and feel like a complete ass. So much for the self-righteous attitude she'd had when storming out on him. She should have just told him the truth.

She locked the dead bolts and shuffled in exhaustion toward her room. Without even taking her shoes off, she dropped her purse on the mattress and allowed herself to fall on to the old knit purple blanket, which her mother had made for her as a baby, years ago. As her body made contact with the sweet softness of the bed beneath her, she allowed herself to sob harder than she ever had before. The smell of talc and baby powder—the scent of her mother—filled her nose as her eyes grew swollen from her tears. She felt like a fool. How could she ever have thought that her life would end up perfect? That she could find the man of her dreams, marry him and live happily ever after?

Maybe she should go back. Was she pathetic for thinking that? After all, David had asked her to stay by his side, and she had been the one to walk out. He didn't even know how hurtful the words he'd said had been right now. If he knew the truth, would he have said those things? If she'd told him afterwards, would he have taken them back?

Allsún shivered and quickly huddled under the covers, then rubbed her hand over her barely rounded belly. It was her first pregnancy, so even though she was twelve weeks along, she was just now beginning to show. Luckily for her, she managed to hide her newly forming baby bump underneath baggy clothes. She'd known for a couple of weeks now, but she'd been waiting to tell David. She'd wanted to give him the news at the perfect moment, but no matter how many different ways she planned to tell him, none of them felt right.

She'd hoped the baby shoes Shelley had given them would be a good intro into telling him that in less than nine months he would be a father.

So much for that.

He'd made it blatantly clear that he didn't want children with her. She rubbed her belly again. She swore it seemed rounder every time she felt it. She wasn't going to be able to hide her pregnancy much longer.

She wondered again whether David would have said those things if he'd known she was already carrying his child. Part of her felt that he wouldn't have, but did it really matter now? He'd already said them, and she'd already left. Even if she didn't go back for her own sake, because despite everything she loved him, maybe she should go back for the sake of the baby. It would need a father. And David would never abandon his own child, no matter how unwanted that baby might initially be.

From behind her, she heard a small creak as someone stepped into her room. She'd been sobbing so hard she hadn't even heard her mother get home.

"Leave me alone, Mom. I just need to be alone for a while." The mound of blankets and pillows she'd buried herself in muffled her voice.

She heard a few more steps, though her mother didn't speak. A warm hand pressed softly on to her shoulder, the touch lingering before suddenly tightening, tightening....

"Ouch! Mom, that hur—"

Without warning, she was shoved backward. Her spine buckled as she slammed into the wall of her bedroom. Pain seared through her as her head bashed against the plaster, sending a warm trickle of blood running through her hair.

Her mother was standing at her bedside, hand out, and holding her to the wall. A distorted voice sounded from her throat. "Mommy's not home."

Allsún's eyes widened, and the little breath left from the initial impact escaped her. The rotten smell of sulfur filled her nose.

Demon.

Allsún writhed against the demon's hold, fighting to free herself to no avail. The demon stepped closer, twisting her mother's normally warm face in a look of pure hatred.

"Well, would you look at that?" A sinister grin crossed the demon's face as it reached out and touched Allsún's pregnant belly.

"David!" she screamed, though she knew it wasn't any use. David was nowhere to be found. He hadn't come after her.

The demon chuckled.

"Please, don't hurt me. Please, have mercy on me. I'm pregnant."

"And that's exactly why I'm *not* going to have any mercy on you."

"No, please, don't. Please. You can come back and kill me once the baby is born, but, please, don't hurt me now. Don't hurt my baby. Please! I'm begging you!"

"You really think pleading is going to save that disgusting unborn piece of filth inside you? That's exactly why I'm here."

Slowly lifting Allsún's shirt, the demon ran a hand over her bare stomach. The familiar feeling of her mother's smooth skin coupled with the evil she knew was behind the touch made her skin crawl. She cringed and tried to pull away.

"*You* may not know it yet, but I can sense you're having a boy. I can already feel his power. He's going to be a self-righteous exorcist just like his father."

"No, you're wrong. He's not going to be an exorcist. He won't have that kind of life."

"You're right. He *won't*—because I'm here to make sure he doesn't have a life at all."

The demon moved as if to shove its hand deep inside her gut. Pain the likes of which Allsún had never known before seared through her body. She screamed and fought against the demon's hold, but it was no use. Tears poured down her face as she felt the monster's hand grip her insides and twist. As if someone had flicked out a light blazing inside her, she felt the baby's life force slowly fade. Blood gushed between her legs, staining her jeans a warm blackish red.

The demon released her as her screams of pain subsided into cries of heartbreak. She crumpled to the floor in a puddle of her own blood. The sound of her mother's footsteps leaving the room pounded in her ears. With every last bit of strength she had, she dragged herself to the end of her bed, pulling her purse down and fumbling inside to find her cell phone.

Her vision spun as she pressed the numbers.

"9-1-1 operator. What's your emergency?"

Allsún tried to speak, but only a weak noise came out.

"Ma'am? Ma'am? I can't hear you, ma'am. Please, speak up."

"Help me," Allsún panted.

Spots massed in front of her eyes before she felt herself pass out.

Chapter 11

Tears continued to pour down Allsún's face as she pushed the horrific memory from her mind. It didn't matter that she knew the events of that night weren't David's fault; no amount of reason could convince her heart otherwise. There had been so many nights when she'd dreamed that, in the moment when she'd screamed David's name, he'd burst in and saved her, only to wake and find no such thing had happened. Each time she woke, David was no closer to saving her than he had been that night.

It didn't matter that there had been no way for him to know what would happen when she left his apartment. All she could focus on was how, if he had just loved her enough to come after her, maybe their son would still be alive. A sense of pure loneliness washed over her as she lay there in David's bed. She hated times like this when she was alone, when she missed not only David but the baby she'd lost, and her now-deceased mother, as well. She wished she could feel good about herself the way she did before losing her son. She should have been able to protect him, but she'd been incapable. She'd failed him as a mother.

It was her own fault, too, for not telling David the truth, for running off instead of facing her problems, even though she'd had no more idea than David had of what was to follow. Years later, she still had so much pain, yet no true target for the blame other than the way she felt about herself.

She lay there, allowing the tears to flow freely until she had no more left. She gave herself the chance to cry not only over her current situation but over everything. The demons who were coming after her, the family that had been murdered, and the awful things Robert had done to her. When she couldn't shed another tear, she wandered into the bathroom and cleaned up her face, using cold water to reduce the puffiness around her eyes. When she was finished, she returned to the bed, but no matter how long she lay there, sleep evaded her.

She lay in the silence, listening for any sound of

David moving around in the living room. She thought about the kiss they'd shared, about how the last time she could remember feeling something so electric, so emotional, was the first time they'd made love. She couldn't deny that she wanted him on a physical level. It was the emotional baggage she wasn't certain she could handle.

Hell, just kissing him sent her into a fit of tears, thinking of all the things she regretted and wished she had done differently. That could only be a sign that sleeping with him was a terrible idea, right? Even if sleeping with him meant she could get her light back.

She tried to convince herself of that, but her heart kept telling her otherwise. Yes, she was crying for so many reasons, but the one that wouldn't leave her was that no matter how she looked at it, kissing David had made her realize just how much she really missed him.

What in Morgana's name was she doing?

Exactly what got me into this mess—not following my heart.

"David?" she called out. When no response came, she swiped the back of her hand over her eyes one last time before she padded into the living room. "David?" she said again.

Through the darkness, she saw David stir.

A moment later he sat up. He rubbed the sleep from his eyelids and stretched before turning toward her. "Hey, Allie. You need something?"

"Yeah, actually, I do. I…uh…I changed my mind."

Before she realized what was going on, he pulled her into his arms and kissed her deep. She fell on top of him, her body pressed flush against his. His tongue met hers, and his erection pushed against her hips. She ground her hips into his, eager to feel him inside her. He moaned beneath her lips and kissed her harder. Slipping his hand around the back over her neck, he cradled her as their mouths met.

An electric pulse, the likes of which she'd only known the first time they kissed, rushed through her. Heat flooded between her legs. His length pushing against her sent waves of heat through her body, arousing her most sensitive flesh and preparing her for his touch. With ease, he ripped the T-shirt from her body. Her nipples hardened in the cool air of the apartment, sending a chill down her spine. The whole situation was all wrong, but damn, did he feel right against her.

Continuing to kiss him, she snaked her hands down his sides until she could hook her fingers beneath the hem of his shirt. He sat up, allowing her to pull it over his head, then wrapped his arms around her and slid his hand down to her behind. He shifted out from underneath her, then scooped her up into his arms, laying her flat on the couch and straddling her. Eagerly, she unbuckled his leather belt.

He kissed her again, sucking on her lower lip, then pulled back and whispered against her mouth, "Not yet. I want to make you come first."

She smiled and kissed him again. She had forgotten what that felt like, a man wanting to pleasure her first, who was willing to take her into his mouth. Tom was too vanilla for oral sex. She found herself blushing suddenly, as if this were her first time.

David stopped midway as he slowly traced light kisses down to her navel. "Am I tickling you?"

She shook her head. "No, I was just thinking about how long it's been since a man has done this for me."

He raised a brow. "Who wouldn't want to? You taste divine."

He trailed more kisses down her stomach until he rested his head on the soft skin of her mons. A wave of heat rushed through her as he gently drew her clit into his mouth. He rolled his tongue over her, and she bucked against him. She reached down and ran her hands over his head, his buzz cut smooth yet coarse beneath her fingertips. Running his hand over her inner thigh, he positioned his fingers at her entrance before easing them into her. She cried out as he immediately began massaging her g-spot. She slickened and rocked against him, moving with the rhythm of his fingers as he brought her closer and closer to the brink of ecstasy.

The flick of his tongue over her flesh sent shivers through her. The warmth of his mouth radiated over her core and heated every inch of her body. He increased the speed of his movements as her arousal rose. She rocked her hips, meeting each thrust of his fingers. The sweet ache between her legs built as she came closer to climax. The vibration in David's fingertips rippled through her, the nerves in her g-spot shooting electric waves all through her body. Her back arched, and she moaned as her pleasure peaked.

"David!" she cried out as she felt herself shatter.

A feeling of pure bliss flooded her, and for the first time in years she lost herself completely in the heat of the moment.

David's cock jerked with need as Allsún's honey flooded his mouth. He lapped up her sweetness like a hungry animal. The warm flesh of her thighs pressed against the sides of his face as she ground herself into his mouth. She tasted like nirvana on his tongue. She gasped when the last shudder of her climax rolled over her. He released her, pushing himself from the couch to strip off his jeans. His pants and belt hit the floor with a thud.

He couldn't wait to be inside her again. It had been so long. How many nights had he dreamed of a scenario like this? He met her gaze and smiled as he lost himself in her gorgeous emerald eyes. Within a heartbeat he was on top of her, their tongues swirling together as he positioned himself just outside her entrance. He dipped his head and captured her taut nipple in his mouth. A small moan escaped her lips as he rolled his tongue over the hard peak. He palmed her free breast. She was small enough that she could fit in his hand, and he loved the ease with which he could cup her breasts and pleasure her. When he released her, he kissed her once more.

"I'm going deep," he said.

A naughty grin crossed her lips, and he took that as a sign.

He sheathed himself inside her, and she cried out as the wet warmth of her walls tightened around him. He filled her completely, pushing her to the max. She threw her head back as he thrust into her. Holy shit, she felt phenomenal. He'd missed this.

"Do you like it deep like that?" he asked as he pushed into her again.

She moaned and bucked against him.

"I'm guessing that's a yes."

Sitting up, he lifted her legs, placing them over his shoulders. He knew exactly what she liked best, and he intended to give it to her. He leaned forward. A low growl escaped his throat as he saw how flexible she was. Man, he loved that. He could bend her like a pretzel, and she always welcomed it. He intended to leave her begging for more.

"Take me," she whispered.

He growled and nipped at her ear. "What did you say?"

"I said take me."

"You don't have to ask me again." He slammed into her, cupping her sweet behind as he moved. His cock jerked with pleasure as he penetrated her hard and deep. Tilting his hips, he aimed for her favorite spot. The one he was certain would make her climax explosive. The sheen of her wetness coated him as he watched himself slip in and out of her. He loved seeing the way she took the full length of him. He felt all her muscles tense as she neared her orgasm.

"David!" she cried out as the first shudder of her release overcame her. He watched her ride wave upon wave of pleasure, knowing his own climax wasn't far behind. Her walls squeezed him tight, the final clench sending him over the edge. He rode the radiating pleasure of his own finish, pumping her full of his seed. As the last shudder rolled through him, he pulled her into his arms.

He wanted to tell her he missed her and still loved her more than she would ever realize, but instead he only kissed her again.

Mistress would welcome this addition to the mix. Seeing the look of terror in the woman's eyes as she pleaded sent a jolt of pleasure down his spine. Sammael existed for this. The warm blood drained from her terrified face and on to the shard of glass buried in her womb. That alone was enough to excite him on a level far beyond what these pathetic humans could know.

Too bad he wasn't wearing one of his victims this time. Using a family member's body to kill the other victims was always so much more fun. The first family had been priceless. But now he was wearing the first family's neighbor, who was being forced to watch helplessly as he became an instrument of slaughter, and that was almost as good.

The woman's pulse quickened, then slowed as she fell further into shock, slowly bleeding out. He enjoyed the husband's stupid, undignified expression as he watched the woman he loved gradually slip closer to death. He snapped a chunk of the glass shard from her abdomen. What fun could he have with this? The look of panic in the husband's eyes as he lay tied up with no hope of saving his wife told him enough. He admired the bloodied shard before slicing it across the woman's open eye just to see the husband cry harder. The woman convulsed. A final gurgle escaped her lips, but he frowned as the last note of the sound was drowned out by the husband's obnoxious caterwauling.

No matter, he wouldn't be making noise for much longer. He had slit the man's liver after binding him. He would bleed out slowly, over a period of hours, forced to look at his wife's eviscerated corpse before him. To take in the grandeur of his suffering. To give him time to question what he could have done differently to save her, whether if he had taken her home just a few minutes later, she would still be alive. For Sammael, the scrumptious second-guessing, self-blaming psychological hell this man was going through was pure bliss.

Black blood. Dirty human liver blood.

It was a filthy, wonderful sight to see him wallow

in it as he died. His favorite parts were the sounds: the squelching, the screaming, the pleading, the wet pitter-pattering of blood on overpriced hardwood flooring. His Mistress would be pleased.

Those pieces of shit, the hunter and his worthless faerie bitch, they would just *love* this. The exorcist, that sentimental little cocksucker, would just boo-hoo as he sat on that fancy motorcycle of his, and it would make this all the more worthwhile. If Aronowitz only knew what he and Mistress were planning.

And then his Mistress would tear them to shreds, and there would be nothing they could do about it.

Chapter 12

David wasn't sure which was worse, the sound of the alarm or the prospect of getting out of the bed they'd moved to at some point in the night. The alarm blared in his ears as he lay there with Allsún wrapped in his arms. He held her just the slightest bit tighter, wishing he didn't have to let her go. Damn these early-morning Execution Underground meetings. He didn't want the night to end. The alarm continued to whine, a constant reminder of the duties he'd sworn himself to perform.

Damn, this sucked.

After thirty more seconds of working himself up to it, he finally eased Allsún out of his embrace and slipped from beneath the sheets. He watched her lie there, peacefully asleep, while he shut off his alarm.

Her ability to sleep through anything had always amazed him. He hadn't expected last night to go the way it had, but there wasn't a single part of him that wasn't grateful. He'd been dreaming of a reunion like that with Allsún since the night they'd broken up. Sure, her initial rejection had been painful, but all the pain had been erased from his mind as soon as she woke him. He glanced over at the alarm in his hand, then back at Allsún.

Yup, it was official—the way she woke him up last night…best way to wake up *ever*.

He grinned. It killed him to have to leave the apartment, but he dressed, put on his artillery and prepared for the day. Grabbing a notepad from the fridge, he scrawled out a message letting her know where he would be. He made certain to shoot the dead bolts and the bottom lock on his way out. She would be safe there, he was certain of it.

Within twenty minutes David strolled into the warehouse with his head down and shoulders tensed. It didn't matter that he'd just spent an amazing night with Allsún; he knew that more than likely the news waiting on him was not of a happy nature. He trudged into the warehouse and flopped into his usual seat at the table. Damon, Trent and Ash already sat waiting.

"Any news?" he asked.

Damon shook his head. "We all hear it at once."

Great. He would be held in suspense until everyone got there, including Jace. "Where's Shane?"

Ash leaned back in his seat, all relaxed. "Teachin' one of his classes. He said if we need him, call."

"I gave him the okay to be absent. If we need him, we'll call," Damon said.

"So we're just waiting on Jace, then?" David asked.

Damon frowned as he nodded.

About ten minutes later Jace kicked open the door to the warehouse and waltzed inside as if he made it a habit to be late to major covert meetings…oh, wait, he did. He was carrying a large brown paper bag.

A scowl crossed Damon's face. "You're late."

"What else is new?"

"What's with the bag?" David asked.

Jace reached inside and pulled out a large bottle of Johnnie Walker Blue Label and a large wooden box.

"What's this about?" Damon practically growled.

Jace flipped up the box lid and removed a large, fat Cuban cigar. He bit off the tip, pulled out his lighter and puffed. He grabbed the Blue Label by the neck and exhaled smoke.

"What it's about, you crazy motherfuckers, is that I'm going to be a fucking dad."

David was pretty sure his jaw hit the floor before he smiled from ear to ear. "J, you crazy son of a bitch." He stood up and grabbed Jace for a handshake that turned into a hug. "Congratulations, buddy."

"You and Frankie are having a baby?"

Jace shook his head. "Not *a* baby. *Babies.*" He held up two fingers.

Trent gawked. "She's having twins?"

Jace nodded.

"Well, I'll be damned." Ash stuck out his hand. "Congrats, man."

David imagined Jace with a family of his own. He knew how loyal Jace had been to his mother before she'd passed and how much family meant to him, which was why the way his father had been had been such a blow in his childhood. Having kids with Frankie was a great thing, giving him something to look forward to. He wished he hadn't been too much of a coward to do the same with Allsún.

David shook his head with a smile. He couldn't be more pleased for his friend. "Wow. That's great news. I'm really happy for you."

Damon stood, walked around the side of the table, and held out a hand to Jace.

Jace stared at Damon's hand as if it were covered in poisonous snakes before he finally lifted his own and they shook.

"Congratulations," Damon said.

Jace gave a single nod. "Thanks."

To David's surprise, Damon didn't demand they all get to work. David had never so much as seen a drop of liquor touch Damon's lips, but all five hunters shared a drink in Jace's honor. David relaxed in his seat, listening to his best friend talk about his plans to move to a nicer area of town, perhaps out in the suburbs, somewhere that would be a good safe place for their growing family. Watching his friend be so happy and his fellow hunters sharing in that joy, with the thought of Allsún lying in his bed at home, naked and gorgeous from the night they'd spent together, for a second, he almost forgot about all the problems at hand, about all the horrible shit he was up against.

When they'd all finished their drinks and stripped off their artillery, they headed toward the control room. The atmosphere immediately changed from one of lighthearted happiness to strictly business. Suddenly it was impossible for him to forget about the shitty news he was sure lay ahead of him.

His suspicions were confirmed as soon as Chris's face appeared on the monitor. Chris was their contact at HQ. "Hey, guys. You're not going to like the news I'm about to deliver. Especially you, David, since it's about your case."

David swore. Damn, he couldn't catch a break, could he? "Rip it off like a Band-Aid."

"Well, I got pretty much nothing from the samples you sent me."

A collective groan from all five men filled the room.

"All the blood samples were normal, except for the father's. Obviously he had an unusual amount of sulfur in his bloodstream, since he was possessed. Everyone else, the infant included, had completely normal tox screens. The only medication I found even traces of was an asthma med in the teen's blood. There were also high levels of estrogen and progesterone in the mother, which probably meant she was still breast-feeding the baby."

"What about the sulfur in the dad's blood? Did you run that through the database and see what type of demon it came up with?"

Chris nodded. "Yeah, I did, and there was no match,

which means whatever you're dealing with, it's something we haven't seen before."

Fuck. That was the last thing David wanted to hear. Pinpointing the type of demon would have given him at least an indication of how to track the monster, not to mention an idea of any special weaponry or specific exorcisms he could use against it.

"But, lucky for you, I like to go above and beyond," Chris said, breaking David's train of thought. "So I took the liberty of running tests not for an exact match but for something similar. And I came up with this." He jabbed a finger on to a single key on his keyboard. Next to his face on the screen, a profile popped up with the word "Abyzu" flashing at the top.

David groaned. "You've got to be fucking kidding me. I knew it."

Chris raised an eyebrow. "What? Do you have something against Abyzus specifically?"

David shook his head, then let out a long sigh as his fellow hunters all looked toward him. "I was afraid of this. Abyzus are some of the nastiest little bitches to track. This pretty much confirms my theory about the crimes."

"What theory?" Damon asked.

"All of this is just intuition, since we have no evidence, but after examining the scenes, a few things indicated to me that the kids were the focus of the murders. An Abyzu's usual thing is that it possesses children to fuck with the parents' minds, and it feeds off the fear. I think something similar is going on here. From some blood I found on a chair at the scene and the positioning of the bodies, the mother tried to save her baby but was tossed aside. My thought is, why not kill her then, if she's interrupting? The only reason I can think of is that the demon needed the mother alive. I think it was performing some sort of ritual, and was using the parents' fear and horror as they saw their children murdered in order to fuel its power."

"That's just fuckin' sick," Ash said. "Some days I'm thankful I deal with ghosts instead of all those crazy beasts ya'll work with."

"I don't know, man. Ghosts give me the heebie-jeebies." Trent shuddered. "I think we've all got some bad shit to deal with."

Damon looked toward David. "Back on topic. Anything else you want to add?"

David shook his head. "No, that's all I have for now. Abyzus like babies—infants, not toddlers—so if this bastard's similar to an Abyzu, the only way I could possibly track it was if I could somehow monitor all the families in all of Rochester with newborns to twelve-month-olds. There's no way that's possible. So basically, I'm fucked." David fought back the urge to slam his fist on to the control panel.

"Chris, there has to be something headquarters can do about this, right? I mean, the shit-ton of media attention two dead families are going to draw is going to send every fucking family in the city and the surrounding suburbs into a panic," Jace said.

Chris tightened his lips for a moment as if he was thinking. "Which one of you handles the tech stuff for your division? Shane, right?"

They all nodded.

"He's teaching a class at the university this morning. You know, all that smart people shit." Jace waved his hand in dismissal.

David rolled his eyes. He and Jace had never seen eye to eye on education. Jace had a natural intelligence he'd always relied on to get by. David had book smarts because he'd forced himself to remain diligent and go to college. Personally, he admired Shane's super brainy ways and the time he spent teaching.

"Well, with Shane's help, I think I have an idea that will allow us to keep an eye on all the families in

Rochester that have babies under the age of twelve months," Chris said.

Shane was smart, but David had no idea what the hell Chris was getting at. How did he think there was any way to pull this off? "How can we possibly do that?"

"Easy." Chris held up his index finger. "One word. Satellite. If I can get Headquarters to agree, we can tap into one of the government's spy satellites to monitor the families."

David shook his head. The idea sounded too far-fetched. "How will we know which families to monitor?"

Chris smiled. "That's where Shane comes in. Get him to contact me as soon as possible. He can hack into the local hospitals' databases, social services… whatever he needs. I know there are women who've had their children outside of hospitals with midwives and whatnot, but at least this covers the majority of the possible targets. It's better than nothing. Get Shane to contact me as soon as possible so we can work out the interface."

David opened his mouth to speak, but Damon interrupted. "Once we get everyone identified, how are we going to monitor them?"

After typing for several seconds, Chris brought up a

new image on the monitor, a screen covered in varying shades of red, orange and yellow. "We'll be able to see the insides of their homes with thermal imaging, since all demons have a high body temperature, especially when they're possessing someone. There are a couple trainees who owe me a favor. They'll be able to monitor from here, so none of you will have to sit and stare at a screen for hours at a time. I'll have them contact you at the first sign of demonic activity."

Damon spoke up again. "David will have Shane contact you in the next hour. Thanks, Chris."

Jace chuckled. "I don't know whether this will work or not, but, Chris, if you can pull this off, I'll personally see to it that David's grandmother sends you all the coffee cake you can eat for the rest of eternity."

Chris grinned. "My pleasure—and I'll look forward to that coffee cake."

Damon reached forward and pressed the button on the control panel that turned off the monitor. Chris's face disappeared.

David leaned forward in his seat. "So, what am I supposed to do until then? I have no possible way of tracking this thing, but I can't just sit on my ass and do nothing. The blood of these families will be on my hands."

Ash clicked his tongue. "David, you oughta know better than to blame yourself like I can tell you're doin'. None of this is your fault. It's them damn demon fuckers that are doin' this. Not you. You're doin' your best."

David couldn't help but smile at the way any time Ash spoke, any form of "your" sounded more like "yer." He was grateful for Ash's support and Chris's efforts, but he couldn't help feeling a sense of defeat anyway, knowing that their plan wasn't foolproof, and any blowback would inevitably land on him. "I know you're trying, Ash, but nothing you can say, short of telling me you know who the demon's next victims are and how I can protect them, is going to make me feel better."

Ash shrugged. "Figured I might as well give it a try."

David sat up and brushed off his negativity. Yeah, the situation sucked harder than a professional porn star, but their plan was better than nothing. "I'll call Shane and leave him a message."

Damon slapped his hand on the table. "Fine. Until Shane's able to get things worked out with Chris, this meeting's adjourned."

David thought about making a comment that for once no one had stormed out before the meeting's end but thought better of it. As his fellow hunters headed off, he pulled out his cell phone and prepared to call Shane. He sincerely hoped that Chris's plan would work and that his grandmother really would need to bake that coffee cake.

Chapter 13

If there was one thing Shane hated, it was students who left their cell phones on in the middle of class. No better way to say "I don't care about school" than answering your phone. The insistent ping indicating an incoming message was only minimally better.

Shane cleared his throat. "Okay, whose cell phone is it?"

The students glanced around the room, looking for the culprit. A freshman girl sitting eagerly in the front row raised her hand and piped up.

"Dr. Grey, I think the sound came from your messenger bag."

Shane looked at the bag on his desk. He pulled out his phone, saw the voicemail icon blinking and realized she was right. He touched the screen and saw that the message was from David. Damn. He faced the class.

"Five-minute break," he said.

The classroom erupted into a roar of chatter as he walked toward the door and stepped outside for a moment. He pressed the Return Call button and waited for David to answer.

Seconds later, David's deep voice rumbled from the tiny speaker. "I need your help."

Shane had figured as much. Not that he ever minded assisting David, but when did his fellow hunters ever call for a social chat? "I'm in the middle of class right now. What do you need?"

"I need you to hack into the databases of all the hospitals in the greater Rochester area."

Shane's jaw fell open. "Why the hell would I—"

"Because it's our only hope of stopping a baby-killing demon," David interrupted him. "Chris is gonna explain what to do with the info."

Shane let out a long sigh. He always got stuck with the grunt work, didn't he? He guessed that was what he got for locating to an area with minimal occult activity—not that witches were really that active anywhere anymore—and being the only one with the tech abilities to do the work.

"I'd really owe you one," David said.

"On a scale of one to ten, how important is this?"

"Ten. There could be another dead family if this plan doesn't work."

Shane paused, thinking ahead and planning his next move. He'd better get back to his office as soon as possible. "Should I call Chris for more information, then?"

"Yup, you know the drill."

"By the way, I haven't found anything on that symbol you gave me yet. I've found some similar markings, but nothing definitive. I'll keep searching." He glanced through the small vertical window of the classroom door to check on his students. They hadn't gotten too restless—yet. "You owe me."

David chuckled. "I always do."

Shane quickly said goodbye and hung up his phone. He took a deep breath before he returned to the classroom. As soon as he walked in, his students quieted down.

He grabbed his messenger bag and started shoving his notes and papers inside. "Something's come up and class is dismissed for today, but don't think this gets you out of your essay. It's still due tomorrow."

The screeches of chairs being pushed back, followed by the sounds of backpacks and bags opening and closing, filled the room, nearly drowning out the murmur of conversation.

"Dr. Grey?" a voice called from the back row.

Oh, God, not her.

Vera Sanders raised her hand. "Are your office hours for this evening canceled, too?"

Every logical part of him wanted to say yes, his hours were canceled, but he owed it to his students to at least keep some of his office hours after canceling class. He needed to get to the secure computers at division HQ before he could hack into any databases, but once he was finished he could return to campus. "No, but they'll begin a little later then usual. I'll send out an email to the class with the new time," he said before he could stop himself.

Shitty decision number one. He knew he probably should have canceled—because of *her*—but he couldn't resist. This was going to be a long night.

Allsún yawned and stretched like a cat, allowing her spine to crack into place. She snuggled deeper into the sheets as she cradled her pillow against her like a lover. Speaking of lovers… She rolled over on to her other side, only to find the spot next to her empty. Had David moved back out to the couch at some point after carrying her in here in the middle of the night?

She kicked off the covers and forced herself to get out of bed despite the pleasurable ache from the night before. Her whole body pulsed with the sweet aftermath of hours of mind-blowing sex.

She grinned. That had been one crazy night.

She walked toward the living room and leaned around the corner of the door frame to check the couch.

No one. Where had David gone?

Immediately she crossed the living room into the kitchen to search the fridge for a note. Just as she'd suspected—and just like when they'd been dating—David had left a note on the refrigerator, underneath the magnet she'd brought him back from a trip to Ireland: a picture of James Joyce and a quote from *Ulysses* about the "snotgreen" and "scrotumtightening" Irish Sea. She pulled the note from underneath the magnet and quickly scanned it.

Allie, went to the EU meeting. Didn't want to wake you. Be back soon. Keep the door locked. Love, David

She crumpled up the note and threw it into the waste bin. She checked the clock. Five in the evening. Man, she'd slept the day away, though she *had* been awake into the wee hours of the morning.

Looking around the apartment, she contemplated turning on the TV, but the dull ache in her limbs convinced her that resting until David returned didn't sound so bad. Just as she snuggled back into the comforting nest of David's bed, she heard the sound of the front door handle being turned.

She lay there in excited silence, waiting to hear the sound of David's motorcycle boots clomping across the carpet and into the bedroom, but the door never opened. She propped herself on her elbows to listen as the handle continued to rattle.

Shite. It wasn't David.

As quietly as she could, she slipped from the bed and tiptoed to the front door. She stood on her toes and glanced through the peephole. A slender blonde woman was standing on the other side. All of Allsún's senses blazed to life. She didn't need to look the woman in the eye to know she was possessed.

Double shite. Was this demon after her or David?

Either way, she needed to act—and fast. The doorknob continued to jiggle as the demon tried to force the handle. No longer bothering to worry about how much noise she was making, Allsún ran into David's bathroom.

A ward. She needed something to make a ward.

She wrenched open the cabinets under the sink and quickly found a can of shaving cream. She popped the cap off and ran to David's bedroom doorway, praying she remembered all the intricacies of the symbol. She dropped to her knees, shook the container and began to spray the foam on to David's light beige carpeting. The rattling of the door handle increased, and a loud bang echoed through the apartment as the demon tried to shove its way through the door.

If only she could remember the combination to David's lockbox under the bed, at least then she would have some manmade power to back up her Fae abilities. She drew the last symbol on the triangular ward and chucked the can to the side. There was one last bang as the demon kicked in David's door.

Shite. Shite. Shite.

Allsún scrambled backward away from the nearly invisible symbol. The demon charged straight toward her at full speed, falling right into her trap. As soon as it hit the triangle, its whole body slammed backward as if it had hit an invisible brick wall.

"What the—"

Allsún picked up the can of shaving cream and shook it at the demon tauntingly. She grinned.

The demon growled and tried to step through the ward to no avail.

She couldn't help it. She was pretty damn proud of herself.

"So who are you after?" she asked. "Me or David?"

The demon scowled. No answer.

Allsún shrugged. "Fine. I see we'll just have to go ahead and proceed with the exorcism."

The demon let out a low feral growl. "You little Fae bitch."

Allsún walked across the room and picked up the potted plant at David's bedside. She hated to smash it, but David would understand. She needed to be connected with the Earth in order to perform a full-on exorcism like this without any aid but her Fae magic. This would drain her, but it would be worth it. She thought about the poor woman the demon was possessing and hoped there would still be something of her left when this was over.

Walking back toward the doorway to stand just out of the demon's reach, Allsún smashed the plant on the floor. The dirt spilled out, covering the carpet in a large dark mound. She had the irrelevant thought that she would have to help David get the stain out. Using one of the shards from the broken terracotta pot, she sliced open the skin of her palm. Pain from the cut shot through her hand, but she ignored the discomfort, pushing forward with the ritual. She mixed her blood with the dirt, chanting the words in the ancient Fae tongue her mother had taught her.

"What are you doing, you stupid glitter-slinging dirt monkey?" the demon hissed.

She ignored the insult, continuing with her ritual. A smile crossed her face as the demon's knees buckled, and it screeched. Already it was feeling the pain of her power. Her chants became melodic, similar to old songs in the Gaelic language of the Irish people, but with slight variations.

The demon fell to its knees. Veins bulged and pulsated over its entire body, nearly glowing beneath its skin before light flooded its eyes.

"No, please. Stop!" it screeched.

Allsún chanted the final words and watched bright white light flood the demon's body. She brushed the dirt off her hands. "You're going straight back to hell where you belong."

A final pulse shot through the demon, delivering the final blow. The woman's body crumpled to the floor. Allsún crawled to the woman's side, pulling her into her lap. After a moment of silence the woman gasped for air, coming to life in her own body again following the exorcism.

"Where am I?" Tears filled her eyes and overflowed on to her cheeks. "Where is that *thing?*"

Allsún stroked a hand comfortingly over the woman's golden hair. "It's okay. Everything's going to be all right. You're safe now."

She held the woman, comforting her as best she could, but a heavy weight pressed down on her chest. The way the ritual had drained her meant she had another problem on her hands. She'd slept with David, yet she still didn't have her light back.

David's casual walk turned into a full-on run as soon as he spotted his splintered front door. Shit. He raced down the hallway, bursting into the apartment, then stopped in his tracks at the sight before him. Allsún was sitting curled-up next to an unconscious woman. Dirt covered his bedroom floor. The potted plant his grandmother had given him had been destroyed and lay to one side, its exposed roots drooping.

David looked from Allsún to the unknown woman on his floor and gaped. "What the hell happened?"

Allsún gestured to the blonde. "A demon came in, but before it broke down the door I had time to draw a ward with your shaving cream. When it came in, it came running straight for me and got caught in the ward."

David eyed the woman. "I'm assuming she's not still possessed, right?"

Allsún shook her head, "No, I took care of it. But I had to destroy your plant and use up most of my energy in the process."

"Damn. I'm so sorry, Allie."

She ignored his apology and patted the crying woman on the back. "Doesn't the Execution Underground have someone who deals with live victims like this or something? I mean, aren't you guys supposed to have a bunch of resources?"

David shook his head for a moment, trying to get hold of his thoughts as he processed the situation. He hadn't expected to come home to something like this. He'd thought Allsún would be completely safe in his apartment. "I'll call Damon and have somebody who deals with victims get out here to help her. Did the demon say anything before you exorcised it?"

She rolled her eyes. "Oh, just the usual, about me being a stupid Fae bitch and all that, nothing interesting. I asked if it was after you or me, but I didn't get an answer. I'm figuring since it knew what I was straightaway that I was the intended target, but I can't be certain."

He examined her closely. She did look weak, as if all her energy had been zapped, which clearly, as she had said, it had been. A familiar feeling of guilt rose in his chest. If he hadn't left her alone, maybe she wouldn't have been attacked. "I'm so sorry I left you here alone all day. I had that meeting, and then…well, you know how it goes."

She waved a blood-and-dirt-covered hand at him in dismissal. "Don't beat yourself up about it. You had no way of knowing they knew your address."

David swore again. "Damn. Well, clearly we can't stay here now. Not without a working door, for one thing."

The mystery blonde let out a groan from the floor. Allsún reached out and rubbed slow circles across the woman's shoulder blades, trying to soothe her.

"Is she okay?" David asked.

Allsún nodded. "Yeah, she's fine. Or she will be. She regained consciousness right after, but then she passed out again."

David pulled his phone out and placed a quick call to Damon, requesting that someone come pick up the victim and take her for any necessary psychological treatment. As soon as he hung up, he turned to Allsún. “Damon said he’ll be by to get her himself.”

Allsún nodded her head. “As long as she’s taken care of. So where do we go from here?”

David fiddled with his keys, thinking, “We’ll get a hotel room somewhere. If they know where my apartment is, chances are they know where yours is, too, and I’m not taking a chance of leading them to my grandmother’s place.”

Allsún tried to stand up, but a wave of dizziness made her think better of it. “Any updates from your meeting? What did they find on the samples?”

David shrugged. “Nothing that gets us any closer than we were before, but we’re trying to set up a way of monitoring the families who could be potential targets.”

Allsún’s eyes widened. “That has to be a lot of families.”

David extended a hand to her. “I’ll explain more once we get her taken care of.” He nodded toward the victim. “Does she have any injuries?”

“No.” She grasped his hand and hoisted herself up with a groan.

A knock came at the door. David glanced over his shoulder to find Damon standing in the doorway.

He raised a brow. “Wow. That was fast.”

Damon gave a single nod. "I was already on my way when you called."

David frowned. "That can't mean good news."

"I got a call from Elliot at the P.D. They found another family."

David and Allsún swore. Shit. They both knew what that meant without Damon saying another word.

Damon reached inside his leather jacket and pulled out a small folder. He handed it to David.

David took the folder without opening it. "What's this?"

"Pictures of the crime scene. We don't have the coroner's report yet—too soon. The place is swarming with policemen. There's no way you're going to be able to get in there without the cooperation of the local P.D., and we've only got two guys on the inside. This will have to do for now."

David ran a hand over his face. He wasn't sure how much more he could take. "So much for avoiding a shitstorm of media attention."

"Chris and Shane have surveillance set up on the families, so just wait for Chris's call and be ready to leave at a moment's notice. We may not have saved this family, but with luck we can save the next one," Damon said.

"Yeah, you got it, chief."

Damon gestured toward the woman curled up next to Allsún. "What happened here?"

"She was possessed, burst in through the front door and ran at Allsún. Allsún exorcised her, but she's upset and clearly confused about what's happened to her."

Damon gave a single nod. "I'll have someone from the New York City office fly up to counsel her. They're better equipped to handle this. The EU will take good care of her."

Allsún crouched next to the woman's side and gently nudged her shoulder. The woman blinked awake and lifted her head.

"Someone's here to help you," Allsún told her, "so you have to go with him now. You'll be safe. I promise."

The woman's lower lip quivered, and she glanced between the three of them, as if she wasn't certain what to do. When she spoke, her words came out tattered and broken. "W-what about that th-thing? Is it going to come b-back and…take over my body a-again?" The last word turned into a sob.

Allsún wrapped an arm around the woman's shoulders and helped her to her feet. The woman's knees trembled, as if they might not be able to support her weight. That was one of the drawbacks of an exorcism.

It left the victim with some serious fatigue. It sure beat the alternative, though.

Damon placed a hand on the woman's shoulder. "You'll be safe with me. I'm going to take you to someone who can help you. What's your name?"

The tears didn't stop, but she stood up straight and looked Damon in the eye. David couldn't blame her for being in rough shape after the ordeal she'd been through.

"Alicia," she said.

Damon nodded. "Come with me, Alicia. I'm going to take you to somebody who can help you, and we'll ensure nothing like this ever happens to you again." He ushered Alicia out the door, pegging David with a stern look just before he left. "You two better get out of here and find somewhere safe to go." He paused briefly. "And, David, I'm sorry I didn't listen to you on this sooner. Next time something like this comes up, you'll have my full attention."

Once Damon left, David turned his attention back to Allsún. He eyed her up and down. "We need to get you cleaned up."

Allsún started toward the door, shaking her head, "We can do that later. Right now we need to get out of here. Who knows whether or not they'll send more demons our way."

"When Jace and Frankie were on the lam, Jace said they stayed at the Imperial Hotel. We could always crash there."

"That sounds like a plan."

"I don't know about you, but I'm starving right now. You want to grab a pizza or something to eat while we look over this file?" He held up the folder.

Allsún raised an eyebrow, "I don't know that I necessarily want to eat while I look at crime scene photos."

"Then we can eat before we look."

"Deal."

Thirty minutes later they stood in the hotel lobby, key cards in hand, waiting for a delivery of their New York–style pizza. Allsún nearly snatched the box straight out of the delivery guy's hands when he arrived. David chuckled. Clearly, she was as hungry as he was. Then he used his key card to authorize the elevator to take them up to the penthouse, and they made their way to their hideaway.

It took them a whole ten minutes to tear through the pizza. Allsún sat back against the cushions of the king-size four-poster bed and sighed. "Man, I didn't realize how hungry I was."

He smiled at her happiness, then turned serious. "I hate to ruin your pizza high, but we'd better get to work looking at those photos."

He didn't like not being able to examine the scene himself and take samples. "It's weird not being able to see the scene. Half the time I'm the first one there."

Allsún placed her hands behind her head. "I hate to say it, but at least this way it seems a little less real. You know, without all the actual blood."

David pointed to the folder. "We can't allow it to stop being real to us. That was a family in those pictures. We need to do our best to get justice for them."

"Yeah, you're right."

David disposed of the pizza box in the garbage can near the dining room table before rejoining Allsún. He sat down on the edge of the bed but paused before opening the folder. "You ready for this?"

She glanced at the folder with a wary eye. "As ready as anyone can ever be to see such depravity."

David opened the folder and removed the crime scene photos. They both let out a collective groan. The things that had been done to this family were no less disgusting than what had been done to the first two. The first couple of shots showed a set of bloody footprints near the door and a broken window, a dark preview of what was to follow. They looked at each other. A bad feeling knotted in David's stomach. The next photo validated their fears. Dried blood, almost black, pooled underneath a man bound with duct tape. From his open eyes, it was obvious he had died conscious and terrified. David knew the darkness of the blood meant he'd bled out from the liver, a slow, painful process. His skin was lily-white, a sure sign the body had been drained.

"Damn." Allsún put a hand over her mouth to stop herself from gasping.

Reluctantly, David flipped to the fourth photo. Somehow it managed to be worse. A woman's face contorted into a hellish death scream. And blood. There was so much blood—bright arterial red splashed across her body. The look of pain in her one remaining eye was too much, even for David. The other eye had been sliced open, probably on some sick whim. Her feathered blond hair lay matted in the pool of dried blood, gluing it to the floor.

Rage built inside David. All he could hear was the sound of his own ragged breathing as he balled all the anger up, shoving it down deep inside himself. As if the first photos of the scene hadn't been sick enough, nothing could have prepared them for the fifth one.

Had their P.D. contact intentionally organized these to be as traumatizing as possible?

The fifth photo showcased the woman's cause of death: the gaping, football-sized hole in her abdomen. Layers of flesh and organs spread out like the pages of a book, as if someone had stabbed her and reached inside the wound to tear it open with both hands. Blood had splattered in all directions from the violence of the attack, streaks spiking out star-like from her body.

David cringed at the sight. Some part of him was thankful that her death had been quicker than her husband's, that they both hadn't had to suffer such a long, agonized fate, though did it really matter now?

David closed the folder and stared at the wall. Allsún pulled her legs up to her chest, holding herself in a fetal position with tears building in the corners of her eyes. They sat in silence for what felt like an eternity, neither one of them able to speak.

Finally David cleared his throat. "We're going to find that demon, Allie, and when we do, we're going to get justice for these people. They deserve that much."

Chapter 14

Dr. Shane Grey didn't date students…or at least that was what he kept telling himself.

He tapped his pen on the edge of his planner and stared at the time. Two minutes, according to the email she'd sent earlier. She would be here in two minutes. He let out a long sigh and sat back in his chair. He tried not to think about how sweet the sway of her hips would be, or how the sight of her high-heeled leather boots made him want to strip her naked—except for the boots. She could keep those on. He wanted to feel the spikes of the heels pressing into the small of his back as she wrapped her legs around him. He chewed on his lower lip and ran his fingers over his ponytail. This was *so* not right. She was his student, for shit's sake. It didn't matter that she was twenty-three and he was only twenty-seven, or that she had the most beautiful, soft-looking lips and the most tantalizing pair of breasts he'd ever seen. He *could* not and *would* not make a move on his student.

A knock sounded on his office door. Was she early? He shook himself off, straightened his clothes, then leaned back in his chair again as if he'd casually been waiting. She couldn't know he was nearly sweating through his shirt at the hot and heavy thoughts he was having about her.

"Come in," he called.

The golden doorknob twisted, and Vera Sanders slipped inside, all long legs and sex appeal. "Hey, Doc." A sweet smile crossed her face as she walked toward his desk.

He swallowed the lump that had formed in his throat and tried not to think about the way his cock pushed against his dress pants. This was too much like every naughty fantasy he'd ever had about her—the ones where in the middle of the night, he'd work late into the evening, and in entered Vera, sexy as ever, who would stalk in as if she owned the place, walk right up to his desk chair, and without a word spin him toward her. She'd strip him naked, until they were both making love on top of his desk.

Yeah, that would be the ultimate fantasy.

"Have a seat," he said.

She did as she was told and sat across from him, her perfect posture accentuating the sweet curves of her body.

"So, we need to talk about your grades in my class."

She shifted in her seat a little as if the topic made her uncomfortable.

"Your grades are substandard, and if you don't start pulling them up soon, the Religious Studies department won't allow me to give you credit for the course. I'd hate to see your money for that part of the semester wasted."

She pursed her full lips together and let out a huff through her nose. "Yeah, that's a problem."

Shane folded his hands together and placed them over his grade book. He lowered his eyes to the pages, trying to pretend he didn't see the ample amounts of cleavage her shirt showcased. What was with him?

He forced himself to focus. "I can tell from the look on your face, the idea of failing my class doesn't please you."

Vera crossed her arms over her breasts and shrugged. "Yeah, I guess you could say that."

Shane nodded. "What can I do to help you, then? How can I help you succeed in my course?"

She didn't respond.

"Vera?"

She dropped her arms away from her chest and let out a long sigh. "I don't know, Dr. Grey. I honestly don't know."

"I don't really understand what the problem is here. Are you struggling with the material? I've seen you in class, and you have an understanding of the subject, way more than a few of your peers, some of whom are even getting A's."

She continued to remain silent.

"Are you going to work with me on this? What can I do to help you? If you need private tutoring, then I'd be happy to—"

"—Yes, I want you to tutor me," she blurted out.

Shane blinked several times, and it took him a moment to find his words. The sexy, somewhat coy, look on her face as she spoke sent a wave of heat racing down his spine, and did not help the situation that was currently escalating underneath his desk.

"I meant another student, not me, but—"

"I'd really prefer if you tutor me," Vera said. "When you talk about the subject I understand it so much easier. I've gone to the tutoring center before, and it's no good for me."

Shane ran his fingers over his ponytail. This was not a good idea.

"Please, would you just tutor me? Just a few times. That's all. I just need to prepare for the final."

Though every molecule in his brain was screaming that was the worst idea he'd ever heard, somehow when he opened his mouth, he said, "Yes."

Lately guilt was becoming David's new best friend. As he glanced over the crime scene photos yet again, he couldn't help but feel as if it was his fault these people had been murdered. Logically, he knew that there had been nothing more he could do to track the demon's next target, but the weight of all those deaths weighed on him nevertheless. He wanted justice for them, and he needed to put a stop to the murders.

"There's one thing that won't stop bothering me about these photos." David was sitting at the huge dining table as he thumbed through the pictures again, still looking for anything he could have missed that could point him in the demon's direction. The only slight clue they'd been given was yet another symbol painted on the wall in blood, a slight variation from the first. He'd already sent the picture to Shane in hopes that it helped in his search.

Allsún scooted to the edge of the bed and joined David at the table where the crime scene photos were sprawled out in front of him. "What's that?"

"When Damon told me about this, he said it was another family, but this was only a couple."

"Some people consider a married couple to be a family. Maybe it was just his word choice."

David shook his head as he continued to stare at the photos. "I think it's something more than that, something I'm just missing." He stared at the photos for a long moment without speaking. "This is making me question my theory about using the parents' fear. If there are no children in this equation, it doesn't fit the profile, even though the use of the symbol means the murders are clearly connected. Yet when Chris ran the samples to determine the type of demon and no true hits came up, the closest match was an Abyzu, and that means a child should be involved somehow."

Allsún leaned against the table and crossed her arms, eyeing the pictures once more. "Maybe it attacked a family with no children in order to throw us off."

David pushed the gruesome photos away from him, unable to stare any longer at all the unnecessary violence. "Somehow I doubt the demon cares whether we're on its tail."

Allsún slid the pictures back toward him. "Don't give up. Somebody needs to fight for these people, David. When we're trying to diagnose an animal at the vet, we look at all the symptoms and then ask why. What could be causing everything we're seeing? Maybe we should take a similar approach. Maybe we're not digging deeply enough into why the demon does what it does. For example, why cut the man's liver? Why choose such a slow method of death for him and a quicker one for his wife? It can't be as random as it seems. And why choose to kill the wife in such a difficult way? I mean, it takes a lot to pull out someone's insides. We need to start asking questions."

David leaned forward to pore over the pictures again. He held up the shot of the wife with her organs spread around her. "One of the things I'm wondering is how long he held them captive before he killed them. Look at her wounds. Even though her stomach is cut up, there's no stomach acid. There are no stomach contents in evidence. Why is that? How long has it been since she's eaten?"

Allsún leaned over the photo, examining it closely. Her eyes widened. "Shite." Her slight Irish accent thickened just a little, always a sign she was distressed.

David pushed back his chair. "What?"

"No wonder Damon said 'family.' That isn't her stomach, David. That's her uterus. She was pregnant." Allsún covered her mouth. "I think I'm going to be sick," she said, her voice muffled by her hand. She ran into the bathroom.

He thought about following her in there straightaway, but he decided to give her a moment to collect herself.

David looked at the photo again and realized Allsún was right. It was so obvious now that he couldn't believe he'd missed it. No wonder the demon had chosen a slow death for the husband. It had wanted him to watch as he killed his wife and unborn child. Sickening. David's phone buzzed against the hard wood of the table. A text message from Chris.

Shane did amazing. Surveillance is up now.

A sense of relief filled David, knowing at least some of the families were being monitored. Maybe he would be able to save someone after all. Though he needed to tell Shane ASAP to do another search, this time to locate and monitor pregnant women, as well. He texted Shane, and received a reply from his fellow hunter within seconds. With that taken care of, he pushed his chair out and went to the bathroom to check on Allsún.

She was sitting on the edge of the tub with her head in her hands.

"Allie, are you okay?"

She wiped at her eyes. "Yeah, I'm fine. Sorry. I know I've been crying a lot lately, but it's not like there's been a shortage of things to cry over."

He watched her reactions in her face as he spoke, trying to get a read on how she was feeling. "It's okay. You've had to deal with all this demon shit, and you still haven't had time to process everything that happened with Robert. I think a few tears are warranted. And if you ask me, you're holding up extremely well, all things considered."

She bit her lower lip. "Thanks."

He had to stop himself from frowning. He knew that look. Allsún was holding something back from him. The way she'd raised her eyebrows when he mentioned Robert made him wonder if that was what she was really upset about. He knew her too well for her to hide something from him.

Forcing the suspicions from his mind, he held up his cell phone to get her attention. "I just got a text from Chris. The surveillance is set up. I also texted Shane to let him know to add pregnant women to the monitor list, so now we just have to wait for a call if this actually works and he can find the demon."

Allsún wrapped her arms around herself, as if she

was trying to hold herself together. He couldn't blame her. She'd been through so much.

A moment of silence passed between them. Allsún fiddled with the handle of the drain. David debated whether to bring up the question he'd been dying to ask and satisfy his burning curiosity about what she was holding back, because he could tell there was something.

Despite everything that was going on, he couldn't help but let his mind wander to the previous night. Their time together had been phenomenal, more than he ever could have hoped for. He'd been dreaming of being with her like that for ages. He knew now was an awful time to ask, but he had no way of knowing if Allsún was going to stick around, so he had to seize the opportunity while he could.

"So…" he said.

She glanced toward him and waited for him to go on. When nothing came, she replied, "So?"

David leaned against the wall of the bathroom and crossed his arms. "I was just…uh…wondering how you were feeling about last night?"

She shot him a look of disbelief before storming out of the bathroom. He fought not to curse. Damn, that was exactly what he'd been hoping she *wouldn't* do.

Couldn't just this one thing go right? Double damn. If Allsún's reaction was any indication as to how the rest of the night was going to go, he might as well throw in the towel now.

Allsún flopped down on the bed. Sometimes she was certain men existed just to cause her misery. She'd been hoping David wouldn't ask about last night's lovemaking, because honestly, she didn't want to think about it. At face value, it had been a fun night reliving some once-romantic times with an old flame.

When she dug deeper though, her heart told her it was more than that, and that thought alone made her sick with anxiety. No matter how great things with David felt, there had been a reason why they'd broken up. He wasn't willing to give her the family she so desperately wanted, and though she knew she shouldn't, a part of her still blamed him for the loss of the child she had carried. She couldn't even think about the photos of that poor woman. She supposed she should consider herself lucky for not having suffered a similar fate. The thought sent another wave of anxiety-fueled nausea rolling through her stomach.

David followed her into the bedroom. "I know the

timing sucks, but I wanted to ask you, just in case I don't get the chance later…did I say something wrong?"

She lifted a hand to stop him from continuing. "I'm not in the mood to talk right now, David."

He walked to the bedside, standing only a few feet away from her. "We're only ignoring the elephant in the room if we don't talk about what happened last night."

She moved over to the far side of the bed to distance herself from him. "Well, we were doing better when we *were* ignoring it."

"*I* haven't been ignoring it. I just didn't have a chance to bring it up earlier."

She lay down and turned her back to him. Maybe if she didn't look at him, he would leave her be. "I'm just not ready to talk about it yet, David. And if I did, you probably wouldn't like what I had to say."

"How can you say that and then expect me to just leave it alone?"

She could hear the frustration in his voice and let out a long sigh. Why did he have to do this? "David, please don't push the issue."

He shifted closer to her on the bed. "I have to, especially since I have to wonder why you're so dead set on *not* talking about it. You're hiding something from me, Allsún, and I deserve to know what it is."

Her head snapped toward him, and she couldn't keep the bite out of her voice. "Don't you dare accuse me of hiding something from you. You don't have a right to every single thought I have, and I said I don't want to talk about it."

He stood, and for a moment, relief rushed over her as she thought he was finally giving up and going back to work. A frown crossed her face when he suddenly rounded the bed and sat down only inches away from her.

"How can you expect to waltz back into my life, sleep with me and then not expect me to talk about it?" She tried to force herself to ignore the pain in his voice. "You avoided me with absolutely no contact for five years," he continued. "Then you show up, nearly get yourself killed, and within twenty-four hours of you getting out of the hospital we're in bed, and we can't discuss it? Now I say I feel like you're keeping something else from me, and you're not even bothering to answer me."

She covered her face with her hands. "I'm not hiding anything," she snapped.

Damn him. How did he know? What had she done to give him any indication she was holding back? The problem was, she *was* holding back, but how couldn't she? Guilt was eating away at her heart. Sure, there had been plenty of reasons why she'd slept with David: for pleasure, for fun. Because, if she was honest with herself, she still cared about him. There was also the fact that she wanted her light back. What a liar she would be if she couldn't even admit to herself that, while not her main motivation, that had been a factor.

"Why are you doing this, Allie? What is there to hide? You know I don't have any sort of ulterior motive. You can tell me anything, because all I want is you." Before she could stop him, he kissed her, and their tongues collided together in a sensual swirl.

When he pulled away he drew her hands into his.

"This is so wrong."

He shook his head, leaning in close, so he could whisper against her cheek. "If this is so wrong, then tell me to stop."

She opened her mouth to tell him again it was wrong, that she shouldn't be with him, but she couldn't bring herself to utter the words, and she knew why. It wasn't true. "You know I can't do that." She couldn't say no to him. She didn't have the willpower.

"You can. If you really wanted me to stop, you could say it, but you won't, because you don't want me to stop. I know you want this, Allsún, so show me." He paused. His next words came out as a sexy rumble. “If you want me, kiss me first.”

As much as she wanted to resist, as much as she wanted to tell him he was a jerk for thinking he knew her so well, he *did* know her that well. She couldn’t stop herself. She leaned in and kissed his lips. When she pulled away, her breath caught, and she saw a fire ignite behind David’s dark eyes. She lingered there, so close she could feel the warmth of his breath on her face. The moment only lasted long enough for her chest to ache with the hope that he would kiss her back.

He did.

The taste of Allsún’s lips against his was sweet bliss. David cradled the back of her head, tangling his fingers in her hair. His mouth captured hers, and he expertly parted her lips with his tongue. The ache in him intensified as she wrapped her arms around him. With his free hand he pressed against her lower back, pulling her body against him. Finally he lifted her and laid her out across the bed. A small grin spread across his face. There wouldn’t be much sleeping going on there tonight.

Before she could protest, he slipped her shirt over her head. Slowly he peeled off her clothes, allowing her to do the same to him. When they were both naked, he pulled her into his arms. She lay with her head nestled against his chest, and they stayed there together, savoring each other's touch for what seemed like an eternity.

Suddenly, with a coy smile, Allsún rolled onto her side, turning away from him. David grinned; he knew what she was doing. She was playing hard to get. He grabbed her by the waist and gently pulled her against him until their bodies were spooned against each other. He wrapped his arms around her, holding her close to him. The feel of her smooth bare skin against his sent shivers of excitement tingling down his back. He leaned into her neck and allowed the warmth of his breath to tickle over her skin as he kissed along her collarbone.

With a grin, she tried to wiggle away from his touch, but he moved closer.

"You aren't getting away from me that easy," he whispered.

He trailed kisses higher up her neck until he captured the edge of her ear between his lips, nibbling on the sensitive skin. Allsún moaned and arched her back against him in pleasure. He ran his hand over the curve of her side before he gently cupped her bottom. She had the sweetest, roundest little ass he'd ever seen. He rubbed his hand over her thigh, massaging her soft skin until slowly he slipped his hand in between her legs.

She gasped as his fingers found her clit. He massaged her sensitive flesh with slow, rhythmic movements until she writhed against him, moving with the motion of his touch. David continued to massage between her legs. She slickened against him, her sweetness dripping on to his hand.

He leaned forward and spoke softly in her ear. "Does that mean you're ready for me?"

Circling her hips in rhythm with the motions of his hand, Allsún smiled over her shoulder at him. "You tell me."

A devious grin crossed David's face as he nipped at her ear again. "I think you're more than ready for me." He positioned his fingers just outside her entrance, savoring the feel of her sweet juices, then eased his fingers inside her, flexing his hand in slow movements as he massaged her core. She pushed her hips back against him, rocking into his thrusts. He touched her for long minutes, working at a gentle pace to prepare her for him.

Her lower lip stuck out in a pout as he pulled his hand away from her. "Don't stop," she pleaded.

He grinned. "I'm not stopping. I'm giving you more."

Using both hands, he parted her thighs, opening her up so he could slide into her from behind. He slid his cock between her legs, rocking himself back and forth over her sweet spot.

She moaned.

"Do you want it?" he asked.

She responded with a coy smile.

He let out a low, playful growl and whispered in her ear, "I said, do you want it?"

A small moan escaped her lips at the feel of his mouth at her ear again. "Yes."

Without another word, he eased himself inside her, pushing deep into her core. He let out a pleasured groan. She was so tight. He rocked against her, slipping in and out of her velvet embrace. His cock hardened at the feel of her soft walls tightening around him.

"David." His name slipped out of her mouth on a sigh. Her pleasure made him enjoy the moment even more.

He snaked his hands over Allsún's sides, running his fingertips over her until he palmed both her breasts. Her nipples had already hardened into taught peaks, and he rolled them gently between his thumb and index finger until finally he couldn't take it anymore. He had to see her beautiful face staring up into his. He slipped out of her, easing her from her side on to her back.

Within seconds he was poised above her. He dropped his head and kissed her deeply, their tongues dancing together in a slow, sensual tango. It took everything he had in him not to plunge inside her. Tonight was made for a gentle touch, so he held himself back, easing into her as he rocked his hips against hers.

She cried out as he pushed all the way inside her. She wrapped her legs around him, holding him close. He focused on her pleasure and brought her closer to the brink of ecstasy with slow movements, but still deep enough to satisfy her and fulfill his hunger to be inside her.

He slipped his hand underneath her hair and cradled her head, holding her in an intimate embrace. He stared into her emerald eyes. The sweet scent of her sex filled his nose. She was beautiful, perfect, divine.

Everything he wanted. How could he ever have let her go?

He was hardly deserving of her, but he wanted her—and only her—anyway. If he could have her like this every night, he would die the happiest man in history. He rocked against her, bringing her closer to her climax. Her tightness enveloped him, their bodies growing more intimate with every thrust. He could feel her teetering on the brink of ecstasy, until the warmth of her center pulsed over him as she came.

She was divine.

He wanted to continue, but knew that the words sitting on the tip of his tongue would stop him from enjoying his own finish to its fullest extent. Slowly, he pulled out of her. She gave a contented satisfied sigh as he drew her into his arms. He opened his mouth several times to speak, but the words refused to emerge.

Finally Allsún reached up, cupping his cheek. "Are you okay?" she asked. "You didn't finish. You could have continued if you needed time. I wouldn't have minded. Just because I was done didn't meant you had to stop."

David nodded. "I'm better than okay," he whispered.

She ran her fingers over the shaved stubble of his hair. "I can tell something is bothering you."

He nodded. "There's something I want to say to you, but I don't know if I should."

She ran her fingertips over his cheek as if cueing him to continue. Before he spoke, he kissed her hard. His heart thumped inside his chest, and a sweet ache filled him. He wanted and needed her in every way.

When he pulled back from their kiss, he lingered, his

lips barely touching hers before he whispered, "I love you, Allie. I never stopped loving you."

Allsún's breath caught. She wasn't sure what to say, or even if she should respond. Her heart ached at his words. The weight of how fully she'd missed him over the years pressed down on her. She'd never stopped loving *him,* either. She thought about speaking, but she was at a loss for words. Part of her wanted to say them back, even if just for old time's sake, but another part of her wasn't ready.

David laid a tender kiss on her cheek. "It's okay. You don't have to say anything. I just needed you to know."

She reached up and placed her hand on his cheek again. She ran her fingers over his slight five o'clock shadow—just enough scruff to be sexy.

He smiled, then kissed her. With all the strength she possessed, she rolled the two of them over so she lay on top of him.

He grinned. "This is a nice change of pace."

She flashed him a playful grin. "I want to do something for you."

His eyes widened as she kissed her way across the rock-hard muscles of his abdomen. She grinned at the shocked look on his face. This was something David had always wanted—he didn't have to say that for her to know—but he had always been too giving to ask for anything that was for his pleasure alone.

"Allsún, you don't have to do this if you don't want to."

She kissed the delicious V leading down to his cock. "But I *do* want to."

Before he could protest again, she wrapped her lips over the head of his dick and slipped her mouth down as far as she could manage. A moan escaped David's lips. Instinctually, she used her hand to work the part of him her mouth couldn't reach. He tangled his fingers in her hair, massaging her head. She smiled on the inside, because even when he was receiving his own pleasure, it was his natural instinct to please her.

"I need to be inside you again."

She released him from her mouth.

"I need to be inside you," he repeated. "Now."

Suddenly she was on her back again, with David hovering over top of her as he used his impressive arms to support his weight. He sheathed himself inside her, and she cried out. He felt phenomenal, filling her up to the max. Wrapping his arms around her, he cradled her against him as he thrust. His right hand trailed down her side until he nestled it between her legs, rubbing her clit to speed her to the brink of ecstasy.

Her core grew slick as she came closer and closer to climax. He penetrated her hard and deep as her arousal increased, matching the strength of his thrusts to her level of pleasure. He was amazing in bed, so good to her and so aware of her needs. She felt him stiffen inside her, coming closer to his own climax.

"Come for me," he whispered against her ears. Shivers shot down her spine as the heat of his breath tingled over her.

He pulsed inside her and cried out as he reached his own climax, the cry fading into a strong feral groan as he filled her up. The feeling of his fingers massaging her most sensitive flesh and the long hard strength of his cock combined with the pulsing sensation of him coming inside her sent her over the edge.

She threw her head back. "David!" she cried out. Wave after wave of pleasure washed over her, reaching every inch of her body. A fire burned inside her chest, and electricity shot through her limbs. As the last shudder of her release rolled over her, David kissed her deep. The sweet taste of his tongue flooded her mouth.

David rolled over onto his side, pulling her flush against him once more. She kissed his cheek, before pulling back to stare into his dark eyes. A feeling of total adoration filled her, and she knew from the smile on his lips that he could see the truth reflected in her face: she'd never stopped loving *him,* either.

Warmth the likes of which she'd never known consumed her, like the sun blazing inside her, shining from the inside out. And that was when she knew. She wasn't quite sure how it had happened, but somehow, her light was back and there was only explanation she could think of. Though she hated to admit it to herself, this time when they'd made love, she'd fallen *in* love with David all over again.

Chapter 15

David could feel it in his bones. Something about the second time had been different, David thought. The first time they'd slept together they'd been making up for lost time, years spent apart. The second time it was as if they'd gotten all the necessary carnal desires out of the way. Instead of wild pleasure, it was about unfaltering love, a love that, though they'd tried to deny it, they just couldn't ignore.

He had never stopped loving Allsún. He'd always known that, and for years he'd questioned how it had been possible for her to stop loving him. After all, how could she love him, yet intentionally leave? Sometimes it made him wonder if she'd ever really loved him at all.

He knew better now.

It wasn't possible for her to stop loving, and she never had. It was only possible for life, obligations and responsibilities to get in the way of that love, because true love doesn't die or disappear. True love was indestructible, even in death.

He laid awake in bed for what seemed like hours, content with the feeling of Allsún's warm body tucked against his. It wasn't until, still sleeping, she rolled on to her side and out of his embrace that he finally got out of bed. He welcomed the brisk cool air of the penthouse. The chill acted as the reminder he needed. As great as things were going with Allsún, he wouldn't feel truly better until he was certain no more families were in danger.

After staring at the crime scene photos again, examining them for any new clue, he stepped away and pulled on his clothes—ready if needed—then went back to the pictures.

After he'd been staring at the photos for a while, his phone buzzed. He picked it up and answered. "Hello?"

Chris rattled off an address several blocks away. "Get there now."

David hung up the phone. "Allsún." He spoke her name in a sharp bark in order to rouse her.

She jolted awake. "What?" she snapped.

He crossed the room and pulled on his leather jacket as he threw Allsún her clothes. "Get dressed. There's been a hit on the surveillance."

She immediately went into action mode, pulling on her clothes in seconds.

Within two minutes they were on the Super Glide, speeding toward the address Chris had given him. David ignored the traffic lights and cut in and out of cars with expert precision. He didn't care about traffic laws right now. The sooner they got there, the more likely they were to save someone. When they pulled up to the apartment building, David rode up into the grass, throwing the bike down as he and Allsún bolted inside. They ran at full speed, bounding up the stairs until they reached the third floor.

Using the heel of his boot, David kicked in the door to the apartment. Pain seared through his bad leg, but he didn't give a shit; he would end this demon motherfucker once and for all. Gun at the ready, he stormed in. The demon stood in the middle of the family's living room, wearing a teenage boy as its meat suit and clutching what appeared to be its possessed victim's identical twin brother by the throat. Two dead bodies lay on the floor nearby. The parents.

David squeezed the trigger and fired one of his custom rounds into the demon's shoulder. The demon dropped the boy as it reeled with the unexpected pain. Normal bullets weren't pleasant for demons, but David's new toys caused a special kind of hurt. Smoke billowed from the wound in the demon's arm.

It hissed, eyes glowing a fiery red as it turned its gaze toward David. "You'll pay for that, exorcist."

With the wave of its arm, David flew backward as if hit by an invisible force. His back buckled as his spine collided with the wall. His head bounced off the plaster in a cloud of dust. A warm trickle oozed down the back of his head, and he could feel the warm blood dripping down his neck.

"Please, don't hurt him! That's my brother!" the newly released boy yelled.

Stupidly, the demon had merely slammed him into the wall, David realized. It hadn't bothered to hold him down, choosing instead to tend to its wound. Big mistake. He fired off a shot, hitting the demon right in the calf.

The smell of burning flesh filled the apartment. The demon fell to its knees.

"Don't fire!" Allsún yelled.

As she rushed up behind the hell-crawler, a beautiful burst of sparkling green light rose from her hands, shimmering in the midst of the bloody scene. But David knew that beauty was extremely misleading.

Holding both hands over the demon, she focused her power until the light was so bright that David had to squint to see. Suddenly the demon writhed on the ground, twitching as if it were an ant being fried under the power of a sunbeam concentrated through a child's magnifying glass.

A sheen of sweat broke out on Allsún's brow as she continued to keep the demon in place. "David, draw a ward and prepare to tie this thing up."

He didn't need to be asked twice.

Impressively, Allsún managed to hold the demon down despite the victim's terrified brother screaming nonstop, until David successfully shoved it into a chair and made certain it couldn't escape. Several minutes later he tied the last knot around the demon's wrist, securing it firmly to the arm of the chair.

The demon looked up at him through the eyes of the innocent teen boy. "I like a little bondage play."

David rolled his eyes. "You do, huh? Bet you're into pain, too."

The demon gave him a smug grin. "You can't hurt me, exorcist."

David smiled. "That's where you're wrong. Let's see

how much you like this." He shoved the blessed serrated blade against the demon's bare collar bone and slowly pressed the tip of the knife into its flesh—the knife he'd just dipped in holy water behind the little shit's back. The demon screeched. It didn't matter that demons weren't actually humans, just imposters wearing their hosts like suits. When they were inside a human, they felt pain the same way their hosts did, which meant that the collarbone and genitals were very vulnerable places. David slowly dug the blade in. The demon continued to scream.

"Please, I'm begging you. Don't hurt my brother. He's in there somewhere," the twin cried out from behind them.

David heard Allsún walk to the boy's side as he continued to focus on causing the demon pain in hopes of driving it out.

"It's okay," Allsún whispered to the twin. "We're going to get your brother out of there. Just let us do our job. I know this is scary, but we're going to save him."

The boy let out a tortured sob. "It killed my mom and dad."

"I know, and I'm so sorry. I promise you that we're going to make this monster pay, and we'll save your brother. Come on, let's go out in the hallway. You don't need to see this."

"No. I want to watch. I want to see it leave my brother's body," the teen protested.

Finally, much to his personal disappointment, David withdrew the blade from the monster's flesh. The demon let out another howl of pain.

David leaned down, nearly nose to nose with the little bastard. "That was fun, wasn't it?"

The demon sneered. "Eat shit, you fucking Holy Roller."

David grinned. He leaned down and waved the knife in front of the demon's face. "If you liked that, wait until you see what I have in store for you next."

The demon winced. "What do you want?"

David's eyes widened. Wow, that had to be a record. "Well, well…we have a talker already. If there's one failing that all you demons share, it's that you have no fucking loyalty to each other. See, that's the problem with your kind, you're only out for your own interests. Believe me, I've met my fair share of humans who are assholes, but even the nastiest displays of human selfishness are nothing compared to what you lowlifes get up to." He paused and placed his boot on the edge of the demon's chair. "If you're ready to talk, I'm ready to listen."

"What do you want?"

David frowned. "You know what I want, you worthless fucker. I can tell you're not the one responsible for all the deaths around here. This doesn't fit the usual pattern. There's no baby, no pregnant woman, so tell me what I want to know."

"I don't know what you want from me."

"This one's not very bright, Allsún." He placed the heel of his boot right between the demon's legs, exactly where he could put just enough pressure to make it squirm. "You really don't know what I want, huh? Information, you pathetic shit. Information. Who sent you to do this, and why? Don't even bother trying to tell me you're doing this on your own. I wasn't born yesterday. Weak little assholes like you are always taking orders from someone. You're no head honcho. And if you were the same demon asshole that's been killing families around here, you would've stuck to the pattern. So, tell me, who sent you to do this and why?"

The demon spat on David's boot. In response David punched the monster with the butt of his blade.

Blood trickled from the corner of the demon's mouth as it spoke. Its eyes blazed red. "You're going to exorcise me either way, so why should I give you information?"

David laughed. He leaned down so he was eye to eye with the monster. "So first you play me by pretending you're going to talk, and now you're acting like the silent type? That's fine, because it's not a matter of whether or not I send you back to hell. It's about how much pain you experience beforehand."

David sliced the knife across the other side of the demon's collarbone and held the holy-water-soaked blade to the wound. Smoke billowed from the cut.

The demon screeched and writhed against its bonds. "I'll tell you what you want, just *stop!*"

A sense of déjà vu washed over David at the way the word "stop" sounded on the demon's lips, and his eyes widened in shock as he recognized the demon sitting in front of him. "Shit. You're the Abyzu demon that was possessing babies a couple of months ago. I thought I sent your sorry ass back to hell. How'd you crawl out so fast? You shouldn't be up here again this soon." He pulled the blade away from the demon's throat.

The demon let out a low guttural hiss. "Look at you, all high and mighty because you're a big deal exorcist. Not such a big deal now, though. I notice you're missing something this time."

David scoffed. Whatever this demon thought it knew about him, it was full of shit. "Oh, yeah? And what's that?"

The demon grinned. Blood stained its teeth a putrid crimson. "You don't have all the power you used to. The faerie light you had is gone."

David raised a brow. What did this hell-crawler mean? He glanced over his shoulder toward Allsún, but she was too busy comforting the host's unpossessed twin to notice the demon's comment.

"Faerie light? What are you talking about?" he asked.

The demon laughed, a vicious sound that made David want to gag. "Your little Fae bitch didn't tell you? You've been carrying around a portion of her power for quite some time now."

David rolled his eyes. Really? This was the sort of shit the demon was going to feed him? He wasn't about to allow this worthless monster to get under his skin. "And how did I lose it?" he baited.

"The Fae in all their two-faced glory only share their powers with those they 'love.' That's the only way they can give it or take it back—fucking. Tell me, have you been fucking around with her nice and good? Because she's sure been fucking with you." The demon's mouth curved into a smirk.

David glanced over his shoulder toward Allsún again. No, it couldn't be. He ignored the monster and crossed the room to Allsún's side. She was sitting on the sofa with the boy wrapped in her arms, crying into her shoulder.

David nodded toward the hallway. "Can I see you outside for a minute?"

She nodded. "Yeah, sure." She turned toward the boy and ran a hand over his slightly disheveled hair. "I'll be right back. You'll be safe right here. That ward stops the demon from being able to move, so it can't get to you. If it tries to talk to you, or tells you to do anything at all, ignore it, no matter how tempting it sounds. That's not your brother in there right now, okay? So if he tells you to untie him, don't listen."

The teen nodded. "Okay."

She followed David out into the hallway and leaned against the wall. "What's going on? Has the demon said anything useful yet?"

"Not that I can tell, but it did say something that's making me wonder."

She nodded, urging him to continue.

"I exorcised this same demon a few months back, and it said I'm different this time, that I'm missing something. It said I had Fae light in me, and now that's gone. You don't know anything about that, do you?" he asked.

Allsún's jaw dropped, as if she couldn't believe he'd asked her that. "What? David, you can't possibly believe that. You *know* demons lie through their fucking teeth."

He nodded. Maybe she was right, but he had to ask. "Yeah, but this lie seemed a little too specific for this dipshit's intelligence level, you know? So, do you know what it's talking about?"

She glanced down and to the left, refusing to meet his gaze. "I don't know, David. I really don't know."

Shit. She wasn't actually lying to his face, was she? Damn it. "Allie, I know that look. That's your I'm-not-telling-the-whole-truth look."

She shot him an angry glare. "Are you calling me a liar?"

David took a moment to collect himself before he continued. "It depends. Should I be? Because you're acting pretty goddamn suspicious."

Allsún scoffed. "You're really going to accuse me of lying all because of the word of some demon?"

"Just answer my question straight, and I won't have to accuse you of anything. Do you know what it's talking about?"

Allsún met his gaze, trying her best to hold a level stare, but she broke quickly. She was horrible at lying. Keeping things to herself was one thing, but flat-out lying was something she'd never been good at. Her lower lip quivered before she finally broke down and confessed. "Yeah, I know what it's talking about."

"And?"

She shrugged. "And nothing. It's no big deal, okay? They're *my* powers, after all."

David's eyes widened. "Wait a second. Your powers? So you *did* take some sort of Fae power from me?"

"Yes, I did, all right? But what does it matter? You didn't even know you had it, and I'd only gifted it to you by accident years ago."

David gaped at her. "It matters because, according to that demon in there, the only way for you to transfer those powers is during sex."

Allsún didn't respond.

No. That couldn't be it. She couldn't possibly have done that, could she? "Did you sleep with me just so you could get your powers back?"

She remained silent.

"Allsún."

She refused to look at him.

"You did, didn't you?"

The pain hit him straight in the chest. For a moment, he couldn't move, couldn't breathe. She'd slept with him to get her powers back. Here he'd been thinking that maybe something was starting between them again, that maybe, just maybe, by the grace of God she was slowly coming back into his life. But, no. That wasn't the case. He'd been duped. Allsún had used him without a qualm.

"It's not what you're thinking. It's not the way it sounds. At first I thought about it, I admit it. But by the time we actually slept together it was more than that. I promise you. I didn't even intend to take my light back. I hoped maybe it would come back on its own, and it just happened."

David pounded his fist against the wall. Damn, this hurt. "What was the point of lying? Why not just be up front in the first place? You know I would do anything for you, anything you asked of me, as much as it would kill me inside."

She shook her head. "I couldn't."

"What do you mean, you couldn't?"

"I just couldn't tell you, okay?"

"Why did you even need your power back? You've lived without it for at least five years, so why do you need it now?"

When she didn't respond, he persisted. "Allsún, why do you need these powers back now?"

She sighed. "I need them to get to the Isle of Apples. If I have all my powers, then I can go to the Isle and the demons won't be able to come after me anymore. I'll be safe there."

David fought back a curse. Shit. Not only had she used him, but she was leaving, to boot? "And when exactly were you planning on telling me this? Not only are you leaving, but you're going to another whole fucking dimension and you didn't think that was important to tell me?"

He stepped closer to her, and she shoved him away. "Oh, don't give me that hurt act, David. If you were so fucking in love with me you would've chased after me the first time."

"I didn't think you wanted to be chased. I actually thought you would come back." The thought alone made his heart ache. "Do you know how much it hurt, hoping for weeks, months, years, that you were going to walk back through that door? The pain of losing you was nearly unbearable."

"Oh, yeah, because I'm the only one who's caused any pain around here." She crossed her arms over her chest and turned away from him.

David shook his head. How could she not see why he'd made the choices he had? "Look, I know I've made my share of mistakes, but joining the Execution Underground wasn't one of them. I should have told you beforehand what I was going to do, but I don't regret joining. I've saved countless lives, Allsún. I made the right choice for the greater good. Besides, the only reason I went ahead with it was because I felt so certain in our relationship that never in a million years did I think you'd leave. I thought it was the right decision for both of us. I'd be better able to provide for us, for—"

She cut him off. "Don't act so self-righteous, like you didn't do anything wrong. *You* were the one who hurt me first by making your choice without even consulting me, David."

"You're right. I was wrong to do that, but *you* were the one who walked out," he said.

She jabbed a finger into his chest. "You *made* me walk out!"

Pain the likes of which he'd only known the first time she'd left seared through his heart. "What are you talking about? I begged you to stay."

She raised her voice, jabbing him harder in the chest. "I couldn't have stayed even if I'd wanted to."

What on earth was she talking about? How could she have thought she had no choice? "Why the hell not?"

"Because I knew you didn't want us!" she yelled.

David paused. "Us? Who—"

"Me and the baby, you insensitive jerk. I was pregnant. I was twelve weeks along, and you practically told me the thought of having children with me made you sick to your stomach."

For a moment, David felt as if his heart had stopped. Allsún had been pregnant? Images flashed through his mind of the possibilities: Allsún holding an infant in her arms, a house with a white picket fence and a nursery. He shook the thoughts from his head. How could she have kept that from him? "Sick with worry, Allsún. Not because I didn't want children. I always wanted children with you. I just wanted them to be safe, and I knew that was something I couldn't guarantee, so I didn't want to have a kid when I knew I couldn't protect it. Why didn't you ever tell me you were pregnant?"

She looked at him as if he were ridiculous for even asking. "Why do you think? I was scared of how you'd react. You tell me you don't want kids, and then you expect me to be forthcoming when I find out I'm carrying your child? I couldn't have stood the pain if you'd asked me to have an abortion."

He stepped toward her. How could she think that of him? That he wouldn't want to keep his child? "I never would've asked you to do that. And you thought telling me now that I'm a dad would be a better idea?"

She shook her head. "You're not a dad."

He paused. "What?"

The tears were already pouring down her face. "I lost the baby."

David's breath escaped in one large rush. He felt as if he'd been kicked in the stomach. "What?" he managed to choke out.

Allsún wiped the tears from her eyes, though they continued to fall. "I lost the baby. I had a miscarriage."

David was at a loss for words. His heart sank to the floor. "Allie, I… What happened?"

"If you had just come after me. If you had just fucking chased after me, everything would've been all right."

"Allsún, what are you talking about?"

"How I lost the baby!" she cried. "I ran home that night, crying my eyes out, and I was so upset I didn't see the warning signs that…a…a…" She choked on her words, barely able to speak them. "…a demon was in the house. It was so powerful that I couldn't fight it. It pinned me to the wall. It knew I was carrying your child and it…it…" She sucked in a deep breath before she let out a strained sob. "It made me miscarry. It reached inside me and just…" Tears rolled over her cheeks. "It was a baby boy. It was going to be an exorcist—like you."

David's whole world spun as the horror of the situation hit him full force. He'd told a pregnant Allsún that he didn't want children, and then a demon had ensured that his son, another exorcist as powerful as he was, was never born. It was his fault the demon had come after her, his fault for not chasing after her and saving her and—oh, God—saving their child.

"Allie, I'm so sorry. I swear I didn't know. If I'd had any idea, I would have…" He reached out to touch her shoulder, but she swatted his hand away.

"Don't touch me."

"Allsún—"

"Just leave me alone, damn it. I was fine—totally fine—until you came into my life again." She stepped backward, inching away from him.

He moved forward, but she retreated even farther.

"Leave me alone. I want you out of my life. For good

this time." She ran toward the stairs, face buried in her hands.

At the sound of the front door closing, David's world shattered.

Chapter 16

Allsún ran from the building, refusing to look back to see if David was following her. She was certain he wouldn't be. He had quite the mess to take care of before he could even think about his issues with her. The romantic part of her still wished that when she'd glanced over her shoulder he had been there, though. She paused as she reached the Super Glide, which he'd thrown on to the grass in a frenzy to get inside. There was no way she could support the weight of that thing on her own. She would need to take a cab, but to where?

A list of possibilities ran through her mind. She could go back to the hotel, but David would find her there, and she would be forced to face him again. That wasn't something she wanted. She couldn't go back to his apartment, because the demons knew where it was, not to mention that the door was broken. And she certainly didn't have any family members she could stay with, since they'd all gone to the Isle of Apples. There was always David's grandmother, but she couldn't go there. Not only didn't she want to put anyone else in danger, but when David was upset he often went to his grandmother for advice. As at the hotel, she would probably be forced to confront him there. The only other option appeared to be to go home. She couldn't go straight to the Isle of Apples, not without arranging homes for her pets. She reassured herself that her sweet little fur babies were entirely the reason she couldn't just leave, though she knew deep down she was really hoping to reconcile with David.

As far as she knew, no demons knew where she lived, only where her mother's home was, so maybe she would be safe at her own apartment, at least for a little while, until she could think of a better alternative. With any luck, David wouldn't think to look for her there. She flagged down a cab, worried that using her Fae magic to steal a free ride home was getting to be a bad habit.

When she reached her locked front door, she was grateful she always kept a spare key taped under the welcome mat. She locked the door behind her and flipped on lights as she went.

One of her many cats, Olivia, a black-and-white former stray, ran through the apartment to greet her. Thank goodness for Mrs. Cole, her sweet elderly next door neighbor, who'd clearly been taking care of the cats in her absence. Olivia let out a sweet meow as Allsún picked her up and cradled her in her arms. She rubbed her cheek against Olivia's soft fur.

"I missed all my babies," she said to the cat, which was purring loudly in her arms.

She carried Olivia into her bedroom and gently placed her on the bed. Two of her other cats came tip-toeing into the room: Olivia's brother, Ralph, and Jack, a three-legged tabby she'd rescued from the side of the road after he'd been hit by a car and left for dead. She lay back on the bed, falling into her mounds of pillows, then allowed her emotions to run free, expecting more tears to pour down her face.

To her surprise, no tears came. If she was honest with herself, the argument with David had been something of a relief, allowing her to finally get all the pain and anger off her chest. A beautifully marked calico leaped on to the bed—Ms. Fit, her slightly angry eldest cat, which her mother had saved from a box of homeless kittens outside a convenience store. She petted Ms. Fit's head before she propped herself up on her elbows, surveying the cats in her room.

She lay there for nearly an hour before she heard a knock at the door. There was no need for her to look through the peephole—though she did it as a precaution anyway—she knew who it was.

She opened the door and stepped aside. David walked in without a word and headed straight for her couch.

He sat down, then cleared his throat. "I wasn't going to make the same mistake as last time and not come after you, so I'm here now, and I'm not leaving until we have this conversation. I think it's long overdue."

She crossed the room and sat down beside him. Even after all the time that had passed, she wasn't sure she was ready for this, but regardless of whether she was ready, David was here now, and he deserved the truth. She twisted her hands together as she spoke. She couldn't look at him yet. "The night we broke up, I was mad about you joining the Execution Underground, but that's not why I left. I left because I was three months pregnant."

David shook his head, as if he still couldn't believe what he was hearing. "Why didn't you tell me?"

"David, how could I? From the moment we got engaged, you had always insisted you didn't want children. I'd known for weeks, but I'd been afraid to tell you, because I had no idea how you would react."

He lifted her chin with his index finger and forced her to look at him. "I would've told you we'd get through it. That we would be great parents, and that I was happy, even though it was unplanned."

"I tried to tell you, but that's not the reaction I could have predicted when I showed you those baby shoes. Instead of realizing what I was trying to say, you just brought up the fact that you didn't want kids. How was I supposed to feel about that when I was twelve weeks pregnant and full of raging hormones?"

He reached out and took her hand in his. The most sincere sadness crossed his features, and she could have sworn his eyes were the slightest bit misty. "I'm so sorry, Allie."

That was when she lost it. Tears clouded her eyes before they poured down her cheeks. "Well, that doesn't really matter now," she snapped.

David ignored her anger and continued to treat her gently. "I should've been there to protect you. I wanted to come after you so badly, but I thought you would come back if you wanted to. Even after a week had passed, I still just thought you were cooling down from being angry with me, and rightfully so. I was such an idiot—I know that now. Then a week turned into a month, and the months turned into years, and by the time I actually accepted you weren't coming back, approaching you seemed impossible. I knew you didn't want me anymore, so I thought it would be best to let you move on with your life."

She shook her head. Move on? Boy, was that a joke. Even with a nice guy like Tom around, she'd never been able to move on. That was exactly her problem. "I've never been able to move on after losing you and the baby at the same time. It's always followed me around like a dark cloud hanging over my head." She paused. "I'd hoped our first would be a boy, you know."

David remained silent, tracing circles on her palm with his thumb in gentle movements.

"The demon said he would be an exorcist, just like you, and that's why he had to..." She couldn't choke out the word, no matter how hard she tried. But then she opened her mouth again and the words fell out as if a floodgate had opened. She couldn't hold them in any longer. "I managed to call 9-1-1 after the attack. An ambulance rushed me to the hospital. The doctors only told me what I already knew the moment I saw the blood. The baby—our baby—was dead. The doctors wanted to put me under anesthesia to have a D and C, a medical abortion, but some part of me just didn't want to give up on him just yet, even though deep down I knew it was a lost cause. I kept praying, hoping, pleading with God to save him, but no answer ever came.

"I wasn't hemorrhaging, and since I wouldn't agree to medical intervention, the doctors sent me home for what they call 'expectant management,' which is really just a medical way of saying you're miscarrying at home and alone.

"The doctors also like to say, 'It's okay. You'll be able to have another.' But all I wanted to do was scream at them and say, 'But I want this one. This baby. My baby. Because I already loved him and would have gladly given up my life just so he could live."

Without warning, David pulled her into his arms. She rested her head against his chest as her tears continued to fall. "Not a day goes by that I don't think about him. I couldn't bear the thought of not giving him a proper memorial, so I paid to have a headstone laid for him at Mount Hope Cemetery. I visit it once a week and put flowers down when I can. Each year on what would have been his due date, I light a candle for him and say a prayer, even though some days I don't have a lot of faith in God after losing him. He would've been four years old now. I named him Michael, like your middle name, like the angel. Michael O'Hare Aronowitz."

David stroked her hair. "It's okay. You can tell me anything. You need to get this off your chest."

"The worst part is when I hear other woman talk about their kids, not because I'm jealous that their babies lived and mine had to die, but because they say things like, 'Wait until you're a mother someday' and I just wish there was some way I could tell the world I *am* a mother." The last words came out as sobs.

David tightened his hold around her. "You're not alone anymore, Allie. The world may not know, but I know. I know now, and I think you sound like the world's best mother, because I can see how much you loved Michael."

Another cry escaped her throat when David said his son's name. No one else had ever cared enough to call him that before, and she could tell by the way he said it that he cared, more than he probably wanted to. "I've never heard anyone else call him by the name I gave him before. It makes him feel so much more real."

David kissed her forehead. His lips were so tender and soft, warming her from the inside out like a favorite blanket on a cold winter night.

He whispered against her skin, "He *was* real and he

is real. I know it may be hard for you to believe, but I know in my heart you're going to see him again someday. *We'll* see him again."

When Allsún had cried all the tears she could possibly manage, she pulled away from David's arms.

"Thank you for coming here. I needed to say all that."

He nodded. "Sometimes all we need to begin to heal is for someone else to bear witness to our pain. I don't know if the pain of losing a child will ever fully leave, but now you have someone to share it with," he said.

A small part of her wanted to tell him everything was different now. That she could feel a change, some sort of shift between them now that he knew everything she'd endured, but she was smarter than that. She needed to think things over still. Needed space. "This doesn't change anything, you know. Not yet."

He tried to smile at her, but she could tell his heart wasn't in it. "I figured that would be the case." Though she expected him to, he didn't get up to leave. "You still need protection," he said. "I can't just leave you, not after everything that's happened."

She stood and gestured toward the door. "You have to, David. At least for tonight. I need some space to clear my head."

He began to protest, but she held up a hand to silence him. "Please go."

His face twisted into a look of frustration, but to his credit, he respected her wishes. She opened the door and showed him out without another word.

As soon as the dead bolt latched into place behind him, Allsún breathed a sigh of relief. Time for herself at last. Her cats came rushing up to her again, and she petted them one by one, snuggling them to her chest.

Wait a second.

One was missing. Another older tabby who had once been an adorable kitten named Mew, but after having an accidental litter of kittens and then getting spayed, was now a fat cat affectionately nicknamed Moo.

"Moo!" she called out.

Silence answered her.

She tried the cat's other nickname. "Moo-ey *bueno!*"

Finally, a small mewing sound answered her back.

"Moo, where are you?"

Another mew came from her guest bedroom. "Moo, what are you doing? Come here." Finally she stood, turning on more lights as she went.

Just before she rounded the corner to her mother's bedroom, Moo skyrocketed out the door, running right past her.

"Moo, what's wrong?" She let out a long sigh. "You weren't being bad again, were you? You better not have been scratching Mama's quilts." She turned into the bedroom and flicked on the light.

She didn't have time to scream before the demon lifted its hand, pinning her against the far wall and knocking the wind out of her.

Shite. How had it gotten inside?

"You really should have put bars on the window above the fire escape," the demon said. It was wearing a man's body, someone she recognized as one of her downstairs neighbors, a man she'd rarely spoken to but had often seen in passing.

The demon stepped toward her. The man it was wearing was middle-aged, slightly overweight, with just a hint of a receding hairline. But knowing there was a demon inside him made his normally innocuous form unbelievably threatening. The demon stepped closer to her. "I promised you I'd be back one day."

Allsún's eyes widened. No, it couldn't be. The demon that had killed her baby? "You sick, pathetic hell-crawler," she spat. "What do you want from me now?"

"Call me Sammael." The demon grinned, managing to twist the face of the innocent man it was wearing into something distorted and evil. "Don't worry, no dead babies this time."

Allsún struggled against the demon's invisible hold. She knew it was no use, but she had to at least try.

"Exactly what you've given me—you." Sammael lifted an open hand, then clenched it into a fist.

Allsún's muscles spasmed as pain seared throughout her body. She screamed before the demon slapped her across the face.

"Shut up," he hissed.

"If you're going to kill me, just kill me already," she gasped.

"By the time I'm done with you, you'll wish all I wanted was to kill you. Unfortunately, I *can't* kill you. I need you. You followed the plan exactly. I planted that demon, and I instructed it to tell David about your light because I knew it would drive you here—alone, now that the exorcist has left you unprotected once again."

"How did you know I'd taken my light back?"

The demon laughed. "Don't be stupid. The whole reason that demon possessed your doctor in the first place is because I needed to drive you back to Aronowitz. I needed you to reclaim your light. That's why I've put every demon under my control on a hunt for you. I knew you'd have no option but to flee to the Isle of Apples, and I knew you and that pussy Aronowitz would inevitably crawl back into bed together. You humans act like you're independent, but you're so fucking predictable."

She fixed the demon with a glare of pure hatred. "What do you need from me if you don't want me dead?"

"Tonight marks the four millionth full moon since my Mistress was cast from the Garden of Eden. Magic is in the air tonight, just as my Mistress ensured before she was cast out, and it will ensure Lilith's rise from hell. And you, my dear, have a role to play. You see, the fear of the parents and the deaths of their children were part of the spell Lilith cast. Consider it her punishment to God for cursing her with infertility when he cast her out. Two infant deaths seasoned with their parents' fear have led to this night, when you're going to help us with our third and final family, the family that will bring Lilith to this earthly plane once again."

Allsún scoffed. "I'll never do anything you want me to, even if you torture me. Believe me, whatever you have up your sleeve, I've been through worse. I can withstand anything. I'm a survivor."

Sammael ran a single finger across her cheekbone. A shiver of disgust and fear ran down Allsún's spine.

Sammael pulled his hand away. "As much pleasure as I'd find in torturing you, I won't need to. Lilith is going to possess you."

What in the world was this hell-crawler talking about? "Lilith? As in Lilith from the Bible? Besides, I'm Fae. No demon can possess me, you sulfur-sucking idiot."

Sammael grinned. "That's where you're wrong, my dear little Fae whore. You see, demons as powerful as Lilith and I *are* capable of possessing you disgusting little Fae. We've done it before, and we'll do it again."

"I'd like to see you try."

"You will, my dear. You will." She cringed as the demon patted her cheek. "All in due time."

Allsún opened her mouth to speak again, but before she could, the Sammael drew back his arm and aimed his fist straight toward her face. That was the last thing she saw before everything faded to black.

Maybe the library wasn't the best place in the world to research the crime scene symbols. Shane rested his forehead on the keyboard of his computer and groaned. Damn it. No matter where or how he searched, whether online or in books, everything was coming up empty. He knew he would identify it eventually, because innocent lives depended on it and he prided himself on never letting his team members down, but he was practically ripping his hair out, and at this rate he was going to go bald before he found the answer.

"You don't look too happy," a female voice said from behind him.

Damn it. No way. He didn't have time to deal with this right now. He looked up to find Vera Sanders now standing in front of him.

Couldn't the universe give him a break for two fucking minutes so he could crack this case?

He collected himself and asked, "What can I help you with, Miss Sanders?"

She rocked back and forth on her high-heeled boots as if she were nervous. "Well, when I saw you sitting here, I was kind of hoping you'd be willing to help with that tutoring we discussed before." Her eyes widened in a look of concern. "I really don't want to fail your class, Dr. Grey," she added.

Damn. He wanted to help her. He really did, and not just because he was attracted to her, but because he genuinely cared about the academic welfare of his students, but this wasn't the right time.

"I'm sorry, Miss Sanders. Right now just isn't a good time. I'm researching something rather important."

She leaned in to look at his research. He slammed the lid of his laptop shut, so she wouldn't see the symbol smeared in blood from the crime scene, but it was too late.

Her eyes widened with surprise and she immediately grew flustered. "Damn, Doc Grey. That's some serious black magic you're getting into. A ritual to summon the demon queen is—" She clapped her hand over her mouth.

Shane pushed back his chair. "Demon queen? What did you say?"

She shook her head. "I'm sorry. I don't know what I was talking about. I need to go now."

She moved to step away from him, but he stood and blocked her path. "Vera, this is really important. What did you mean when you said 'the demon queen'?"

She tried to step around him again to no avail.

"Vera, please. Lives may depend on this," he pleaded.

She shook her head as if she couldn't believe what she was saying. "Lilith. The demon queen. She's in lots of folklore, you know. I saw it on TV"

Oh no. Shane wasn't falling for it. He wasn't stupid by any stretch of the imagination. "Vera, how did you really recognize that symbol?"

She met his eyes with a stricken look, then dodged

past him at last and practically bolted for the front door of the library. He grabbed his textbooks, shoved them into his bag, and ran after her.

The cold Rochester air prickled against his skin as he sped out the door in her wake.

"Vera, wait!" he called.

She ran without looking back.

And then he knew. It was so clear that he wondered how he could have missed it.

Vera Sanders was a witch.

When Allsún's eyes flickered open, it took all the self-control she had not to scream. She tried to move, but her hands were bound behind her back. She wiggled her feet and discovered that they were tied to the chair where the demon had placed her. Her eyes darted around the room as she took in the scene before her. A mother, father and son lay on the floor, tied up just as she was and also gagged.

A house. She was in a house. What had to be the family's home. The bindings on her hands and feet bit into her skin. The terrified expressions in the family members' eyes struck a terrible chord in her mind as she remembered the carnage she had so recently seen.

For now the family was safe, but they were frozen in fear and reduced to the occasional whimper.

"Have a good view?" a familiar, disgusting voice whispered behind Allsún.

She tried to turn and see who was speaking, but the ropes limited her movement. It didn't matter. She knew that foul voice. She didn't respond, instead pulling harder against the restraints.

"You really should save your strength." The neighbor's normally bland voice turned snakelike and poisonous when the demon spoke.

She felt its hot breath on her neck as the words slithered into her ear. It was close, very close. At that moment, an unfamiliar woman entered the room. Allsún felt the brief urge to warn her, tell her to run for her life, but when she saw the cold, dead-eyed expression on the woman's face, she knew any warning would be pointless.

The clearly pregnant mother whimpered something from behind her gag. The female demon kicked her hard in the stomach, causing her to curl into a fetal position, eyes welling up with tears. The son writhed in impotent agony at seeing his mother in so much pain.

"Now, now, there will be time enough for that," the

demon behind Allsún purred, "when we have our little Fae bitch to do the kicking for us."

Allsún wanted to hurl at the thought that she was intended to be the instrument of their torture and death.

She struggled against her restraints again, the taut ropes rubbing her flesh raw at her efforts.

The demon stepped in front of her and grabbed her by the chin, jerking her face to meet its lifeless eyes. "You've got fight in you. I respect that." It lashed out, slapping her hard enough across the face that her mouth filled with the metallic tang of blood.

"That one was from me. Consider the rest to be courtesy of Lilith," it snarled.

Allsún defiantly locked eyes with the demon. "You can go straight back to hell you piece of shi—"

The demon grabbed her by the back of the head and with one swift move locked its mouth over hers. Allsún immediately felt a chilling sensation slinking through her body. A cold, numb tingle floated down each leg and then back up again—a slow paralysis.

She heard a strange, eerie noise as the neighbor's mouth performed what felt like a demented form of CPR. A cold gaseous substance entered her lungs. Her motor control started to fail.

Her senses remained as sharp as ever, but her ability

to control her arms, her legs, was lost. She saw and felt the hand at the end of her arm clench, but it could not be hers, not in an objective sense. She screamed and then realized no sound was coming from her mouth.

Her body was lost to her, invaded by the demon. Somewhere in the back of her mind she heard laughter—a sick, high-pitched giggling, like a disturbed child dismembering a small animal. The demon had her. She tried screaming again, to no avail. The giggling continued like the hellish refrain from a nightmare, reverberating somewhere in the confines of her consciousness.

She felt her limbs flexing against her will, the hell-beast taking her for some kind of demented test drive. She remained defiant, screaming silently in her own mind, *Get out of me, you fucking coward. I will never do what you want me to do.*

Her face smiled, and she heard the distorted voice reply directly in her brain, in the most bloodcurdling horrific language imaginable, straight out of hell itself, with no body to filter it through, no host to dilute it. It was a choked, malignant hiss of a voice, fashioned out of knives and suffering.

We'll see what little Allie can and can't do. The voice giggled again like some kind of evil clown. Allsún's mind flashed back in vivid detail as the demon controlled her memories.

It blurred back to the day she'd walked out of David's door and fled to her apartment. It made her remember every fading heartbeat of the baby she'd lost, made her relive every second of that anguish. She snapped back to reality to find she'd been untied by the demon's accomplice.

The voice rang in her brain again. *Do you really want to keep defying me?*

Allsún didn't respond. She felt the demon's power coursing through what had once been *her* body.

While this really is fun, Allie, we have more important matters to attend to. Like the question of which of these people will you kill first?

Allsún fought with what little strength the demon had left her to try to stop her body from moving toward the family.

Hmm...that boy sure didn't like seeing what our friend did to his mother. Perhaps her first?

The female demon-host put a large butcher knife into Allsún's hand and sat in an armchair to watch, rapt, its eyes filled with sick fascination.

Let's see what happens next, shall we?

Allsún knelt down by the mother and grabbed her by

the hair. She pulled the gag away and forced the woman's mouth open with the flat of the knife. She slowly inserted the blade into her mouth, making sure the son and father were watching. The two men writhed and wailed beneath their restraints.

Allsún pulled the knife out slowly, nicking the corner of the mother's mouth into a little half smile.

No…not enough pain in their eyes yet. No. No fucking way. There was no way she would allow the demon to hurt these people using *her* body. Allsún focused every ounce of mental energy she had on redirecting her own limbs. Her whole body was trembling, but the hand that held the knife slowly began to drop.

The demon hissed inside her head. *No, what is this? How are you doing that? You filthy faerie whore.*

Suddenly, her mouth was hanging open and the gaseous white substance that had invaded her earlier was escaping in a frigid cloud. Once again she was in control of her own limbs, but before she could process what had happened, the other demon seized her from behind. She struggled against its hold, attempting to elbow the monster in the ribs to no avail.

The body Sammael had previously abandoned was now animated again as the demon sidekick began to tie her up. In one last attempt to save herself, she threw her head back, bashing the top of her skull into the demon's nose. The demon let out a muffled grunt, and she felt the warmth of blood pouring down the back of her shirt.

"You stupid whore." Sammael crossed the room and backhanded her across the face. The sting in her cheek was nothing compared to what she planned to do to him someday. No demon was going to take over her body and live to tell the tale, at least not for long.

Sammael leaned into her, their faces so close their noses nearly touched. "You're going to regret that little stunt, because the pain I'd planned to cause those humans using your body will be nothing in comparison to the pain I show them now."

Allsún spat straight into Sammael's face. The sneer that crossed his features was staggeringly foul, and then he pulled back his fist and punched her straight in the stomach.

Between the self-inflicted blow to the head and the lack of oxygen from being punched in the gut, her vision swam, pulsing dots clustering before her eyes, until finally, everything faded to black.

Chapter 17

The rest of the night passed in a blur for David. He barely felt the joy he normally experienced in exorcising a demon. His follow-up call to Damon to check on the arrangements to sanitize the scene had been almost mechanical. He was still trying to wrap his mind around everything Allsún had told him. All he wanted now was to get back to where they'd once been before he'd failed her in so many ways. He wanted to be the man she loved once again, but after all the pain he'd caused her, he wasn't certain if she would be able to love him again or not. The thought of losing her all over again was agony the likes of which he'd never known.

Pregnant. She'd been pregnant with his child, and he'd told her he didn't want to have a family. No wonder she'd run off when she'd shown him the baby shoes and he'd reacted the way he had.

Suddenly it all made sense. Her sudden anger over a situation she'd long before known his feelings about, followed by her not speaking to him. She blamed him for the baby's death. He could feel it in his bones, and honestly, he couldn't fault her for feeling that way. The thought that maybe, if he'd gone after her, he could have saved their unborn child killed him inside.

How had he been so blind to the changes going on with her in the weeks leading up to their breakup? He'd been so focused on his plan to join the Execution Underground that he hadn't even noticed what must have been subtle but still obvious changes in her. His mind played those thoughts and worse on constant repeat as he went through the motions of his job, returning to the crime scene to assist Damon.

When he arrived, the clean-up crew had just shown up, and Damon had already placed the two boys and their infant sister into HQ's custody.

David tried not to think about the difficult adjustments that lay ahead of the twins. As tough a life as it could be to hunt the paranormal killers of the world, it was one of their better options. The Execution Underground only recruited men who already knew about supernatural creatures, and often the way the regular population found out about the supernatural was by losing someone they loved. The twins would be a recruitment target. HQ loved to find potential hunters with what they termed a "personal passion" for fighting the supernatural, which was really just a bullshit political way of saying they liked it when hunters had a personal vendetta that fueled their training. If they chose, both boys would both become hunters for the Execution Underground, be trained in combat for years until they were ready for the serum injection that gave them increased and strengthened capabilities. After that they would be sent out for field training. He was rare in his recruitment as an exorcist. That was the one gift the Execution Underground hadn't given him, though at the moment he wasn't loving the abilities he'd been born with any more than those he'd been given or, in fact, his job.

Damon aided him in gathering data from the scene and taking photos to show to the fellow members of their team. Damon agreed to send the samples off to Chris immediately, but David knew they would be no help to his case. That wasn't the demon that had been behind the previous murders, and he told Damon as much. He'd continued to interrogate the demon before he'd chased after Allsún, but the little shit had refused to give anything up. David was no closer to solving the crimes than he had been a few hours earlier. This incident had only managed to raise more questions.

Clearly, whoever the head-honcho demon was, it had been hoping David's encounter with the Abyzu would throw him off, but he couldn't possibly fathom why. What was the point? Why change its M.O. now and send a surrogate to do its work?

Once he'd finally finished up at the scene, he returned to the hotel. A deathlike numbness had washed over him after his conversation with Allsún, but as soon as the hotel door closed behind him, he let loose. Anger and guilt pulsed through him as he bashed his fist into the wall. A garbled yell ripped from his throat. Damn it all. What the fuck kind of man did she take him for? How could she ever think he would ask her to abort her child? His child. *Their* child.

He'd always known how much she wanted a family. How could she have thought he would ask her to end her pregnancy? And if she'd only told him sooner, he could have helped her through the pregnancy. Instead, it had ended tragically, all because she'd kept him in the dark, so he hadn't known she needed extra protection. It was *his* fault, because he hadn't protected her, but damn it, why hadn't she told him?

After he'd fumed in anger for so long he couldn't stand it anymore, he lay awake in bed for hours, unable to sleep at the thought of her alone in her apartment. Finally he decided that, come morning, he would go to her place. He needed to be there to protect her, whether she liked it or not. He didn't expect them to get back together. He was far past hoping for that. But that didn't mean he had any intention of staying away.

Not again.

David woke the next morning to the awful sound of his phone's ringtone. He knew it couldn't possibly be Allsún calling him, which could only mean one thing. He picked up the phone with a grumble. "Hello?"

Damon's voice sounded from the other line. "Sorry to wake you."

"Let me guess: bad news? Another dead family?" David asked.

Damon let out a short sigh. "Unfortunately, yes."

David swore. "How could the demons have possibly gotten around the surveillance? Why did no one call me?"

"They hit a family outside of the surveillance. From

the intel Chris was able to gather, the family used a midwife and their birth was only on record with the state department, not with any of the hospitals or social services."

"Shit."

"You have a few hours before the police show up. Get over there and collect your samples, investigate the crime scene. The media is in a total frenzy. We need to end this soon, David."

David wanted to scream into the phone that he wanted to see Damon end this soon. How could they expect to make any progress when the system they ran their samples through came back with no answers? He bit his tongue and refrained from bitching out his leader. "Yeah, I'll get over there." He hung up the phone, but he needed to make a personal stop first.

Twenty minutes later David was knocking on Allsún's door. When there was no response he knocked again, harder. Still nothing. Desperate to get inside, terrified that she was there and too injured to call out—he refused to consider the even worse possibility that raced to mind—he pulled out a credit card and jimmied the lock.

"Allsún?" he called as he entered, then paused just inside the doorway.

Everything looked normal. Her living room was pristinely clean, as usual, and everything appeared in place. He called out her name again and received no answer. With careful movements, he crept down the hallway toward her bedroom. When he reached it he flicked on the light.

Shit.

Her bedroom was a mess, piles of laundry scattered across the floor, drawers pulled out of the dresser and dumped, and a knocked-over water glass no one had bothered to clean up.

This wasn't like Allsún.

In all the years he'd known her, she'd been a total neat freak. Back when they were dating, she'd even gone so far as to clean his apartment on a regular basis, because, according to her, she couldn't stand the mess of his bachelor living space.

Something had happened here. Something bad.

He called out her name. "Allsún?"

No response and no sign of her. Wherever she was, it wasn't here, and he was frighteningly certain that it wasn't good.

Panic rose in his chest. What the hell had happened to her and where the hell was she?

Just as he was preparing to call her and pray she answered—because if she didn't, he was calling Shane to put a tracker on her cell—his own phone vibrated. Allsún's name flashed across screen. He let out a sigh of relief as he answered the call.

"Hey, babe," Allsún cooed.

David raised a brow. Babe? Since when did she call him babe? He pushed the thought aside. He was over-analyzing things. "Where are you?"

"Oh, that doesn't matter right now," she said. "Maybe I should be asking you the same thing."

David frowned. What the hell was up with her? Why was she acting as if everything was fine between them? "I'm in your apartment," he said. "Looking for you." He paused, then asked again, "So, where are you?"

"I just decided I needed to go out and get some fresh air."

Some fresh air? "You mean you're not still mad from last night?"

"Nah, I'm over it."

Over it? Over blaming him for the death of their child? Something wasn't right. He was certain of it.

"I'm glad to hear you're not mad."

"How could I be, silly? You know I can't stay mad at you for long."

Bullshit. Even Allsún herself would admit that she

had a temper; it was in her nature, part of her pixie bloodline. For a second the thought that he might not actually be speaking to Allsún crossed his mind. Had she been possessed?

He shook his head. No, that couldn't be. The Fae weren't capable of being possessed. Then again, Allsún was only half Fae. Could it be? No. She was just behaving oddly after their fight. That was all.

"I have bad news," he said.

Silence. He took that as his cue to continue.

"Another family has been killed."

"That's unfortunate."

David raised a brow. Unfortunate? She was referring to the brutal murder of a family as *unfortunate?* Something wasn't right, and he needed to figure out what. He also needed to get over to the scene before the police descended on it. "I have to get over there right away. Why don't you meet me?" He told her the address. Once he saw her, maybe her behavior would reveal what was really going on with her.

Allsún was waiting for him outside the house with a calm smile on her face. David's suspicions were immediately confirmed. And her behavior once they were inside wasn't any better. He took in the monstrous scene around him with a mix of fury and nausea, yet Allsún barely blinked. All the signs pointed to possession, but he still hadn't figured out how it was even remotely possible for a demon to possess a Fae. He'd never heard of such a thing before, even for a half-breed. He carefully examined the crime scene, trying to determine which family member had died first.

Judging from the state of the bodies, blood pooling and stage of rigor, the teenage son had been the first to go. Dark, dried blood formed an ominous halo around his head. Figuring out the cause of death was easy. His throat had been slit.

Judging by the corpse's lividity and the lack of blood, the next victim had been the father. His death was disturbing in a different way. It had been clean, almost clinical in nature, as if the demon had decided the man was too annoying to deal with, and had just shut off his life force like a light.

He took samples from the first two victims, even though he suspected they would be completely useless.

Knowing the M.O. of the killer, he was certain the baby had been the next to die, with the poor mother left for last and forced to watch her family being murdered before her eyes.

Unlike with the previous scenes, the infant's body

had been left intact. He noticed that everyone else's hands and feet had been bound, the victims gagged, as well. The demon had possessed an outsider, using someone outside the family as the murderer.

"I'm surprised the baby's in such good shape," she said in the same blasé tone she might have used to say she was surprised it wasn't raining.

David's jaw nearly fell open. It took everything he had in him not to turn to Allsún and ask, "What the hell's wrong with you?"

He nodded, trying not to let his suspicions show. "Yeah, I was surprised by that, too."

He wasn't sure what it was. Maybe it was the look on her face, the blank stare devoid of any sadness or anger at so much atrocity, but no matter what, he knew he had to get her out of here while he figured out what to do.

He cleared he throat. "Why don't you head home like you usually do, and I'll collect the rest of my samples?" He wanted to see her reaction to the blatant lie about her usually going home. "I'll give you a call in a few hours. Sound okay?"

She nodded. "Sure, sounds fine."

David fought to keep his face from revealing his thoughts. The Allsún he knew would never sit still for being excluded from an investigation. He walked her to the front door and opened it for her. She smiled, then leaned in and kissed him on the mouth, grinding her lips against his in a parody of passion.

His muscles tensed, but his body was as certain as his brain that this wasn't Allsún, and his blood ran cold at her touch. The very thought of kissing Allsún's body while there was a demon inside her made him sick to his stomach.

She pulled away with a grin that was flippant and carefree. "See you later," she said lightly, before waltzing out the door.

As soon as David closed the door behind her, he pulled out his phone.

Jace picked up on the first ring. "Yeah?"

"I think I have a serious problem on my hands."

"You care to elaborate?" Jace asked.

David shook his head, though he knew Jace couldn't see him. Habit. "Not yet. I need you and Shane to meet me at my apartment as soon as possible. Can you track him down?"

"Yeah, I can do that. No problem. See you soon."

David hung up. Once he finished taking photos and gathering his samples, he quickly ran out into the cold Rochester air and threw himself on to his motorcycle. He was going to get to the bottom of this, and if a demon was possessing Allsún, he would make the fucker pay.

Jace and Shane were already waiting for David in his apartment when he arrived. David was grateful to see that the landlord had fixed the door, and Jace had used his key to get in. David found the two of them sitting on the sofa. Jace picked up the romance novel from the coffee table and shook it at David.

"Romance, dude? Really?"

David closed the door behind him and waved a hand in dismissal. "Whatever. I don't have time to hear you harp on me about my reading habits right now. There's some serious shit going down."

Shane leaned forward on the couch. "And I have some serious shit to tell you in return. I've been researching all night. You first."

David stared at the floor, unable to meet his fellow hunters' eyes. "I think Allsún's been possessed."

"What?" Jace barked. "No fuckin' way. She's Fae. She can't be possessed."

Shane's eyes widened. "Shit. It all makes sense now."

David pegged him with a sharp look. "What are you talking about?"

Shane met David's gaze. "When Jace called me, I was just about to call you. I figured out where the symbols from the crime scenes are from. They're not occult. They're biblical."

David didn't like where this was going. "What are demons doing fucking around with symbols from the Bible?" he asked.

"I think you already know what I'm getting at. The fixation on infant victims, the similarities to the Abyzu DNA. I just didn't know she was anything more than a myth, but this is clearly some sort of biblical summoning ritual for her," Shane said.

Jace lifted his hands in a questionable shrug. "What am I missing here? Fill me in."

David looked at the floor with a thoughtful expression. "According to Jewish belief, Adam had a first wife, a disobedient wife, before Eve. Her name was Lilith. She was cast out from the Garden of Eden and is now better known as the mother of demons. Specifically, she's said to have spawned the Abyzus. I thought she only existed in biblical lore, and apparently Shane did, too, but if Shane is right about those symbols from the crime scenes, the demon that's been murdering those families has been trying to raise Lilith from hell."

"Why would it want to do that?" Jace furrowed his brow.

Shane shook his head. "Why do demons want to do anything? To be evil assholes."

David nodded in agreement. It all made sense now. The demon that targeted Allsún and caused the miscarriage. That was what Lilith was known for, causing miscarriages, infant death and SIDS, because she was jealous and infertile after being cast from the Garden. If Allsún had been the target all along, there was only one reason he could think of for why Lilith would choose her. "If Allsún is possessed, the only demon I know of that would be strong enough to possess a Fae is the mother of demons herself. And if Lilith specifically targeted Allsún, I can only think of one reason why. Allsún is the last Fae outside the Isle of Apples, where all of demon-kind's enemies are residing. It takes a Fae to open the portal. That's what she's going to use Allsún for."

Shane and Jace fell silent for a moment, as they processed everything David had just said.

"Are we jumping to conclusions? Can we even be certain she's possessed?" Jace asked.

David groaned. "I'm not certain. I don't have proof without doing something to try to hurt her. I just have a feeling, because she's acting beyond weird." The thought of Allsún possessed by Lilith, the mother of demons herself, caused bile to rise at the back of his throat.

"What was the tip-off?" Shane asked. "What made you think she's possessed?"

"A bunch of things. But the most obvious one was her complete lack of reaction to the crime scene. Although you'd think even a demon would have some kind of reaction. Maybe glee, but still…a reaction."

"Maybe it didn't react because it's already seen it. Maybe it's its own work." Shane gave David a questioning glance.

David immediately went on the offensive. "You're suggesting Allsún killed those people?"

"No, not at all, I'm suggesting that the demon inside her killed them."

David tried to think of Allsún committing murder, possessed or not, but he just couldn't picture it. Shane interrupted his thoughts.

"I know someone I think can help us. She can look at the scene and envision exactly what happened. She's a witch."

Jace looked toward David. "I think that's the best option we have right now."

David nodded. Though he didn't want to admit it, Jace and Shane were right. This was their only choice. It wasn't as if he had a better plan. He could barely think straight at the thought of Allsún being possessed. "Yeah, okay," he agreed.

Shane nodded. "All right, I'll go track her down."

Shane stared at the screen of his laptop in disbelief. He just couldn't catch a break, could he? He glanced at the profile again. Nope. Definitely not. If there was one thing he didn't want to do, it was introduce David and Jace to Vera. In a strip club.

Which was exactly what he was going to have to do.

"Did you find her?" David's deep voice rumbled from over Shane's shoulder.

Shane jumped. Damn it. He reached forward and slammed his computer shut. "Uh, yeah...I found her."

"Then, what are you waiting for? Let's go." David clapped Shane hard on the back before he grabbed his leather jacket and headed for the door. Jace was close on David's heels. Shane let out a long sigh. Pulling his coat off the back of the chair, he stood, slipped the coat on and followed his fellow hunters down three flights of stairs to David's Escalade.

The three men got into the vehicle, David in the driver's seat, Jace riding shotgun, and Shane behind them. A minute later they were on the road, speeding down the street in response to Shane's directions. The multicolored lights of Rochester flashed past them.

David kept his eyes focused on the road. "Where to, Shane?"

"Turn right." Shane pointed at the next stoplight.

The look on David's face was grim, and Shane could tell from the slight tension in his posture that David was in rough shape. Shane knew his friend well enough to understand that he wouldn't be himself again until Allsún was safe.

David turned right and raced down the road. Music from the satellite radio pounded through the car, Asia singing "Heat of the Moment." Shane grinned. David was a classic rock fan, and somehow the song seemed fated.

Jace turned the sound down. "So, where the hell are we going and who are we going to see?"

Shane bit his lower lip. Damn. Might as well get this over with. He knew the heckling was going to come sooner or later. "Her name is Vera Sanders. She's one of my students, and like I said, she's a witch. We're going to see her at her job." He knew his face was giving him away. His fellow hunters were perceptive, and he could tell from their knowing expressions that they'd figured out just how he felt about Vera.

"Which is where?" Jace asked.

When Shane didn't answer, Jace twisted in his seat to look at him. "Come on. Spit it out, kid."

Shane covered his face with his hand and muttered the name under his breath. "Soft Tails."

Jace chuckled. "Holy fuck." He let out a long, low whistle. "Damn. Shane, you dog. Your girl's a stripper?"

David pushed down harder on the accelerator and raised a brow at Jace. "Why am I not surprised you know it's a strip club?"

Jace rolled down the passenger window as he pulled his pack of Marlboro Reds from his trench-coat pocket. He lit up and took a long drag before blowing the smoke out the window. "Frankie may be the only woman on my mind now, but I didn't magically grow balls the night I found her in that alleyway. A man's got his needs, and the girls at Soft Tails really know how to show a guy a good time." He flicked ashes out the window.

Shane could feel himself blushing several shades of crimson. He tried not to imagine how tempting Vera would look nearly naked, stiletto heels accentuating her long legs as she swung around a stripper pole. Or better yet…

Nearly naked wouldn't cut it. He wanted to see her topless, but for his eyes only. He damned himself for thinking that way. It was wrong on so many levels. Vera was his student, for fuck's sake.

Shane straightened his glasses nervously. "No, she's not a stripper. She's the bartender."

Jace scoffed and glanced back at Shane again. "The bartender at a strip club, who—judging by the look on your face right now—is smokin' hot, and you think she never takes a ride on one of those poles?"

Shane shook his head. "I checked the place out online. Her uncle owns the place. No way would he let her get up on that stage."

Jace flashed Shane a look that said *Maybe in a more decent world.*

A few minutes later they wheeled into the parking lot of Soft Tails. The neon pink sign blazing the club's name glared against the darkness of the winter night. Another flashing sign out front declared *24 Beautiful Girls...and 1 ugly one!* Shane frowned. Bartender or not, Vera certainly wasn't the one ugly one. David pulled the car into an empty parking spot and switched off the ignition. The three men exited the car on the run and headed toward the entrance.

Jace clapped Shane on the back. "I have to hand it to you, man. Finding a woman who not only bartends, but at a strip club? Daaamn. That's impressive."

Shane blushed again. "She's not my woman. I already told you. She's one of my students."

Jace dropped his cigarette on the ground and ground it out with the heel of his boot. "Who gives a flying fuck? Student or not, you're interested in her, right?"

Shane knew his blush was all the answer anyone needed.

David's and Jace's eyes widened as they stepped into the strip club. The place was packed, busy even for a Saturday night. Loud bass-heavy music thumped from the speakers, and a round of cheers rang out as a stripper on the main stage slowly slid down the pole headfirst. She reached the bottom and flipped herself over again. Her see-through platform heels enhanced the length of her legs and angled her ass provocatively as she shook her long red hair over her shoulders. Sliding down into a split, her back to the audience, she bounced her ass cheeks up and down, her firm flesh barely covered by her hot pink G-string.

Jace elbowed Shane in the ribs. "Twenty bucks says she's a natural redhead." He chuckled.

Shane couldn't really say he was impressed. After spending most of his evenings throughout his childhood and teenage years backstage in Las Vegas, with naked women surrounding him as far as the eye could see, it took a lot to get him riled up.

"Where's your girl?" David asked.

Shane scanned the club until he spotted the polished wood bar. Vera was standing behind it, a bottle of Absolut Citron in one hand and a bottle of Jack Daniel's in the other. She poured the whiskey into a customer's glass as she poured the Citron into the mixer. He pointed in her direction.

David and Jace turned toward the bar and paused. "Holy shit," they said in unison, and Jace let out a low whistle.

He shot Jace and David a look and said, "Behave yourselves. She's my student."

Jace shook his head as if he wasn't certain what to say. He cleared his throat. "She's your student who works in a strip club, bartends and gives Marilyn Monroe a run for her money—a student who you want to jump into bed with. I think she's the exception to a lot of rules."

David shrugged. "Or she's the reason rules were made in the first place."

"Would both of you just try and keep your mouths

shut and follow me?" Shane snapped, then ignored Jace's and David's laughter and made his way over to the bar. He snaked his way through the groups of drunken patrons and watched Vera as she poured a shot of Bacardi into a mixer.

One of the dancers approached Vera and spoke into her ear, then pointed to the table where she'd been entertaining. The men raised their glasses, beckoning Vera for another drink. Shane walked closer to the bar and called out her name, but she didn't hear him over the thumping beat of the music. She nodded to the stripper, abandoned the bottle of Bacardi and snatched a silver bottle of Patrón from the liquor shelf, then headed to the table.

As Vera walked around the bar, confident in her fire-engine red stilettos, a man nursing what appeared to be a gin and tonic reached out a single sleazy paw and hooked it through her belt loop. He wrenched her backward, pulling her off balance, and she fell into the bastard's lap. She elbowed the asshole in the gut and was on her feet again before the drunkard knew what hit him.

Red clouded Shane's vision, and without thinking, he suddenly found himself standing behind the offending patron. He gripped a chunk of the bastard's greasy brown hair and pulled his head back.

"Hey, what the—"

Shane cut the man off midsentence by slamming the dickhead's forehead into the bar with an audible crack. Then he watched as a trail of blood oozed down the guy's temple.

Shane growled, "Touch her again and I'll cut off your balls slowly with a dull knife. Got it?"

The man groaned in pain. Without another word, Shane released him. The idiot crumpled on to the bar in a bloodied drunken heap. Shane glanced at Vera. She was standing completely still, shock written on her face. He could have sworn that the look in her eyes was one of awe and admiration.

"We need to talk," he told her.

As gently as possible, he reached out and took her hand. Goose bumps prickled up his arm at the feel of her soft skin against his. She was like a live wire. The electric current she sent through his body was indescribable. Still holding her hand, he led her out the front door of the club and into the cool Rochester night. She didn't say a word as he led her out to the car. When they reached the vehicle, he slipped off his coat and placed it around her bare shoulders. "I need your help."

"Dr. Grey, I don't know what you could possibly need my help for but—"

"Call me Shane. This isn't school-related."

"Okay…uh, Shane, I don't know how—"

"I know you're a witch, Vera."

She paused. Her eyes widened, and she bit her lower lip, then glanced away. "I don't know what you're talking about."

"Listen, I've worked in the occult long enough to know a witch when I see one. I didn't realize until after you made that comment about Lilith, but it all makes sense now. And that comment really helped me, by the way."

"I have to get back inside." She moved to step around him. "My customers are—"

Shane blocked her path. "All I'm asking is for you to listen to what I have to say." He stared straight into her eyes. "Please, I'm desperate."

Footsteps sounded from behind them. Shane glanced over his shoulder to see David and Jace approaching. He quickly turned back to Vera.

Her eyes widened, and she took a step back. "Oh shit. You guys aren't what I think you are, are you?"

Apparently she took his silence as a yes, because her eyes widened even more, and she said, "Oh, no. Not again. You're not dragging me in for questioning again. I—"

Shane stepped toward her, and she swung at him.

He ducked out of the way. When she swung again, he grabbed hold of both her wrists.

He held her still and tried to keep the frustration from his voice. "Listen. I don't care whether you practice light magic or dark magic. That doesn't matter to me right now. I just need someone who has magical abilities. A friend of ours is in danger, and without the help of a witch we won't be able to save her."

Vera stared at him suspiciously, clearly still uncertain.

Jace stepped closer and cleared his throat. "The incentive for you is that none of us will haul your ass into headquarters right now if you help us."

Shane shot him a look.

Jace shrugged. "What can I say? I know that look when I see it. That look says what the fuck's in it for me?"

Shane ignored Jace and turned back to her. "Vera, please. We really need your help."

She bit her lower lip and met his gaze. The streetlights highlighted her green irises, and he saw just the smallest hint of fear there. She glanced back and forth between him, David and Jace. "You really won't collar me?"

David nodded.

Vera let out a long sigh. "Okay, I'll help you. Just

let me tell my uncle that he needs to get someone to cover my shift. I'll tell him I'm not feeling well." She brushed past Shane and walked back toward the strip club. She paused halfway and turned back to them. "I just want to say, Dr. Grey, that if you hadn't brought hunters with you, I would have helped you without asking for anything in return. I'm not heartless enough to ignore someone in need. It's hunters I don't like, not helping people."

Shane sighed. "I *am* a hunter. It's part of my job."

"What? You're kidding me?"

Shane almost swore. Just because he had a lean build instead of being some over-muscled slab of beefcake… "What's so unbelievable about it?"

Vera crossed her arms over her chest and shrugged. "Simple. You never struck me as a douchebag." She looked straight at David and Jace, her mouth drawn into a tight line, before she turned and walked the rest of the way into the club.

"A douchebag, huh?" David smiled grimly. "She can call me a douchebag all she wants, as long as she helps me save Allsún."

Chapter 18

Despite everything that was running through his mind, David had to admit he was impressed by the way Vera dealt with the crime scene. She'd admitted to them in the car that she'd never seen a murder victim before, much less one whose end had been so gruesome, yet she handled it quite well. Sure, she gasped and tears filled her eyes for a moment, but once she'd taken in the scene, Shane set her straight to work.

He cleared his throat, as if he were lecturing, and turned to David and Jace. "What I'm going to have her do is a projection spell. Basically, it's going to allow us to see how the murders occurred. If Allsún was the killer, we'll see her image committing the murders." He flashed David a concerned look. "You might want to leave the room for this. It may not be something you want to see."

David shook his head. "You're right. I don't want to see it, but if that's what happened, then I *have* to see it. I have to know without a shadow of a doubt." If Allsún had been possessed and murdered the family, he had already mentally played out what the possibilities for dealing with the situation looked like. He would have no choice. If Allsún really was possessed by a demon as strong as Lilith, he would be forced to either kill the demon and kill Allsún in the process or sacrifice an innocent in order to save her, because a demon as strong as Lilith could withstand a regular run-of-the-mill exorcism. No matter how he looked at it, the thought of having to hurt, let alone kill, the woman he loved tortured him inside.

He prayed and prayed that she hadn't actually committed these last murders. He knew he wasn't strong enough to handle that. But even if she hadn't, she was almost certainly possessed now, which meant his choices were still the same.

"I don't know if I can do this." Vera's words jolted David back into the moment.

"I know you can," Shane said. "I can feel the strength of your powers."

David stepped between them, towering over her. "Look, the woman I love is in danger. If you don't do this, if you can't help me find out what happened here, I can't save her. So, either you tell me, or I'll drag your magic-practicing ass back to Execution Underground Headquarters."

Vera sighed. "Fine. But don't blame me if you don't like what you see."

"I'm sure I can handle it." David's eyes were unflinching and confident.

"Suit yourself." Vera shrugged, then she raised her hands. A fluorescent purple light formed around her fists as she repeated a series of incantations. Slowly the light grew, gaining more and more strength, until a blast of it filled the room. When it faded, an ethereal image of Allsún sat in the middle of the room as if on a chair. David watched in horror as slowly, her image stood. The look on Allsún's ghostly face was horrifying—one of evil and demented anger. David had been wrong. He couldn't watch. He knew from that look alone that his suspicions had been correct. Allsún was possessed by a demon he wasn't sure he could exorcise. David turned and left the room. He couldn't watch, he just couldn't. He'd never be able to look at Allsún the same if he saw her image commit those crimes. He heard the sounds of Shane gasping and Jace swearing behind him and knew he had made the right decision when he had turned away.

A moment of silence passed, before Jace called out to David. "You can come back in."

"Thanks, Vera," Shane said when it was over. He had gone pale and tried to shake off what he'd seen.

Vera, visibly moved by the experience, started making her way toward the door. "Can you take me home now, please?"

Shane nodded. "Yeah, we'll take you home." He turned to David. "Allsún didn't kill them."

Relief so powerful his knees felt weak washed over David. His heart beat rapidly against his chest. Thank God. As shitty as the situation was, at least there was that small bit of good news.

"I need some air," David said.

Without another word, he stepped outside, welcoming the cold night air against his face.

His phone rang a second later. Allsún's name flashed across the screen.

He hesitated, staring at the display, then hit the talk button and forced himself to act as normal and unsuspecting as possible. He couldn't let on that he knew there was a demon on the other end of the line. "Hey, Allie."

His greeting was met with a demented laugh. "Don't play coy with me, exorcist. I know the magical games you're up to. You thought you could hide your activities from me? You're pathetic."

David grasped the phone so hard that his hand hurt. "If you hurt a single hair on her head I swear I'll—"

"You'll what? Exorcise me? I would love to see you try. Exorcising a demon like me would kill your lady love in the process. You know very well that a demon as powerful as I am can withstand an exorcism ritual, even one performed by the likes of you. I suggest you let me go about my business."

"And what exactly would that business be?" He fought to stay calm, to keep Lilith talking until he could get her to reveal something—anything—that could help him.

Lilith let out another laugh—a sick, twisted version of Allsún's normal, cheerful giggle. "So far behind with the program," Lilith taunted. "It's no coincidence I chose to possess the last Fae outside the Isle of Apples. This cold war between us and those faerie cowards hiding away in their own private dimension is over. Your sweet Allsún will be the perfect vehicle for me to reach the Isle. I'll have Fae to slaughter as far as the eye can see. It will be…delicious." Lilith let out another twisted laugh. "Goodbye, exorcist. And for the record, you're quite the kisser."

David resisted the urge to empty the contents of his stomach into the garden. Instead, he pocketed his phone and stood there in silence, immobile and stunned.

A moment later, Jace stepped outside. "You okay, man?" He put a hand on David's shoulder.

David shook his head. "It called me. Lilith called me."

"*What?* David, what did it say?"

David stared off into the distant night, unable to focus. "I was right. She's going to use Allsún to get to the Isle of Apples to start a war with the Fae."

"Fuck," Jace swore. Then he pulled out his cell phone and dialed Damon.

Somewhere in the recesses of David's mind, he was vaguely aware of riding with Jace and Shane to an emergency Execution Underground meeting after they'd dropped off Vera. He stared straight ahead, completely zoned out as his fellow hunters debated the possibilities of what to do about Allsún's situation. He ignored them all, instead opting for tunnel vision as he put together his own plan. If there was one thing he knew, it was that he needed to follow Lilith. And that meant he needed to get to Ireland, where Allsún had always told him the portal to the Isle of Apples was located. Luckily, the demon wasn't smart enough about technology to turn off the GPS on Allsún's phone, and Shane had been able to track her…it…whatever the hell it was. They could tell that she was somewhere over the Atlantic.

They needed to get to Ireland quickly. If Lilith was able to reach the Isle of Apples, there would be no way for them to stop her. She would be out of their reach unless she chose to return to this dimension. Because of Lilith's strength, she would cling to Allsún's soul and body, and a normal exorcism wouldn't do any good. Even if he managed to catch Lilith off guard with an average exorcism, it would be like tearing her from Allsún's body. That could potentially kill Allsún, or worse, leave her in a catatonic state. The thought sent a shudder down his spine. He couldn't let that happen, but he also couldn't let the demon continue to possess her and steal her away from him just when there was finally a hope of rekindling their relationship. The only kind of exorcism that might be strong enough against a demon like Lilith would require a blood sacrifice, which would weaken Lilith and make her unable to cling to Allsún during the exorcism like the demonic parasite she was. Yet he knew Allsún would never want an innocent person to die to save her. He paused. His fellow hunters' voices buzzed in his ears. He forced himself to ignore them, and that was when it hit him.

He would be the blood sacrifice.

He would die so Allsún could live, so her entire race could live.

He pondered the possibility for a moment before a smile crept over his lips. That wasn't a bad way to go, all things considered, dying to save the entire Fae race and, more importantly, the life of the woman he loved.

"David. David? You with us?" Jace waved a hand in front of David's face.

David snapped to attention and focused on the present. "Yeah, I'm here. I have a plan of sorts."

Damon nodded as if to say "go on."

"We're going to need a jet from HQ in order to get there fast enough. As you all know, a regular exorcism isn't going to be strong enough to get rid of Lilith, at least I'm not expecting it to be. But at the moment, that's the only possibility we have. When we find them, I'll try it, but if Lilith's too strong, then we're just going to have to take her down in a group effort, find some way to hold her—maybe a powerful ward of some sort—until we can figure this out. That's all I've got." He clenched his fists until his knuckles turned white. Damn, he hoped they'd all get on board. He knew very well there was no way they would be able to take Lilith down with physical power alone, but if he could convince them that he believed it, maybe they would, too. Then, he would be free to go ahead with his true plan—the one he knew they'd never approve of.

Trent shrugged. "I agree with David. It's not a great plan, but it's the best we've got, and we don't have time to waste."

"Agreed," Damon mumbled. He straightened to his full height, prepared to take leadership. "In order to get a jet that fast to save only one person, I'm going to have to call in a favor, but I'll take care of it. Shane, go ahead and map out our flight route and continue to monitor Allsún's GPS. The rest of you, prepare to leave, and if Shane tells you to jump, then jump."

Damon indicated the entrance to the control room with a nod. "David, come with me."

Icy rain poured over Rochester in a thick heavy sheet. The kind that couldn't make up its mind about whether it wanted to freeze into snow or melt into real rain. Ultimately, it sucked worse than either. Cold and wet, David and Damon trudged across Franklin Street to the Temple Building Apartments, the same building where Allsún's ransacked apartment was.

Once the two hunters were inside Damon's lush bachelor pad, Damon nodded for David to follow him down a narrow hallway. He punched a code into a keypad beside a door, waited for a small beep, then pushed the door open. He stepped inside, and David followed.

Damn. David let out a low whistle, stunned by the communications system Damon had rigged up.

"I came to Rochester with the intention of hunting alone," Damon said. "Becoming head of a division was an accident."

Despite everything on his mind, David couldn't help but chuckle. "Well, aren't you a loving mother hen? Telling your babies they weren't planned. . . ."

Damon ignored him, flipped several switches to start the system, then sat down in the desk chair and typed in a code.

Moments later Chris, their division operator, appeared on the screen. "Hey, Damon. What can I help you with?"

"Can you connect me through to the sergeant?" Damon asked.

The guy on the other end of the screen swore under his breath. "You must be in deep shit if you're calling the sergeant instead of waiting for him to call you. What's going on?"

Damon gave him a dismissive look. "Nothing that concerns you. Just put me through."

Chris rolled his eyes. "Jeez, aren't we in a pleasant mood?"

"He's always an absolute peach," David said.

Damon glanced over his shoulder. "Don't speak unless you're spoken to. Got it?" he snapped.

"Yeah. Fine. Got it."

A moment later a silver-haired man appeared on the screen. "Why in shit's sake are you calling me?"

"I'd like to request your help, sir."

The older man's eyes widened. "My help? What in the blazing hell gave you the idea that you would get *my* help?"

Damon didn't respond.

The sergeant crossed his arms over his chest. "Spit it out, operative."

"One of my division members—one of his loved ones is in danger, and we need a faster jet than anything HQ has access to. We need a military-grade jet and clearance into Ireland, fast."

"Balls." The sergeant frowned. "Why the hell do you think I'd approve that?"

"Because you owe me for that time I saved you and your whole team in Brooklyn, not to mention that we can't afford to have another team member lose a significant other. It's…bad for morale."

David saw the sergeant's face soften slightly, almost as if he pitied Damon? Had *Damon* lost someone? That would explain a hell of a lot about Damon's attitude to a lot of things, now that he thought about it.

The sergeant cleared his throat. "I'll take care of it, operative, but don't expect any more favors from me in the future. This evens the scales."

Damon gave a single nod. "Yes, sir."

The screen went black, and the rigid set of Damon's shoulders relaxed. He waved his hand in dismissal. "There. You have what you need. Call your team members and tell them to be prepared to fight outside their normal parameters. I'll call you with further instructions."

"Thank you."

Damon didn't respond.

David cleared his throat. "You have no idea how much I appreciate this. The thought of never seeing her again… I'm just so glad I told her I loved her before everything happened, you know?" He paused, waiting for Damon to respond, but he still didn't say anything. "Anyway, thanks again." David turned toward the door.

"David…" Damon said.

"Yeah?"

A long moment of silence passed before Damon finally spoke. "I know what it's like to lose someone, and I wouldn't wish that on anyone. I missed my chance to tell her I loved her, and I'll regret it every day for the rest of my life."

David's breath caught in his chest, and he couldn't manage to say anything else, so he just nodded and left. The pain in Damon's voice was enough for David to know one thing: whatever had happened to Damon was the reason the man always had a look of anger and pain behind his eyes.

Chapter 19

David paced over the tarmac as the jet pulled to a stop. The deafening thrum of the engine drowned out the steady beat of his heart. Even though he knew he was headed to an early grave, he'd never been more sure of his course. Anger and nausea filled him at the thought of the horrors Allsún was enduring, but he gathered every ounce of mental strength he had and forced himself to remain focused. All six hunters boarded the plush private jet. In less than five minutes they were airborne.

A strange sense of calm enveloped David all through the flight to Ireland. He felt a sense of satisfaction in knowing that his death would save the woman he loved. He had to be honest with himself. As a hunter, he'd never expected to live to old age anyway. He'd always figured he would be lucky if he managed to reach sixty, like the sergeant had. And if it meant saving Allsún, he would welcome death. He knew he hadn't always been perfect. Hell, he'd made loads of mistakes, and he certainly hadn't been what you would call religious, but somehow he felt a sense of peace.

He took solace in knowing that he was ultimately a good person, or at least someone who tried to be. And for his own sanity, he needed to believe that when he reached heaven, God would deem that enough.

"The GPS tells me we're getting close to her location," Shane announced.

Ash tapped David on the shoulder. "Just where are you expecting us to land?"

Shane spoke up. "There aren't a lot of options, but I think our best bet would be—"

Jace interrupted with a grin. "No, that's not what we're doing. I have a better plan."

"What are you talking about?" Shane asked.

"I'll show you." He stood and walked to the back of the plane. A moment later he returned, carrying several large packs in his arms. He tossed one pack to each of the men.

David caught his and examined it. A parachute. "I'm not sure I like where this is going." The last thing he wanted to do before he marched to his own suicide was jump out of a plane.

Jace smiled. "Let's go skydiving, motherfuckers."

Trent grinned from ear to ear. "Hell, yeah. I only got to do this a handful of times when I was in the army—fun as shit."

Ash shook his head. "Aw, hell, no. No way I'm jumpin' outta any damn plane."

Jace threw him a questioning look. "Why not?"

Ash tossed the parachute back to Jace. "Cause only idiots with a death wish willingly jump outta planes, that's why."

Damon gave Ash a stern look. "You won't be doing it willingly. It's an order. Jace is right. This is a better plan."

Silence fell over the group. Ash was the first one to speak. "Hooooly fuck."

Trent's jaw dropped. A moment later he recovered and said, "Hell must have frozen over. Did I just hear Damon say Jace was right?"

Damon glared. "Don't make me say it again."

Jace sat down, leaned back and propped his boots on a table. "I'm savoring this moment."

Trent laughed. "You sure you can't say it one more time so I can record it?"

Damon frowned. "Shut up, all of you." Jace opened his mouth to speak. Damon pointed a finger at him and stopped him before he got the chance. "Especially you."

Everyone but Jace and Damon chuckled.

Once the official plan was in place, they continued the rest of the ride in silence. Only the roar of Shane's furious typing accompanied the sound of the plane's engine. David sat back in his seat. He wasn't quite sure if the weight of what was about to happen to him had fully sunk in yet.

"We're nearly there. Time to get ready," Shane said.

All six men stood, strapping on their parachutes and preparing their weapons, making sure everything was secure.

Jace clapped David on the back. "You ready to save the woman you love?"

David nodded. "Always."

"Five minutes," Shane called out.

David checked his parachute one more time. Five more minutes. That meant that it was probably less than twenty minutes until he met his death.

Damon told the pilot to open the door. The sound of metal shifting over metal echoed through the plane as the door slid open. Miles and miles of what David assumed to be green Irish hillside lay below them.

"Don't jump until my cue!" Shane yelled.

David shifted his parachute on his back. He'd always hated doing this in basic training, but this was for Allsún, and he was willing to do anything to save her.

"On my count," Shane said. "Three. Two. One. Jump."

David didn't think twice. He threw himself from the plane, allowing the cold Irish air to whip past him as he free-fell down toward the countryside. He admitted to a feeling of relief when he pulled his rip cord and the chute opened above him.

David hadn't expected that Shane would be landing them in the middle of pure demonic chaos, and as the others landed nearby he briefly wondered if Shane had expected it, either. Then there was no more time for thinking, only action.

He slipped off his parachute as fast as he could before wrenching his knives from his boots. Lilith was far from the only demon they would be battling today.

A small army of at least fifteen demons surrounded a small hill. At the top of the hill, Allsún stood, hands raised in the air, Lilith already using her to recite a Fae incantation to open the astral gates to the Isle of

Apples. David's only goal was to get to Allsún's side and exorcise Lilith from her body. Any other demon that stood in his way was merely cannon fodder.

He and his fellow hunters charged forward with a roar. Each man went hand to hand with one demon after another, punching, slicing, fighting with the holy weapons David had given them.

The first hell-crawler to approach David died within seconds as he plunged his blessed blade straight into its heart. He spared a brief thought for the human body that died with the demon, then moved on. The second sulfur-sucking beast was not deterred so easily. It dodged David's knife, throwing a punch that landed square on his jaw. Pain seared through him, but he didn't care. His only focus was saving Allsún. He threw his own punch straight into the demon's gut, and the monster doubled over in pain, giving him the perfect chance to slash straight through the thick artery in its neck. Blood spurted, staining his clothes. No matter, he would be dead soon anyway. He threw a roundhouse kick at the next demon that approached him, knocking the vile bastard upside the head and straight on to the ground. He used that moment to plunge the blade of his dagger straight into the demon's stomach.

He looked up. Allsún stood at the top of the hill, just

a few yards away, still under Lilith's control. He ran forward as fast as he could, pausing only when yet another demon threw itself at him. He smashed the creature straight in the jaw, knocking it backward and off its feet. He didn't even stop to kill it. He needed to save Allsún, and he needed to save her now.

He ran full-speed ahead toward Lilith and tackled her to the ground. She fell into the grass beside him, the demon inside her cackling with laughter.

"Silly exorcist, do you really think you can stop me? Think again. Try to exorcise me from the one you love and see what happens. I'll kill her. You're too weak to touch me." Lilith forced Allsún's body to stand, returning to her incantations and ignoring David as if he were nothing more than an ant beneath her shoe.

"That's where you're wrong," he said. "See, the problem with you demons is you have no loyalty. Not a single one of these cronies of yours will give themselves up to save you. We have you beat there." He lifted the blessed blade in his right hand. Before he could think twice, he slashed it across the skin of his left wrist, then quickly switched hands and slashed the right in turn. He had to hurry before he lost the strength in his fingers. Blood poured down his arms in thick, warm streams as he sank to his knees, lifting his arms into the air and reciting the ancient ritual in Latin.

Suddenly Lilith paused mid-chant.

"What? No!" Allsún screeched in the demon's voice. Veins began to bulge at her ankles, snaking up her legs and undulating up her body.

David continued to chant, though his words grew sluggish as the blood drained from him.

"No! Don't!" Lilith yelled.

She fell to her knees, writhing in pain, as David reached the last lines of the exorcism. Black dots floated in front of his eyes, and his vision began to blur, but he kept chanting. He needed to do this for Allsún, for the love of his life.

As he reached the last words of the ritual, they fell from his lips in a barely intelligible mumble. He was losing blood so quickly. And the cold… He felt so cold, as if his insides had been drained of every ounce of warmth. His vision remained clear long enough for him to see the bright flash of white light as Lilith exited Allsún's body and was sucked back down into the pits of hell. He smiled. He'd done it, he'd saved her. All in all, his death had been worth it because he had given her life. His vision continued to blur, until finally the world faded to black.

* * *

The electronic humming and beeping of machines pounded in David's head as his eyes slowly flickered open. Bright white light blinded him. He blinked several times, waiting for his pupils to adjust. This was some weird-ass heaven. He stared up into the light as his vision cleared—overhead fluorescents, hardly warm and welcoming. Holy shit. Was he still alive? Immediately he sat up, eyes scanning the room. Panic rushed through him. Allsún. Where was Allsún?

A small hand pushed against his chest, "Whoa, easy there, tiger."

He allowed the gentle touch to push him back. Thank God. He knew that gentle touch and allowed himself to relax.

"I thought you were going to be out for a couple more hours."

He turned to find Allsún sitting beside him, a closed book resting on her lap.

"What happened?" David asked.

"I think you know perfectly well what happened, since you were the one who caused it, after all."

David thought back. It only took him a few minutes to remember what he had expected to be his last moments on earth. "But why am I here? I slit my wrists in order to save you."

"That's right." She set her book to the side before reaching out to grab one of his hands. "Thank you for that."

David shook his head. "You must have known I would. I'll always come for you."

Allsún nodded. "I know that now."

"When Lilith possessed you, you present after that? You know, like awake?"

"Some of the time. I was fighting my hardest to get it out of my head. Believe me. I didn't make things easy on it."

David gave a single nod. "Good, that's my girl."

"I'm sorry about our fight. I know we've already talked about it a little, but I shouldn't have sprung the news about the miscarriage on you like that. It wasn't fair. You couldn't possibly have known I was pregnant, much less that anything was going to happen to me that night. Maybe if you'd been there things would have been different, but it's not your fault you weren't there. You didn't know."

"I'm so sorry for everything I said that night. I've always wanted a family with you, Allsún. I just didn't feel that I would be able to protect that family. But if I had known you were already pregnant, I would have done everything in my power to keep you and the baby safe. I realized I was wrong to think that way. There are no guarantees in life. I shouldn't have denied you what you wanted out of fear of losing it. I'd love to have children with you someday, if you'll let me back into your life."

"I did a lot of thinking while Lilith possessed me. I thought I was going to die, so it was like my whole life flashed before my eyes, all my mistakes and shortcomings. One thing I couldn't let go is the fact that you would never again hear me tell you that I love you."

Before David could reply, a knock sounded from the doorway. Jace poked his head around the corner. At the sight of David a wide grin spread across his face. "Hey, hey. Look who's awake."

David smiled. "Come on in."

Jace motioned over his shoulder, and within a few seconds the whole team was standing in David's hospital room. A chorus of "Glad you're awake, man" and "So happy you're okay" created a buoyant energy.

Jace walked over to David's bedside and placed a hand on his friend's shoulder. "Well, if nobody else is going to say it, I will." He fixed David with a pointed glare. "You ever do that again and I'll kill you myself."

The whole group chuckled.

"Consider yourself officially warned that Damon will have you in therapy so fast your head will spin," Trent added.

Damon nodded. "He's right."

Ash ran his fingers through his mane of blond hair. "You came pretty damn close to meetin' your maker there, bud."

Jace nodded. "I'd ask you what the fuck you were thinking, but I think we all know where your head was at."

They all glanced at Allsún and she blushed under the weight of all their combined gazes.

David waved his hand in dismissal. "All right already. All you idiots get out of here and find out how soon I can get out of this damn bed."

"Since when do you give orders?" Shane joked as they all moved toward the door.

"Since I want to be alone with the woman I love and you all won't leave. Get your sorry asses out." David winked at them as they exited.

Once his fellow hunters had left, he turned back to Allsún. "Back to our conversation." He reached out and took her hand. "I was terrified, Allie. I kept worrying I'd never hear you say those words again, too."

She smiled and leaned in closer to him. "Well, now you don't have to worry about never hearing them again before you die."

He squeezed her hand. "I know this is kind of spur of the moment, but, Allsún..." He took both her hands in his. "...will you love me again?"

A smile lit her face as she leaned in to kiss him. "I never stopped."

Epilogue

Two years later

The smell of fresh flowers delivered from friends and family filled David's nose as he held tight to Allsún's hand. She smiled at him, glancing around the hospital room at all the colorful arrangements before her gaze dropped back down to their little miracle. She held their tiny newborn daughter to her breast. At the sight of his two girls, tears clouded David's eyes. He'd never seen a sight more beautiful. The love of his life, the woman who, despite everything they'd been through, had agreed to become his wife, nursing their sweet baby girl. He couldn't think of a happier moment in all of his life.

After a moment's silence Allsún sighed. "I'm so happy, David." She stared into their little girl's wide blue eyes, and he could practically feel the warmth, pride and love radiating from her. She would be a perfect mother. "I'm so happy," she said again, "but I'm still so scared."

He shook his head. He'd already told her she didn't need to be scared, but he would always be there to reassure her. He moved his chair closer to the hospital bed and squeezed her hand. "Allsún, we've already talked about this. There's nothing to be scared about. Everything is going to be fine. Jessica's here now. She's safe in your arms, and I'm going to keep you both safe. I'll be by your side the entire time. I won't let either of you out of my sight. You'll be safe and so will she. I won't let this happiness be taken away from you."

Allsún smiled. She released David's hand and ran her fingers over Jessica's cherubic cheek.

When Allsún didn't speak, he gently placed his forehead against hers. "She has your eyes, and your nose, and your lips." He kissed each body part as he named it. "And, well...your everything, which means she's perfect."

Allsún laughed quietly before reaching up and touching the memorial necklace David had bought her two years earlier, a pendant with what would have been their son's birthstone. "I miss him."

David nodded. "I know you do. Even though I didn't know him the way you did, I do, too."

Another silence passed between them before Allsún spoke again. "Thinking about him still makes me sad sometimes, and I miss him every day, even though we have our sweetheart now." She glanced down at Jessica still suckling on her breast.

David placed his hand on Allsún's arm in reassurance. "Tell me something about when you were pregnant with him that you've never told me before, something happy."

A small near-smile crossed her lips, though it wasn't enough to reach her gorgeous emerald eyes. "Well, the reason I kept ordering carryout from that seafood place that used to be around the corner wasn't because I loved their fish so much. I was craving tartar sauce with lots of pickle in it. When you weren't home, I'd eat it on everything. Whenever I would eat it, I'd talk to Michael out loud and say, 'When you come out, your skin is going to smell like pickles from all of these crazy cravings you're giving me.'"

David chuckled. "That sounds like a nice memory."

She nodded, though he could see tears gathering in

his eyes. "Even though they're happy memories, they're sad to think about, because of how things ended, because I never got to hold him in my arms, like I can with her." A tear slid down her cheek. "I'm so excited and happy Jessica's here now, but I just can't help but miss Michael. I feel like I'll always be sad over him."

Jessica unlatched from Allsún's breast and began to coo, sweet happy noises that melted David's heart. She was so beautiful, just like her mother. Allsún wiped the tears from her eyes and kissed Jessica's forehead with a smile.

"You're my little miracle," she whispered to the baby.

David wrapped Allsún in an embrace and cradled her and Jessica close. He laid a kiss on Allsún's cheek before she nuzzled her head onto his shoulder. "I know it may not feel like it now, Allie, but soon, even though you'll always miss him, you'll be able to remember without being sad. One day you'll even look back on the memories of carrying him and be able to smile."

* * * * *

Acknowledgments

Some books flow easily from a writer's fingertips. *Immortal Hunter* was not one of them. This novel was created from blood, sweat, lots of tears and an overwhelming amount of heartache, and it has more connections to my own life than I care to admit. At its core, David and Allsún's story is about fighting personal demons, not the physical demons they battle in the book, and for me, this book was exactly that, a fight against my own demons.

Because of that, this book took shape courtesy of my personal support network. If it weren't for the following people, I might have given up on writing it. I'd like to extend a huge thank you to the following people:

To my editor, Leslie Wainger, for helping take this story to the next level and giving me the guidance needed to make David and Allsún's story something worthwhile.

To my agent and friend, Nicole Resciniti, for her constant support of me and this series, for being my plot buddy when I was stuck, for being a great editor, and for telling me it would all be okay, even though I wasn't certain it wouldn't be.

To all the readers and the Execution Underground Street Team for promoting this series and helping build a fan base. Special thanks goes to Carla Gallway from

Book Monster Reviews for her never-ending kindnesses; to Jenese Leon from Readers Confession and Laura Moore from Little Read Riding Hood for helping me get my promotional start; to Sabina at Sabina's Adventures in Reading and Jenese (again) for being great beta-readers; and to my friend and fellow author Gena Showalter for taking a chance on this newbie as both a friend and a writer, and for being a beautiful person, a fellow sister in Christ.

To my dad, for sitting me in front of him on his Harley long before I even started preschool, and for always being a great provider. To my mom, for keeping on me about my deadline, even when I didn't want to hear it, and for always being my best friend, the one person I can count on and my biggest fan.

To my husband, Jon, for being the true unsung hero of this story, for making me believe in happily-ever-afters, for always being both the man I need and the man I want, and for holding me close every time I need it.

To my aunt Cindy, for understanding my pain and for telling me that though it would always hurt, I'd look back someday and smile. You were right.

And lastly, to you. You know who you are. You shaped this story, even though we never found our happily-ever-after. For a long time, I wished you could have been the kind of hero David Aronowitz is, but now, I know better. I'm glad you weren't. Thank you.

Dear Reader,

Thank you so much for picking up this book and for taking a chance on me as a writer. I hope you enjoyed *Immortal Hunter*, and that David and Allsún's story stays with you long after you've finished reading the novel. The content of these pages is dark, particularly in its themes of child loss, miscarriage and grief, and I want to share with you part of my own story and my connection to the material.

When I first began writing David and Allsún's story I knew there was an element I hadn't quite figured out yet. Allsún was hiding something from both me and David, and I had no clue what that secret was. It wasn't until I reached the midpoint of the first draft of the novel that I realized what Allsún had been hiding: a tragic miscarriage she'd experienced years earlier. At the time, from an author's perspective, the pain her character had to endure seemed to fit seamlessly with the main plot of child loss in the story. Strong, craft-focused writers know that putting our characters through hell is the only way to allow them to really shine and show their true selves. And losing a child was the worst kind of hell I could imagine for poor Allsún, or for anyone, especially considering I was pregnant with my own first child at the time I was writing this book.

Four days after I finished writing *Immortal Hunter* I experienced the hell I had written about firsthand. My husband and I lost our first baby. Even now, months later, it seems like a cruel twist of fate that the worst kind of trauma I could imagine for my fictional character would become my own struggle, but unfortunately, that's the way things turned out for me.

There is no greater pain in the world than that of a mother losing her child, no matter whether they are a beautiful and sweet infant, a curious toddler, a rebellious teenager, a full-grown adult with a family of their own or a small still-growing baby in the womb. I wanted to take this space in the novel to say to every mother reading this who has ever lost their baby, their whole world, that I understand your pain and that I hope you feel that in this novel I've managed to accurately portray the grief you and so many others have had to suffer through. This book is not intended to trivialize your pain, but to recognize it.

With love,
Kait Ballenger